# CLIMBING MOUNT IMPLAUSIBLE

## Borgo Press Books by DAMIEN BRODERICK

# CLIMBING MOUNT IMPLAUSIBLE

## THE EVOLUTION OF A SCIENCE FICTION WRITER

by

Damien Broderick

THE BORGO PRESS

*An Imprint of Wildside Press LLC*

MMX

# CONTENTS

# DEDICATION

To the young science fiction writers
of the 21$^{st}$ century.

May you scribble your way
to the stars—and beyond!

# FOREWORD

## BY RUSSELL BLACKFORD

Formidably talented, a prose stylist and a polymath, Damien Broderick has long been at the leading edge of science fiction in his native Australia. In 1963, a local religious magazine published his first short story: a non-sf piece entitled "Walk Like a Mountain," about a pious, sturdy farmer who lies dying after a horrible tractor accident. "Walk Like a Mountain" is included in this collection, as is "The Mirrors of the Sea," published about the same time in a Monash University student magazine. But Broderick's real break-through came with a much longer story—also included here, and definitely science fiction this time—"The Sea's Furthest End." He received the acceptance for this ornate, Oedipal space opera when he was only nineteen, and it soon appeared in the UK, in the first of John Carnell's *New Writings in SF* anthologies (1964).

Broderick's own introduction to "The Sea's Furthest End," in the pages below, is self-deprecating to say the least. Despite the author's youth, the story is far more than an adolescent power fantasy (though it surely is that as well). It has outrageously melodramatic touches, and its style is unremittingly purple; yet, it is rich and clever and memorable. The characters and their problems appear vividly to the reader, while the pacing is suspenseful—and every element joins to create a sense of inevitable fate, or other powers, carrying the drama to its foreshadowed cataclysm.

"The Sea's Furthest End" launched Broderick's international literary career, and I am tempted to claim that he never looked back. That, however, would be doubly misleading. First, because financial exigency kept him selling mainly to Australian markets during the 1960s, then led him into a career as a journalist and magazine editor. Second, Broderick actually does look back. He returned to "The Sea's Furthest End" many years later, altering and elaborating the far-future culture portrayed in the original version, re-naming most of the central characters, and introducing new subtleties into their motivations. In Australia, this was published as a novel aimed at the Young Adult market: *The Sea's Furthest End* (1993). Later, a version of the story appeared in the US as "The Game of Stars and Souls."

This exemplifies an important and recurrent feature of Broderick's literary career: although he has always pressed on, finding new interests and experimenting with ideas and forms, he also treats his hoard of published words as metal to work and rework. He often finds opportunities to deepen, extend, and update earlier narratives, giving them new significance. The reflective, retrospective collection that you're reading is itself an exercise in looking back.

It's difficult to see his achievement whole, though *Climbing Mount Implausible* will certainly make it easier. Part of the problem is Broderick's dual status as an Australian writer but also a science fiction writer on the international stage.

On the one hand, he belongs to Australian letters, and undoubtedly appreciates recognition in his home country. His successes in the 1960s placed him in the company of a small group of Australian sf writers who'd gained footholds in the international markets of the time: among them, Wynne Whiteford, John Baxter, and Lee Harding. He has since been active in Australia's science fiction community, as well as its general literary community, and he is currently the fiction editor for *Cosmos*, a Sydney-based popular science magazine. However, his nearest peers are not the other Australian science fiction writers whose professional oeuvres were published during the same four or five decades—and nor are they Australian mainstream authors. He belongs to a worldwide community of writers who employ science fiction's devices to serious literary purpose. He has always identified strongly with sf as an international literature of ideas, and he has now lived for several years in the United States.

Almost half a century after his career began, Broderick is now a distinguished novelist with an impressive body of published work. During the 1990s, he also emerged as a major commentator on the implications of advanced technology, and on the complex boundaries and relationships between literature and science. Indeed, he holds a Ph.D. from Deakin University for his dissertation on the semiotics of literary and scientific discourses, with particular attention to science fiction. Here lies another reason why it's not so easy to see his achievement whole—many readers who know Damien

Broderick the futurist, for example, may not be familiar with his science fiction or his literary criticism.

In recent decades, Broderick has shown an ever-deepening interest in scientific, literary, and philosophical theories. His considered views about science fiction itself, supported by close analyses of the work of Samuel R. Delany and many other luminaries of the genre, are consolidated in a critical-theoretical monograph, *Reading by Starlight: Postmodern Science Fiction* (1995), and in subsequent books such as *Transrealist Fiction: Writing in the Slipstream of Science* (2000). Elsewhere, he laments that much poststructuralist literary and cultural theory is in tension with the scientific realism that he advocates fiercely. A relatively short exposition can be found in *The Architecture of Babel* (1994), while a more concerted and focused critique of poststructuralism, *Theory and Its Discontents*, appeared in 1997 (and immediately attracted controversy). Broderick's work combines genuine intellectual authority with the intensity and engagement of a good journalist, whether his subject is the new new physics and humanity's place in the Universe, or the new new literary criticism and the author's dispossession from the text...or simply the newest news in the field of science fiction.

Any attempt to come to terms with his overall achievement, then, must locate it within both Australian and international literature and ideas. It will also require an understanding of his extraordinary breadth of reading and concern, not to mention a sympathetic awareness of themes and trends in the professional world of speculative literature, what Robert Scholes terms "the fiction of the future." A full critical study would examine Broderick's legacy as a radio dramatist, journalist, critic, theorist, and public intellectual. The totality of the work is breathtaking. But for all that, the productions that have most defined his career, and perhaps his self-understanding, have been his novels and short stories.

No matter how far he engages in other forms of writing, Broderick always returns to this central concern. Not only that, he shows a strong sf sensibility even when writing journalism or more mainstream narratives. There is always the implicit presence of an author who can be imagined strutting triumphantly through acres of scientific speculation quite perpendicular to our mundane experiences of place and history. Picture an almost intimidating, vaguely demonic figure—tall, gaunt, sharply bearded, hiking about a fabulous intellectual landscape where brave, austere minds are at home. On Broderick's turf, a new style of asceticism is required, a rigorous devotion to science and reason—but certainly not a mortification of the flesh. Here, Derrida, deconstruction, and discourse theory are analyzed under the same burning light as selfish genes, speciation, and superstrings. The strategies of nuclear disarmament, the tactics of psychotherapy, and the game plan for teaching literature are all insistent priorities. James Randi, Julia Kristeva, and Jim Morrison demand equal time with J. G. Ballard, Fredric Jameson, and James Tiptree, Jr.

Broderick's early stories tend to be somewhat rudimentary in development and a little smug in tone, but they are remarkable for their concision, a certain relentlessness of emotion—whether the tone is that of a tear-jerker, black joke, or leering anecdote—and for the fact that they are all so well-crafted at the level of pacing and plot, even though their author was very young. It's as if Broderick-the-writer sprang into birth fully grown like Athena, and with a hard-wired literary grammar of all the basic plot transformations and their emotionally manipulative potential. Over time, however, he has grown as a storyteller and wordsmith: he has developed a greater sophistication of technique and a deeper vision. He's also kept abreast of the latest ideas in science and fiction; he's shown that he can write in swift cyberpunk prose, that he can imitate the joke-building techniques of the masters of comic sf, as in *Striped Holes* (1988), and that he always has something fresh to communicate.

Though, to my mild surprise, it does not show up well in this selection of short fiction, Broderick's narratives often depict extraordinary travels in space and time, with a particular interest in the paradoxes of time travel and intertemporal communication, and in related themes such as parallel or altered realities. Something of this can be seen in "The Sea's Furthest End" (and its later variants), where there is a kind of split-level reality; but it is most apparent in such novels as *The Judas Mandala* (1982) and the more recent diptych of *Godplayers* (2005) and *K-Machines* (2006). Often, the emphasis is upon interactions between human or alien characters from different realities or time zones.

However, Broderick is also deeply imbued with mainstream literary values, and his fiction is remarkable for the many techniques and voices that he has employed to express his vision. His first-person narrators range from the bitter and twisted death-note scribbler of "Drowning in Fire" (in this collection), to defiant, subversive Maggie Roche of *The Judas Mandala*, dignified and tragic Xaraf Firebridge of *The Black Grail* (1986), and young, smart, irrepressible Jenny Kane of *Zones* (1997; co-authored with Rory Barnes). *Striped Holes* is told by a sardonic omniscient narrator ("The Interior" uses a similar, but not identical, voice), while complex narratorial strategies are deployed for other works, such as *The White Abacus* (1997).

His fiction can be enjoyed for its clever accounts of extraordinary adventures, for the author's ever-deepening personal philosophy, and most certainly for his gift of humor: I've emphasized Broderick's serious concerns, but many of his stories are surprisingly funny. "The Interior," for example, may be read "straight" as a kind of utopian socialist manifesto, but its ironic point is that its characters bring to utopia the same dreams, sorrows, idiosyncrasies, and limitations that they'd have shown in a more mundane and familiar setting. Funny that, though sad. It's the harsh, deflating-yet-amusing truth about utopia. And what more can, or should, you say, when a recent story ("Cockroach Love") begins with the following laugh-out-loud sentence?

> When Kay got home, tired and unhappy from her grueling flight halfway round the globe, she found her husband Elwood fucking a cockroach the size of a cocktail waitress.

Over the years, since his precocious beginnings as a hungry *enfant terrible*, a teenage wordwolf, Broderick has developed a mastery of style, technique and voice. He renews his central themes each time he takes them up, and displays a versatility that marks him out as a writer of exceptional value and interest.

This volume shows that writer's growth.

# FOREWORD

Mount Implausible? Where is it, anyway? Let us set off on an easy preliminary climb up the foothills of Mount Improbable, an adjacent peak in the Darwinian landscape.

A favorite Patrick Hardin cartoon shows a familiar panel of evolutionary advance across the eons. A gasping fish with webbed fin-flippers drags itself out of the brine, thinking "EAT. SURVIVE. REPRODUCE." Evolution proceeds remorselessly, left to right, each subsequent creature more formidable than the last, each musing "EAT. SURVIVE. REPRODUCE." At the far right a *Homo sapiens* specimen stands with hands thrust into his pockets, stares at the sky and wonders yearningly, "WHAT'S IT ALL ABOUT?"

Another, by the incomparable Kliban, shows a Mitteleuropean gentleman at his club dining table consulting a large menu, accompanied in the opposite chair by an enormous housefly. He tells the imperturbable waiter, "I'll have the gazpacho, leeks vinaigrette with shrimp, orange mousse, a bottle of Côtes du Rhône Rouge '59, and bring some shit for my fly."

It can be argued that those two toons pretty well exhaust all the metaphysical depths ever plumbed by men, women, and Musca domestica.

A lucid, rather more solemn but graciously informative study of how we're here, if not why, is Richard Dawkins' *Climbing Mount Improbable*, a cleverly developed metaphor explaining how the world's glory of bacteria, plants and animals developed without a deliberate designer. It provided me with an appealing image for the strange, craggy path awaiting any hopeful science fiction writer.

Here's Dawkins' metaphor, which I will shamelessly bend and spindle: We stand at the peak of Mount Improbable—not just us humans, but all the superbly adapted bugs and cold viruses—because, in the process of development, random mutation has been culled by contest and a one-way ratchet that preserves good ideas and sends them into the future.

True, you couldn't have got *here* in one leap from way down *there*, if *there* is the brute primordial slime. But step by infinitesimal step, across quadrillions of lives working together and snacking on each other, tiny changes in the genetic recipe built bodies of which some did a slightly better job, on the whole, than their rivals, so it's their template that is preserved and passed upward on the endless climb toward the peak of Mount Improbable.

Not that there *is* a peak, a target, a perfect goal—that's the old backsliding enticement of superstitious thought. Still, up here in a biosphere more than three billion years old, we're a pretty snazzy and good looking group of critters. Well, when we're not poisoning or killing everything in sight.

Darwinism makes it clear, though, that it's populations of genes that evolve, not individuals. New Age pieties drone that we are here on earth to foster personal evolution, souls perhaps recycled in every generation until we are *evolved enough* to escape the wheel of karma, or return to the sky in UFOs, or mingle in a psychic group mind not accessible to the crass and worldly. Well, who knows? Maybe it's so. But to call any of these processes *evolutionary* is a misuse of long-established scientific language. Not that the language police are liable to haul you down to the lexical lockup and beat the soles of your feet for your thought crime. It's more likely, alas, here in the futuristic twenty-first century, that you'll be shunned and despised just for *using* a godless word like "evolution," which we are often assured is a foul plot to pollute our minds and drag us down into Satan's grasp.

For science fiction readers and writers, misapplying "evolutionary" as if the adjective can apply to a single lifetime is as wicked and contemptible as abusing the Second Law of Thermodynamics, and I hope none of us would consider *that*. Ever Homer Simpson is insistent on this score. As it turns out, I don't care. I've called this book, in my subtitle, "The Evolution of a Science Fiction Writer," because it can be argued that ideas, concepts, plans of action, competences *do* evolve, quite literally, inside the ecologies of our minds, which are just our embodied brains at work rather than coasting. The best grappling hook for ideas the human brain ever evolved, helping us all EAT, SURVIVE, and REPRODUCE, has also been named by Dawkins: the *meme*. Strictly speaking, the meme is a slippery meme, not nearly as well-defined and nicely behaved as the gene, but we do need a crisp word to convey the idea of, well, an idea that can easily infect other minds and spread with contagious ease, mutating as it goes into variant sub-species but retaining a ruthless grip on the mind that hosts it.

Each of us is a gorgeous work of art built by vast colonies of genes—at least 20,000 of them—but our brains are specialized to provide support for all the memes that fit, especially those that take up residence in childhood and reshape the very architecture of our thinking and feeling, certainly our emotions (shortcut guides to action) as much as our cognitions. We learn a great deal at our mother's knee, but quite a lot as well from the bullies in the playground, the friends we forge into small support groups bonded by totally arbitrary chants, games, rivalries, fun, fear, moments of shared joy or fright. The memes cultivated by machinery orchestrating this self-becoming wax and wane, struggle inside each head for dominance or at least compatibility, carve up the mind-space into kingdoms, satrapies and small cozy nooks, often run on quite contrary principles but getting on grudgingly for the sake of going on.

For nearly all kids, the memeplex, the megameme, the megatext of magical fantasy, and sometimes its recent offshoot science fiction, is a serious builder of the landscape of the emerging mind and personality. Frequently derided by adults who have forgotten its tremendously exciting lure, its unrivaled satisfactions to a child suffocating in powerlessness and complexity, it can stamp a susceptible mind with an imprint so profound that one's life is altered forever. In the most extreme cases, almost impossible to dislodge or cure, the infection leads to a lifelong devotion to fantasy and science fiction, and in its most virulent form to the overwhelming desire to *create worlds* in this mimetic arena of the mind.

That happened to me. I'm here to testify, brothers and sisters. And I'm not ashamed! Well, only a little bit. Even in this age where two out of three massively expensive movie or computer games are based on science fiction or fantasy notions, characters, settings and tropes, I have the sense that sf fans are still despised as *geeks* or *nerds* or *anoraks* or *otaku* (and it must be admitted that many are bulgy card-carrying members of the Asperger's community, although I thought it was regarded as uncouth these days to make easy fun of people for their quirks).

In any event, it is not an easy task to ascend the mountain of science fiction writing, and has been growing more difficult for at least two generations, since the fabled Golden Age of the late Forties and early Fifties brought a certain rigor to the craft. Like acquiring any strange language with its idiosyncratic grammar and vocabulary, learning to appreciate science fiction, in particular, is hard work, but luckily most enthusiasts acquire the necessary reading skills in childhood or early adolescence when our brains are still plastic, resilient and hungry. We ducked our homework to swim deliriously against sf's shocks and buffets, not realizing that it took as much effort as memorizing stanzas of Middle English poems or tricky feats of algebra—even if it sometimes invoked both.

Above all else, sf was *fun*.

Teaching yourself to *create* sf—at any rate, the kind other people will sit still to read and perhaps even pay for—is much, much harder. I dragged my first awful novel out of me, week after week, at the rate of about half a page a day, stopping now and then to write a men's magazine article to put food on the table. Unlike physiological phenotypic evolution, which built our basic bodies and brains by climbing torturously and tortuously up Dawkins' Mount Improbable, scaling the face of science fiction means venturing upon the even more threatening heights of Mount Implausible.

The very subject matter of these fictions is, strictly speaking, unbelievable. Has anyone ventured into the future yet? No, except for the brief span of a single unfinished lifetime, and at the same rate as everyone else. Do we have any prospect of meeting up with stern, battle-trained members of the Time Patrol or the profound psycho-historic thinkers of the Galactic Empire? No, not unless UFOs really are time machines from Zeta Reticuli or the Singularity. Can we read minds or the future? Well, a little, and blurrily, if the findings of parapsychology are valid, but we won't be seeing teleporting criminals or law enforcement precogs soon, unless what I learn from the former operatives of CIA's Star Gate program is just the disinformation face of the military paranormal.

So sf is the literature of sheer, if disciplined, imagination, of the rationalized absurd, of metaphor embodied in a kind of *faux* naturalism under the sign of science. It is the imagination of Mount Implausible.

I wanted to clamber up there and hack my own name into the pinnacle, alongside Clarke and Le Guin and Russ and Brackett and Dick and Heinlein and all the others who lived in that high place.

☼

Isaac Asimov published a book of his early fiction, *The Early Asimov,* with the subtitle "Eleven Years of Trying." Even this future Grand Master, with his ingenious if somewhat wooden early contributions of Golden Age science fiction ("Nightfall"! Positronic robots and their Three Laws! The Foundation!), took his time attaining mastery of the mode. Don't suppose that even with these brilliant mentors lighting the trail ahead it took me less time than that. In my case it was more like a decade and a half of trying, after my first brief attempts made it into print. But I did learn, step by small step, and I retrace that path here for the amusement and, perhaps, I hope, the instruction of readers who wondered how you went about *starting to be an sf writer*. The answer, as any successful scribbler will tell you, is to write, and write, and write, and read, and read, and read, and do as many interesting things as you can in the company of people you love (with luck) and observe it all with a cool, playful but reserved part of your meme machine, your writerly heart, your cannibal soul.

So I trace some of the byways I pursued, here in the real world where you need to make a dollar to survive, up the craggy and minatory face of Mount Implausible. Follow me, if you will, and I hope you don't grow discouraged, or fall off, pitons flying, because it all works out quite well. Surely, though, I cannot ask you to trudge directly into my beginnings, that would be too disheartening. So I start with my most recent published tale in *Asimov's*, "Dead Air" (funny, I hope, and horrifying as well), a tribute story to the genius of Philip K. Dick, the crazy, madly fluent, exciting, hilarious emblem of today's twin worlds of science fiction: the high literary landscape of postmodernism (he is immortalized in several volumes of the prestigious Library of America, publishers of Tom Paine, Thomas Jefferson and Philip Roth) and the mass mind of gaudy sci-fi (half the movies in the genre still seem to bear his mark, even if, after *Bladerunner,* hardly ever with much fidelity to his spirit). I lead you, then, up the long ascent to a kind of artistry, I hope, and close with a *jeu d'esprit*, "Cockroach Love," written in 2008 with an American pal, Paul Di Filippo, one of Phil Dick's natural sons (as it were). A long strange trip indeed, climbing Mount Implausible toward the stars and galaxies that await the children of the children of Mount Improbable and even, who knows, some of *us*, if the Singularity comes in time, Lord willing and the crick don't rise.

# DEAD AIR

## (2010)

Jive Bolen exited his cramped office inside the two hundred story zeugma complex in the heart of nouveau Manhattan. Summer's noon sun was a blurry disk high overhead, easily visible even through the crowding skyscrapers. The size of a ten dollar coin at arm's length. Or so he'd read in the paper during morning coffee break, hoping to ferret out some lively snippet to throw into his next abortive conversation with Jolene, the building's peripatetic Vogelsängerin, with whom he had been desperately smitten for at least the last four thwarted months. Jive fished a coin from his pouch pocket and held it up. Not quite; the frayed edges of the immense nanotech-spun soletta, stationed out at Earth-Sun L1, extended like a reddish ghost corona beyond the rim of the plastic currency unit. The literal meaning of his ghost analogy stung Jive somewhere in his cerebellum a moment too late to repress it. Shuddering, he folded the coin back into his pouch.

Something rushed directly above him. The sort of uncanny buffeting rush of air, it seemed to him in a vivid recollection from childhood, that a falling ten-ton safe creates in a toon as it tumbles from a high window to flatten a furious two-dimensional and villainous puddytat. In disbelief, Jive glanced up past the rim of his Brooks Brothers tropical pith helmet. By the living lord Harry, it *was* a safe plunging toward him, or a plausible simulation. No, light winked from the front of the thing. Leaping back, terrified, Jive tripped on the curb, fell full length. With a splintering detonation, the thing flew apart into shards of broken glass, trailing wires, microcircuitry from the previous century, plywood and tasteless veneer. Another damned TV set, hurled from an upper window by a cit driven to despair.

Jive scrambled to his feet, retreated, lifted his eyes again. A moment later something long and large with flapping limbs flailed down to slam atop the fractured television receiver. The soggy crump of flesh striking concrete, the spatter of blood, twisted Jive Bolen's mouth in disgust. He felt a sort of remote sympathy. Another day, another 'ratische Augen, as the Kraut socialists dubbed them. Square eyes. Mort victims of the visible dead, supposedly. Kind of ironic.

A siren was already sounding as a mortuary truckee, alerted by gossipgrrl watch, raced to claim the corpse. Jive shrugged, settled his hat about his ears. Mortuarian was a job, distasteful or not. It was a living—and there was another *soupçon* of irony. A more socially useful job, he reproved himself, than his own dead-end post with Industrie Globalisierung, AG. Day after oppressive day, representing the shareholders on the board of management oversight, his nominal post with the Aktiengesellschaft, seemed ever more meaningless. A political contrivance. Even if it paid the bills for himself and Aunt Tilly, god bless her, and his damned wife and the kids off on the far side of the continent in Orange county. Camouflage is what it is, though, he thought, for the great owners whose blocks of stock overwhelmed the protest votes of all the small stakeholders. In effect, he was a mere stalking horse for corporate greed.

Stepping around the corner, with some difficulty putting the corpse from his mind, he bought a liverwurst brat snacker from a sidewalk multimat. Jive consoled himself with the reflection that without such immense and unthinkable concentrations of wealth and power, the sun-blocker could never have been emplaced in orbit between Earth and Sun, mitigating the greenhouse threat that would have wiped 92 percent all surface life from the globe within a mere thousand years. According to petacomp spreadsheet calculations, at any rate. Even though they had been known, historically, to be wrong.

He hurried along Eighth Avenue, munching his sliver, and had disposed of the degradable wrapping before he recalled that he was meant to be meeting Delphine for luncheon at the Quick Brown Pig, given five full stars by Eric in the *Times* Eats Guide. These days, since the divorce, his wife worked for the Consumer Advocacy and spent a day each month at the New York offices of Rand Nader. Probably she gets to eat free at the Pig, he thought morosely, but Del will insist on my paying for us both anyway, as if I'm not already squandering danegelt on alimony and school fees. His homeowatch peeped from his wrist, reminding him belatedly and uselessly of the lunch date. Fool of a thing, its programming bollixed by the same virus that had munged all the music records in the world except for those CDs carefully wrapped and hoarded by a few thrifty collectors like himself. Could that, he thought, abruptly wildly excited, be the doorway to Jolene's singing heart? Did he dare risk humiliation, and the possible emetic degradation of his slender CD hoard?

A lovely young Chinese woman in clinging neck to heel sharkskin cheongsam bowed as he entered the dim luncheon palace. He checked his pith helmet, took a slip. With a hush of tiny slippered steps, she led him directly to an alcove where Delphine sat forward pertly, sipping an alcohol-free Manhattan and reading her own homeowatch. It projected a display directly onto her retinas, which danced like running lights in the lowered illumination of the booth. Jive slid in on the other side of the classic sparkly Formica eating bench, hearing the genuine red leather creak under his buttocks.

"Sorry I'm late."

"Oh, hi. That's all right, Jive. I had some research to catch up on before the plenary this afternoon." Del switched off her data feed and looked at him, perfectly relaxed. She wore a pillbox hat spun from Martian crab grass, which flourished only under the light of the twin hurtling moons of the red planet. He had given her that hat as a Kwanzaa gift two years ago, as their marriage took its final dive into the dumpster. Was this her notion of conciliation, or a final turn of the knife in his spine? "And how's dear Auntie Tilly?"

"Matilda's about as well as can be expected," he said. "Morbid, actually. She's got her nose stuck in that damned old TV set my Poppa gave her for her twenty-first birthday, the one he found on the curb and fixed up with vacuum tubes he scrounged heaven knows where."

"They're the best for picking up the thays, those old ones, I hear," Delphine said absently. "I have to say, the children are still obsessed by it as well, although I notice you don't ask after them. I have to—"

"The children!" Jive said, voice roughening. "What the hell's wrong with those kids? They won't answer emails, their IM messages are totally incomprehensible, they *refuse* to pick up when I phone them."

"For heaven's sake, don't exaggerate. At their age—"

"Ex*agg*erate! Watch and learn!" He keyed the virtual board of his homeowatch, fastclicking his children's phones. The holographic privacy display showed an instant red, with the words: NOT AVAILABLE AT THIS TIME. PLEASE LEAVE A MESSAGE, OR TRY AGAIN

LATER. He turned his wrist so his former wife could witness his humiliation.

"Jevon, you're losing your bearings. It's three hours earlier on the left coast. The kids are both at morning class. You know full well they're not allowed to use the access during scholastic hours."

Deflated, Jive shook his head and reached for the menu. He wasn't hungry; the brat sat in his guts like lead. I will be conciliatory, he decided. Isn't that alleged to be one of my prime work-related skills? Isn't conciliation the doctrine of Sister Grace of Magdalene, pastor of his house of worship, the Wee Baptist Kirk i' the Glen (Scottish Rite)? To the slash-eyed lovely waitron, he said, "Get me a real Manhattan. And whatever my wife...the lady is drinking, get her another. What would you like to eat, Delphine?"

"I ordered en route. You really should eat something if you're going to drink—"

"Why do you let them watch that crap?" he asked vituperatively. "They should have their heads down to their books."

"Jive, Angelina is eight and Barack is only five, let them enjoy a bit of childhood before you start cramming—"

He slammed his fist on the table, making the cut-glass soy dispenser jump. "Watching alleged dead people is *enjoying childhood?* Christ, you're an intelligent, educated woman, Delphine, you must know it's just a barrage of vicious propaganda beamed down on the cit sats from those goddamned *Chinese*—"

Showing her perfect white teeth, Delphine hissed, "Lower your damned voice, you oaf. In case you hadn't noticed—"

Faces had turned their way, hiding shock behind bland contempt. The waitron stood with their drinks.

"I didn't mean.... Oh, please, just put them down." He gestured to the great acrylic patriotic flag above them, pinned to the four corners of the room, fifty white stars on deep sky-blue, three more blue stars clinging at the inner edge of the top white stripes: New Zealand, Australia, Taiwan. "I know *these* Chinese are our loyal allies, our fellow *citizens,* but it's obvious to anyone with his damned ear to the ground that these...these fake *dead* people are a plot to undermine the confidence of our nation. I'm *insulted,* Delphine. It's *our* people they are targeting especially, you know that, the Chinese think we're still a damned superstitious bunch of primitive jungle...."

"Shut *up,* you fool." His wife was on her feet, seething yet containing her fury. Holding her handbag against her breast, she said,

"You can get the check. I should have known better. And give the kids a call at a time when it suits them, not you."

His head had started throbbing. He threw back the Manhattan, coughed. To the impassive waitron, he said, "Get me another. And a soluble ginseng antacid."

His head echoed like a jug kicked by a steel-tipped boot. Ensconced again in the refitted storage room that was his office, Jive Bolen groaned. He was drinking too much. Two Manhattans on a stomach with nothing in it but a brat sliver, it was self-destructive. His tongue rolled again and again against his lips, trying to dispel the over-sweet taste of cherry and burned orange peel. He noticed what he was doing, and recoiled in disgust. This was the tic that had disfigured poor Gran Bolen as she subsided inch by inch toward the grave. Tardive dyskinesia, the medically induced disorder of the nervous system inflicted by early-generation antipsychotic drugs, those barbarously crude neuroleptics such as metoclopramide. Induced supersensitivity to dopamine in the nigrostrial pathway, damaging the D2 dopamine receptor. Or so he'd been told by the apologetic physician who finally had changed the old lady's regimen, but too late, far too late. She had thought to see the dead, Jive recalled, with a shudder. Her erratic thought disorders, that late turn to Buddhism, to the belief in the Bardo Thodol and afterlife demons. As if the word of the Lord Saviour were not enough.

He fumbled off a cap of cuffee, heard the hiss as it self-heated, drank it down with a trembling hand. What's wrong with me? he wondered. It's this damned cramped work space, he thought, staring peevishly at the wall to his right, the racks of classic Barbie dolls still in their virginal packaging.

Without knocking, his Uzbek secretary, Hammerlock Ganji, poked his head around the door jamb. "Christ, you look terrible, chief. You're drinking too much."

"Shut up," Jive said. He took another swig, but the cap was empty. The foul taste of the synthetic lingered on his lips, and he felt his tongue once again begin its bovine rotation. "It's these quarters, Ganj. Undignified for a man of my station."

Neither said anything further; it was simply a fact of life that in these straitened times the great multinational corps must impose the most severe restrictions on their senior factors, and be seen to do so. Ganji entered the office, squeezed past Jive's desk, stood examining, as he often did, with a perfervid fascination, the fantastically-expensive collectible Barbara Millicent Roberts manikins in their plastic and cardboard cages. There was not a single Ken mounted on the wall.

"You need cheering up," Hammerlock said at length. His eyes darted back again to the dolls in their pristine boxes. If one of them ever went missing, which was unlikely given the covert security features in situ, Jive would know where to turn.

"I hear Jolene is in the building. I'll have her drop by. A professional call," he said hastily. "It's part of the building code, as you know, Chief."

"If you wish," Jive said, foraging ostentatiously in a pile of hard-copy documents. "Go away now, I'm busy."

It could only have been ten minutes later when he heard her cheerful birdsong soprano carol his name at the open door.

"I told my secretary I'm too busy for therapeutic melody today," he said gruffly.

"Never too hectic for a heart-filling tune, I hope," she said, and perched herself on the edge of his desk. "What's it to be? Cole Porter? Wit *and* a jaunty air. Something from the Beatles collection? I love 'Here Comes the Sun,' although people have gone off it, and I suppose we mustn't blame them."

"'Come again,'" said Jive, decisively. Jolene had the power and sweetness of a young Linda Ronstadt, it was possible that she could meet the demands of Dowland. If she knew his work.

"Come again?" she said, grinning.

"It needs a lutenist to accompany the lyrics," Jive told her. "John Dowland? Turn of the seventeenth century?"

"Sorry."

"It's the most perfect music I've ever heard." He cleared his throat and sang, well enough to convey the tune, if not much more, reverberant in the small office, "Thy graces that refrain, To do me due delight." He took a deeper breath, knowing how it should be done, even if it was beyond his capacity to build the energy across the octave, note by note, phrase by phrase, to a gently controlled crescendo and release conveying the doomed sense of one long, last breath, one sigh: "To see, to hear, To touch, to kiss, To die...." His baritone broke, and shamefacedly he finished, in a growl, "With thee again, In sweetest sympathy."

The young woman was thunderstruck.

"Oh, Mr. Bolen, that's just...that's— Beautiful. Is there a recording...?"

Jive gazed at her, refreshed, his headache eased. "As a matter of fact, I have probably the last uncorrupted CD pressing of Sarah Brightman and Andrea Bocelli singing the duet. One of the last Deutsche Grammophon Gesellschaft releases before the emetic plague erased— Do you think you'd care to visit my apt and hear it on my classic eMachines CD player?"

Instead of answering, she sang the fragment back to him, with luscious honeyed fragrance, effortlessly soaring. He felt his eyes dampen.

"It's about the thays, that song," she told him guilelessly. "To die again. I wonder how that composer knew, so long ago? In sweetest sympathy. Although they don't look terribly happy."

Jive frowned.

"You're not, I hope, speaking of—"

"Did you see Leno & Letterman last night? It was hilarious. They had the top ten thays, you know, live feeds from viewers' homes."

"Don't call them that. It's all a vicious—"

"Oh, but they *are* disconnected thetans, it's been scientifically proved." Sweet Jesus, Jive realized, she's a 'tologist. Probably second or third generation. But no more eccentric, he decided, than a Mormon or a Moonie. She leaned forward, and light gleamed below her throat, at the open neck of her bright daffodil-yellow blouse. In that moment, he felt entirely prepared to overlook her 'tology belief structure, even forgive the golden—or gold-plated—icon nestled in Jolene's small ripe cleavage. The icon, he noticed suddenly, hung from a fine gold chain linked to a pair of bolts in the saint's neck. Like those terrible old Frankenstein movies. Out burst a guffaw. After a moment of uncertainty, the friendly smile was gone from her face.

"What."

Oh Christ. Risk everything on one wild throw of the die? What the heck. The thick Germanic neck of the iconic Church bust (speaking of busts) was turned outward, its coarse features nuzzling at her. "I couldn't help notice where your Divine Founder has his face buried," he said jovially. "If a man was ambitious, he might hope...." He trailed off.

The sängerin stared at him, speechless. Then a hesitant smile. A shudder of relief jolted through him. Where innocent ribaldry entered freely, soon more joyful bawdry might follow.

"Hey!" she said, then, suddenly frowning. "Are you mocking my faith?"

Jive shook his head piously. "I wouldn't dream of it, darling."

☼

Inside the cosy plastic-shelled condo apartment high above what had once been the Hudson River and was now a stack of mighty water-pumping carbonoid pipes buried below the condo struts, he found Aunt Tilly eating a boiled Raptosaurus egg from both ends. The edible DNA-recovered commercial product rolled unsteadily on her blue-etched dining plate, spilling white albumen and deep orange yolk on the tablecloth. The dignified old lady, dressed formally for dinner in moth-ball reeking black and white, kept her eyes fixed on his near-wall-sized HDTV display. At her hand, the remote shined its merry red activation light. On the screen, a morose peasant face of Asian mien gazed out hopelessly at them both. Others wandered in the ill-defined monotone background, as if peering in at the living-dining quadrant, shaking their heads, moving on. Damn it, he thought, my half senile charge has changed the channel again in my absence. He had warned her repeatedly. Maybe he needed to invoke a Parental Warning lock-down code. But, to his chagrin, he realized that he did not know how to do that.

He picked up the remote, fiddled with it impotently. He changed the channel to a repeat of *Baywatch,* but, to his fury, the fully electronic selector switched it back. The Chinese civ sat radiations, he thought indignantly; they've hijacked my HDTV digital set. Swearing under his breath, he switched it off. Tilly moaned, looked reproachfully at him. She had yolk smeared over the bright red clown's mouth of her lip gloss. In his hand, without his intervention, the red pilot light flashed on again. The screen filled with its voiceless parade of woe.

He threw the useless piece of junk down on the table, and went to the small kitchen sink to find a wash cloth. The newscasts were correct, then. Not just the old pre-digital sets were vulnerable, though they provided the best registration of the images, apparently. Any set with a remote-control was now susceptible to manipulation by these spurious dead, or more properly their Potempkin-style manipulators, who channeljacked it instantly to their interface feed.

Creating the impression, at least in the gullible, of departed souls searching endlessly for the living they had left behind.

It was more than he could take. Jive threw the dampened cloth down into the sink, left Tilly dully viewing the propaganda, and went into his bedroom. Behind a matched, leather-bound set of the

*Left Behind* novels Tilly had given him four or five birthdays ago, before her deterioration had proceeded to its current sorry state, he found a half-empty bottle of Jack Daniel's. He uncapped it, entered the half bath alcove, poured a healthy slug into his tooth glass.

I have to stop drinking, he told himself, feeling the burn. After a time, though, his depression faded away. An image of that lovely little birdsongstress filled his heart with growing elation. He'd have to dispose of Tilly for the evening. Maybe the two middle-aged ladies on the floor above, a long-term lesbian couple if he recognized the signs, would look after the senile old thing for the night. He couldn't imagine that they'd take any liberties. Not, at any rate, the kind he planned for Jolene. He wondered idly if the girl had a surname. Must have, stood to reason. Social Security stamp, the whole ID apparatus. Christ, really it didn't matter. He poured another shot.

> "Sweet love doth now invite,
> "Thy graces that refrain
> "To do me due delight,"

sang Ms. Brightman's simulated voice, admittedly not representative of her peak but glorious still. Jolene sat decorously on the edge of his large formerly marital bed—he'd cunningly moved the CD apparatus out of the living room and into more congenial surrounds—and listened intently. Her eyes, he was happy to see, shone. As the next verse began, she read ahead from the printout he'd prepared, and sang in perfect counterpoint to Bocelli:

> "Come again,
> "That I may cease to mourn
> "Through thy unkind disdain
> "For now left and forlorn."

He might as well have not been in the room. Song was her passion, that and her oddball faith. But now, after that heartbreaking pause, she turned her eyes on him and sang with the two reconstructed voices, male and female:

> "I sit, I sigh,
> "I weep, I faint,
> "I die, in deadly pain

"And endless misery...."

Her eyes were bright with pain.

Perhaps, Jive thought, too late, this was not the best choice of song for a seduction. But the ravishing beauty of her voice, so much richer in this room, singing these old words, was so much more enthralling than in the light ditties she cast upon the conditioned air of the zeugma structure where they worked. He waited, spellbound but sorrowing, as she sang the rest of the verses.

"Deadly pain and endless misery," she said, finally. "That's what the thays are showing us." She clutched hopelessly at her pendant icon, and burst into tears.

He packed away his precious, irreplaceable recording while she visited the bathroom, and then, trying to hide his irritation and painful sexual arousal, escorted her home.

Jive was half in the bag as he slipped a farecard across the turnstile and joined what seemed a substantial proportion of steaming, sweating New York on the 50th Street subway platform. Why didn't I get a cab? he asked himself. Is this my pathetic way of punishing myself? Is my thalamic function overriding my essentially sane frontal brain, driving me into some sort of deliberate confrontation with the world of the Arbeitnehmer, the common workers I'm meant to be representing? He squeezed his eyes shut against the buffeting of the train as it pulled in to the station, grit and oil-scented air flying up like some Biblical plague of insects. He was jostled getting aboard, and held his tropical helmet with one hand as his homey popped on and reminded him in its high-pitched child's voice that he had an appointment at two, with the engineers at the new Thane of Cawdor thanatorium labs. He snapped the homeowatch off with a grunt. Fool thing, where the heck did it think he was headed on this damned crowded train? And what did the idiots at Industrie Globalisierung, AG, think they were doing, sending him to oversee the so-called findings of this bunch of palpable crackpots?

They sped under old Manhattan. The conditioning was on the fritz, hardly unusual. Imagine how life would be without the soletta, he thought. If this was actually the true greenhouse effect everyone was suffering, rather than an attenuated, sunlight-blocked ghost of— He caught his own thought again, snarled at himself. Those things, those mechanical interruptions on the screen, they were not ghosts, not the dead. It was a filthy political stunt, a sort of techno-brainwashing. No matter what foolish Tilly maintained, glued hour after hour in her darkened room, anxiously watching the dead, as she supposed them to be, marching behind her cathode ray tube, peering out, gesturing, their mouths moving silently.

Jesus, wasn't it obvious? Whatever that dear little professional virgin Vogelsängerin believed. Most of them must be Chinese actors, you could tell at a glance. In those tasteless Mao suits, or old fashioned wrapping of one kind or another. Or Indians, not redskins, dark featured and gaunt from the Indian subcontinent, or Pakistan, or Bali, or whatever. A fashion show of faux-starved mummies from hell. He shuddered, rocking as the train thudded over tracks loosely fixed to sleepers unrepaired for years. Every spare cent was required for the big boosters shoving up the materiel to spin the soletta into being, there at the Lagrange libration point 900 thousand miles from Earth. That, or the planet would be roasted. Not immediately, true—but in another millennium. Was that why the dead were suddenly hanging about, shoving their damned stupid faces into people's prime time viewing—

Jive caught himself with an audible obscenity.

"No call for that language, sir," a young blonde mother said, rebuking him with a scowl as she turned her child away.

Apologize? Damn it, no. He was furious with himself, with the way he'd allowed the absurd obsessions of gullible people to draw his unconscious into betraying what he knew for a fact. The train was pulling into Brooklyn; he pushed his way to the door. One consolation: if he'd taken a cab he'd have been cooler, yes, and the ride smoother, but he'd still be trapped somewhere in traffic-lock, probably.

The so-called thanatorium was walking distance from High Street station. His headache was easing, and his dyspepsia.

A long-jawed, raw-boned specimen in a stained lab coat introduced him, the head of engineering, Dr. Samuels. Bart Samuels asked him to say a few preparatory words on behalf the oversight entity of their funding body.

"Very well, gentlemen. And lady," Jive told the assembled nerds and geeks in the traditional garb of their professions or trades. "Let me make one thing clear. I don't want to hear any claptrap—and I believe I speak for the Aktiengesellschaft in saying this—about discarnate souls, or crossovers, or unnucleated thetans." The nerds lounged as if they were taking an authorized anti-stress break, sucking their Prozac spansules, and stared at him without interest, dully. The one woman scientist or engineer actually rolled her eyes. Then, to his disbelief, she poked out her tongue, not at him but for her own entertainment, rolled it as well, and stared cross-eyed at its purplish tip. This was impudence beyond his capacity to cope. He took his seat abruptly, turning his back on most of them. Samuels signalled a bored audiovisual geek to activate the bank of some twenty antique television receivers arrayed like something out of the Apollo project command room three-quarters of a century earlier.

The screens took an agonizingly long moment to come alive, as tubes warmed and electrons skittered about inside magnetic fields. One by one, then, the gray screens lit up with images: two repeats of *I Love Lucy* and one of *Gunsmoke*, broadcast on the free-to-view channels, and a maddening diorama of meaningless, unscripted, silently parading men, woman and children. The Family of Man, Jive told himself, half-hysterically, recalling a book his Grandma had loved and made him leaf through every time he and his sisters visited her in the nursing home. Gone these two score years, God bless her. And here were the same faces of every nation, peering out into the drab humming, shuffling and rustling of the ad hoc, modified media lab.

One of the nerds came forward to a podium. "We've had trained law enforcement lip readers examine the images, Mr. Bolen," he said in a bored, impudent tone. "Most of them are speaking Mandarin, Cantonese and dialectal variants. There's an admixture of other major languages, of course including German, Arabic, English, French, Spanish—"

"Chinese, you say!" Jive cried.

"They seem to be lost and looking for their families. The popular rumour that they are so-called 'thays' or thetans is not borne out by synoptic analysis of the recorded utterances to date. The more articulate among their number are asking for our aid, the assistance of living scientists. Hence this briefing. We are not authorized to—"

"Aid? Aid? Crap! A scheme to divert our remaining resources to ideological lunatics who wish to see the planet's climate disrupted, to their own sectional advantage." Although what benefit could accrue to anyone other than the Inuits he couldn't imagine. Least of all those closer to the tropics.

"Sir, we do have a few ideas about what's causing this manifestation," said Bart Samuels. "It seems likely that the soletta structure is intercepting or even enhancing insolation in the cerebral theta range. Despite racist rumours of a geopolitical flavour—"

Jive cut him off. "Listen, don't give me no moralizing hocus-pocus and run-around," he said angrily, remaining seated but raising his voice so nobody in the room would miss his import. "Three weeks ago, I saw a man throw himself from a ten story window, driven to desperation by these preposterous...*things.*" He flung one hand at the screens. "First he'd torn his TV set off the wall, and thrown it into the street, where the goddamned thing nearly killed me. Then he jumped after it, and did kill himself. This is not a new furtive viral advertising campaign. It is not a political ploy by some misguided faction of the American *Unterschicht* or *sotto classe.*"

He rose, faced the useless pointy-headed drones, then looked back up in rage at the drifting images of despair. If what the screen displayed was truly hell, or some other version of the afterlife, as Tilly and Jolene claimed, it undercut everything a man could believe, could work toward in his career. How could you bring children into a world if this abomination was their destiny? "*No,*" he roared, with the deep-throated power of a Baptist choir baritone. "A fraud! These are computer-generated engrams projected into our living rooms on stolen citizen satellite channels by the Chinese national zaibatsus. Or, if not them, revanchists in the Saudi peninsula. They can't be...." His voice drained away, suddenly, as an image caught his eye. Bile rose in his throat. "Oh my dear god. Granny Bolen? Can that be you?"

An old woman's face peered down at him from the closest orthicon tube display, and in a series of snapping jumps copied itself across all of the banked monitors. The muted mutter of Desi Arnaz and James Arness were wiped away. Jive Bolen stared up at his dead grandmother who looked back in terror at him from twenty gray windows. Her wrinkled hands pressed the inner edges of the screens, and her mouth moved, again and again, in a sort of voiceless screaming supplication. Jive felt his own lips mimic the movements of her mute mouth. *Help me*, he mouthed back, mirroring her cry. *Get me out of here, little Jevon.* Aloud, Jive said, softly, "Help me." Tears ran down his cheeks.

Hammerlock Ganji reached Jive on his phone as he waited impatiently in the research thanatorium lobby for his cab back to the city.

"You're better off waiting there until things calm down, chief," the secretary told him, licking lips nervously.

"Tarry in Brooklyn? Don't be absurd, Ganji." A small red gypsy cab pulled up outside the plate glass lobby. God, is that what we've sunk to now, in our effort to attain a low fiscal profile? Through the dirty vehicle window he saw a villainous wild-haired import from Turkestan or points farther east apparently shouting into an old-fashioned mic with a helical cable. A moment later the cool receptionist crossed the carpet and murmured that his ride awaited. Jive gave her a reflex smile and nod, and went out into the soletta-muted sunlight. A disturbing tang hung in the air. Wood smoke? He coughed, suddenly. Something more toxic than that.

"Get in, mister, you want a ride," the dryback driver told him, pushing the passenger door open from the inside. "We gotta move fast, before anyone catches on we're coming from this science place."

"What?" Jive had no chance to buckle in before the cabbie took off with a screech. They tore through a small crowd of scowling citizens who loitered at the gates of the lab. What the hell? There was a thud, and another. "For the love of sweet Harry," he cried, "those fools are throwing *rocks* at you."

"Not me, professor—you." He gunned the little car's hybrid engine, flung it onto the feeder to the bridge. Jive ducked his tall head, wound down the filthy window. Streamers and pillars of smoke were slowly drifting upward from the Manhattan skyline, billowing into the damaged sunlight. "Blogs are saying kill all scientists."

"I'm not a scientist, I'm a...a high-status administrator." For some reason, saying so made Jive Bolen feel profoundly ashamed. "It's part of my duties to oversee the efforts of bona-fide researchers in the domain of—" He broke off. "Christ, why am I explaining myself to a gypsy hack? Just get me to the zeugma, and step on it."

His homeowatch and phone were both peeping; he shifted his mind into high, concentrated gear. A thudding racket ahead pulled up his head. A laden moving van had ploughed into two or three cars illegally stopped at the edge of the feeder. The 'stanner cursed or prayed vehemently, perhaps in the name of Allah, and jerked them to one side, skidding past the pile-up. God almighty, men stood by the side of the road with rifles and shotguns. The windscreen starred; the side window shattered, fell in fragments. Ganji said, faintly, like a voice of conscience, "Bolen, the thays want all the scientists dead. The streets are clogged with crazies who agree with them. Just get the hell off the road and lay low for a—"

Impact jarred his teeth. The door beside him sprang open, and Jive tumbled bruisingly to the road surface. Pain tore up his right arm as his hand broke at the wrist. He lost consciousness. The pain was gone. He lay in the silent, empty street for minutes or hours, passing in and out of clarity. People were moving past him. Nobody stopped to help. The damn world's gone mad, he told himself. It's been a powder keg ready to go bang ever since the hothouse shock really struck home, when we realized we need to spend every penny the world makes putting up that shield in space. And Christ knows what that's done, in addition. He seemed for a moment to be back in the Wee Kirk i' the Glen, hearing obese, powerful Sister Mary Magdalene belt out the verses of "God of Earth and Outer Space," that sprightly Baptist hymnal entry by the Welshman Joseph Parry. He smiled in the gray twilight. A lot they knew about outer space back then, in the nineteenth century. Sister Mary powered away as he piped along in the choir, with his sisters singing lustily. Where are they, he asked himself. Where are my sisters? At length Jive stumbled to his feet, holding his brutalized right arm tenderly with his left hand against his breast. Now that he was home again, he could get it looked at by competent medical practitioners. After that terrible near-accident, escaping from it shakily, stumbling inside his apt, he found Aunt Tilly absent. Of course, she was staying for several days upstairs with those pleasant dykes. A nice couple, for all their gene-reproductive dysfunction. He walked through the house, and with increasing alarm found that his wife and children were also gone. Plaintively, he called their names. "Angelina, where are you, honeypie? Barack, you scamp? Come out, come out." Silence, and the rustle of strangers inside his home. "Delphine, you bitch!" He found himself on the ground floor and wandered in the smoke-filled streets. Others were drifting along as if dazed, staring into windows, some in the middle of the streets. Why was the traffic stalled? Someone caught his sleeve, spoke urgently, but he couldn't seem to hear the man's voice. The man raised a crudely wrought sign, rendered in thick black marker pen ink on the back, evidently, of an advertising poster: SEND THE SEINTISTS OVER, THEY HAV 2 HELP US. A flicker of motion caught his eye, reflected in the side window of a motionless Hyundai sedan. Behind the curved window, half-seen, the driver sat, listening to his phone. Reflected in the glass, faces passed, jumbled and unfamiliar. Terrified, Jive shook his head in denial. He sat edgily in his favourite armchair, activated the HDTV to distract himself and settle his nerves. The machine wasn't working right. A new emetic virus attack? His daughter's monochrome face contorted in the wide frame of the image. He lumbered to his feet, went to the out-of-order plasma image. The child rushed away behind the screen and returned with his wife and son, who peered in apparent horror at the camera. When was this home movie shot? He couldn't recall. Where is Tilly? In the monochrome, silent background, he watched Delphine turn her head, walk with her head clasped in her hands like a white-face mime doing an impression of Edvard Munch's *The Scream*. Gentle love, he thought absurdly, recalling Dowland, Draw forth thy wounding dart. She opened the front door. Upheaval in the background, black and white gouts of flame and smoke. People were running, striking each other. Two cops stood, hats in hand, unhappy, bearing bad news Jive Bolen could not bear to hear.

*TO PHIL'S MEMORY, OF COURSE*

# THE FIRST STEPS UP
# MOUNT IMPLAUSIBLE

You might say that I was bushwhacked or "blackbirded" at the age of fifteen, although with the best of intentions.

I was the eldest of eventually six surviving children born to toolmaker Frank and housewife Betty (Pamela Beatrix) in what was then the raw new working class outer Melbourne suburb of Reservoir. My mother's family, the Bartels, were a bit better off than working class, and she'd gone to the moderately upmarket Catholic Ladies College (CLC), where she'd become head prefect and perhaps founding editor of the school magazine *Caritas*, which I believe she named (launching a tradition I would continue elsewhere). Betty was born in 1920 and in the late 1930s dropped out of university, where she was studying to be a teacher, at the end of her first year. My father, three years older, was as a young man a sports fan and parish tennis player who'd left school at fifteen during the Great Depression. (He said his entire class, or perhaps year, was deliberately failed, to relieve pressure on the education system or perhaps the work force.) They met, I gather, when they worked together in a factory making munitions or the devices for measuring the devices that made munitions. Frank was in a "reserved occupation" and never saw combat or any sort of military training or service. Even so, I suppose that makes me a war baby.

I had some tiresome physical defects as a child—one eye never worked properly, after a squint repair in infancy, and I suffered fairly badly from asthma, for which there were then no effective drugs. In 1950, when I was five years old, nearly six, my tonsils were removed at a small hospital several miles from home, reached in the rain on my father's bicycle (he never learned to drive, and in those days couldn't have afforded a car). This was the depths of the polio scare, with one sad infected child after another being clapped into "iron lungs," potentially for the rest of their lives. I managed to evade polio (unlike my luckless friend John Foyster, and my guru Sir Arthur C. Clarke), and caught rheumatic fever instead, a streptococcus inflammation of the heart that leaves you with a murmur and an enhanced chance of further infection and earlyish death. Still a matter of concern as my aging body inexorably loses its recuperative zing.

I was exiled for what seemed rather a long time to the Royal Children's Hospital for observation, and then dispatched to the farther ends of Melbourne, hours away by train for my overstretched parents (so I rarely saw them), to a convalescent hospital. Weeks of boredom and terror ensued. I had my sixth birthday there, and a miserable time was had by all, except for the older boy patients who (according to my uncomprehending reports to my aghast and perhaps disbelieving mother) spent many happy hours buggering each other. I was moved to another room, where I invented the movie projector, inveigling a nurse into providing me with a long strip of translucent greased paper (on which I drew a series of stick figure frames), a bare light bulb on an extension cord shining into a used cardboard toilet paper core (the projector), and a box into which I cut slots and a projection hole with blunt-tipped baby scissors (no easy task). At length, trembling with excited anticipation, I dragged the images swiftly downwards through the slots, hoping to cast images on the wall fast enough to create the illusion of movement. The nurse thought this was a daft idea, but humored me. I couldn't understand my failure; I had never heard of lenses or shutters. Unlike those geniuses who we're told can read fluently at two or three, I was still having trouble with the alphabet, and besides the hospital didn't run to encyclopedias.

I emerged eventually from that unpleasant place, badly out of synch with my Reservoir parochial school classmates, and in some respects never quite caught up. Five or six years later I was reduced to inventing the rail gun with some friends, at least in our own minds; we never had a realistic hope of getting our hands on powerful enough portable batteries and magnets to fling steel nails via electromagnetic propulsion at our enemies. And like all school kids we certainly had enemies. Our foes were, of course, the strong, the stupid, the reckless: *them.* L. Sprague de Camp wrote a blistering vengeance fantasy about the bitterness of childhood for kids too smart to emulate ordinariness convincingly, and we'll come back to that theme a bit later.

All this made me rather a disappointment to my father, who never had any fondness for books. Still, hoping to give me a head start out of our Housing Commission neighborhood, my parents sent me at great expense to St. Patrick's College, a sort of second level blue granite Jesuit school then located in East Melbourne next to the magnificent spires of St. Patrick's Cathedral, the premier Catholic site in Victoria. (My parents had been married there by the Archbishop.) It was not as snazzy as Xavier College, which turned out Catholic medicos, barristers, barristers and more Jesuits, but apparently was deemed superior to the local Christian Brothers. I stayed there from grades four through seven—aged nine to twelve—and dithered hopelessly in the middle ranks, chattering and giggling in class, struggling with homework that I found utterly meaningless. I suspect I suffered from the now fashionable attention deficit disorder and could have benefited from, precisely, rather more attention, of an intelligent, targeted kind. No such luck. When I was twelve, the Principal informed my parents that I was a dud—had they considered a more suitable future for me, one like my father's position in a factory, perhaps?

Stung, they enrolled me in St. Joseph's Technical College in Abbotsford, then a sleazy inner suburb, today chic, expensive and gentrified. I studied there through Intermediate certificate, more or less ignored by the teachers because I was hopeless at athletics and had declined to join the cadets; my asthma at least got me off that hook. Eventually I was taken somewhat under the wing of one brother who nurtured a small group of pious boys. I'd always been excited by theology and its paradoxes; Religious Studies was the only subject I ever aced repeatedly. I'd been an altar boy for years, at my mother's goading. Many years later she started a theology degree herself, but died of ovarian cancer before she graduated (God moves in whimsical ways: my father's many siblings had dropped like flies; one of the few survivors, his older brother Ron, became a Christian Brother and was stung to death in Queensland waters by a lethal jellyfish.).

So at the start of my final year at the trade school, prior to the final slog toward apprenticeship or work as a street sweeper, all the students were obliged to take a Commonwealth aptitude test, including a rudimentary IQ scale. Ructions and alarums followed, parents were called in. I was informed later by my mother (but I have no evidence for this) that I scored in the too clever by half range. *What's* he doing *here?* Get him to the Christian Brothers school next year, have him do Matriculation there the year after, and get him a proper clerk's job in the public service. (I wasn't very good with my hands, although I did make a dandy wooden coat hanger and, of course, a book shelf.)

This news came as a crushing burden to my parents, with their ever growing family; their fifth son (today a professor and expert in nuclear-related media) was on the way that year. I suppose I'd been expected to enter the workforce in 1960, at fifteen, and help with the family costs. Now I would be a financial drain: fees, new uniform, books, food. For my part, I was horrified at the idea of going cold into a pecking order long established. I knew I'd be destroyed. Something lateral was needed, a cunning plan.

Luckily, God came to my aid. My classmates suffered a ferocious fire & brimstone retreat around the end of first term. I was purged of my sins and saw the light.

A religious vocation! Yes! Maybe I had a vocation! If I were smart enough after all to study for Matriculation, maybe I wasn't too stupid to master Latin. Maybe God wanted me for a priest! Well, or at least a brother.

I saw that I had a choice. Obviously one ought to take the low humble road: I could be a Franciscan. (The retreat, I feel sure, had been conducted by guileless men of that order.) But wait! Wasn't everyone saying I'd been pissing away these intellectual gifts so cavalierly that people assumed I was slightly retarded? I should become a Jesuit, a course from which I had been so mysterious derailed!

I'd been visiting a Blessed Sacrament church in the center of the city, St Francis's, notable for its gaudy sentimentality and industrial rows of confessionals, and put this question to a random confessor, who suggested I should make an appointment and talk it over. Nervously, I rolled up one afternoon, and this bluff honest fellow explained that by a stroke of luck both my desiderata were met in the Blessed Sacrament congregation, with their Mt. Eymard Juniorate in the town of Bowral, six or seven hundred miles to the north, some distance from Sydney. God had surely sent me directly here! This could be no accident. (The policy appears to have been "grab 'em while you can," given their eagerness to recruit both me and a school pal. I was told many years later that one of the older priests at St Francis' said he only once casually mentioned that he had thought about becoming a priest and the next thing he knew he was on the train to Bowral.)

When I revealed this truth to my parents, they were pleased as punch, although they'd still have to pay for my season in the seminary (something I didn't know then; I thought I'd got them off the financial hook). The local parish priest endorsed my vocation in his incomprehensible Irish brogue. Off I set by train to Bowral, in the high country of New South Wales, accompanied by my somewhat impressionable pal from Abbotsford Tech, John Sutton. And there I stayed for the two years that, you know, made a man of me. Not quite the man I'd have preferred to be made, there being very few girls on the premises, except when sisters of my fellow students came to visit, and nothing in the usual way of socialization skills, except when I talked some of the guys into sneaking out late on battered old monastery bikes, riding in the dark into Bowral to watch a movie. It was rather like a 1980s' teen movie, without the naughty scenes.

Despite these drawbacks, I found it a wonderful place to spend a couple of years. But then I might have been in an unusual situation. At home I'd felt oppressed and limited, didn't get on with my father—typical enough thus far, granted; Bowral allowed me to develop as an individual (each of us had a separate "cell," for a start), and to learn to kick a football (very badly) without being bullied, and join healthy biking excursions up the steep road of nearby Mt. Gibraltar and into the bush. My asthma went into abeyance.

The distinctive tone of Mt. Eymard was governed by the fact that we had all chosen to be there (leaving aside the, ahem, benign manipulation), and did so in a voluntary spirit of self-sacrifice and charity. So people, to my astonishment, tended to be *nice* to each other. The monastery's great L-shaped building in its acres of trees and lawn was marvelous, with one wing closed off or at least unused. The original house was built in the 1920s for the shipping magnate Howard Smith; the inaugural novice master from 1947-58 was an ex-naval lieutenant. Smith's architect had used a rakish plan and a few portholes. The building has subsequently been refitted as an attractive and no doubt madly expensive retirement home, with beautiful gardens. In some of those deserted rooms I found curious items: a thick pile of sermon notes from one dead priest (which I tried to edit into a book, a practice I would hone to a fine art later in life), and a first edition of a Norman Lindsay collection of writings and engravings that I wish I'd been able to keep; it would be priceless now.

The grounds were superb as well—places to walk with other people, places to get away by yourself. We mowed the large lawns, helped a bit with weeding and planting. The recreation room was stark but had a gramophone; music! What a treat! Each month we got a new World Record club 33 RPM long-playing record or two.

This working class kid learned to love at least the more obvious kinds of "classical music." We played intensive table tennis, read; in my case I wrote a bit (typing on a battered old machine I'd found somewhere and was permitted to haul up to my room), drew. Eventually I managed to get away now and then by bike into Bowral to meet up with John Baxter, a local who happened to be one of the nation's most accomplished enthusiasts of science fiction, my obsession since the age of ten or twelve. I return to this remarkable coincidence later in this book in my interview with Russell Blackford. I noted once: "Such was my craving for sf that I'd reached an accommodation with Father Superior: by a special dispensation I was permitted the monthly purchase of *New Worlds*. Once I clapped eyes on poor Baxter's imported sf collection I rather exceeded my prescribed dosage, escalating finally to the point where I secreted entire borrowed cartons of the stuff under my monastic bed."

If life at Mt. Eymard was by ordinary standards eccentric, mine was more so than usual; none of the other men sought such exotic and worldly (not to say otherworldly) pleasures.

☼

Why didn't I stay? I found nothing to drive me away, although the long periods of meditation and "adoration of the Eucharist" that was a specialty of the Order struck me as akin to self-hypnosis (although maybe I'm retrojecting this realization). Increasingly, though, I became aware that I needed more lively intellectual company, a broader access to knowledge (I'd appointed myself librarian at one stage, and spent a lot of time going through the shelves of books, reading in French theologians when I wasn't reading Cordwainer Smith), and some female company. I found that I was not cut out for either celibacy nor obedience; as for poverty, that seemed to stick, and in the subsequent half century I've managed to get rather a lot done in all the free time I've had available because I never wasted time making pots of money, driving a car or dressing expensively.

Still, the seminary was as much fun as a non-stop scout jamboree, I suppose, except that I never did learn the knots. I ate prodigiously and shot up about three inches in a year. I came out wearing some other guy's discarded sports jacket, and stumbled head first into Monash University, where I lived for the first year in a Hall of Residence that daringly housed both males and females. I was shellshocked and hapless, and remained so in one way or another for some years. I grew to detest the arrogance, insensitivity and ruthlessness of any system that will allow a kid of fifteen—or even thirteen or fourteen in the case of some of the unformed worms in the De La Salle Brothers' Juniorate at Burradoo, several miles from Bowral, where I'd studied during the day—to cut himself off from the ample richness of human existence. Not many years later I hitchhiked with Rory Barnes, later a frequent writing collaborator, off the main road at dusk to the Juniorate, en route to Sydney to conclude a deal with my first book. The brothers were new to me but they fed us supper, while small boys goggled at these bearded weirdoes, and generously provided a lift back to the highway. On the outskirts of Sydney, around Parramatta, we snored beside the highway in sleeping bags. The absurd antics of youth, without a penny in your pockets.

Mt. Eymard was primarily intended at the beginning of the 1960s to provide a transitional education upgrade for "late vocations" with inadequate schooling in Latin and French, tutored by a dear old retired pedant, Mr. Swan, who lived in a small cottage on the grounds and was excellent on Thucydides and enjoyed deploying the tactics and strategy of ancient Greek and Roman battles. To that extent the seminary avoided the worst of that crime of kidnapping children for God; most of the other men had work experience and were in their twenties. One had been in retail trade for a year or two. He struggled terribly with his required essays; I tried to help out by loaning him a thesaurus I'd found. He read his new effort aloud and everyone burst out laughing when he described how his mother's house was surrounded by a bloodless barrier. A *what*? He was hurt and sent me a wounded look, for I had betrayed his trust with this evil book. All he'd wanted was a more memorable way to express "white fence," and the thesaurus had said.... In later years as an editor, I would often encounter this sort of word blindness, utterly alien to me.

Of course, the way I use words has always been a source of innocent merriment, if only to me. Father Superior became caught up in one bizarre interlude. My mother and I had long shared a whimsical word-playing, game-playing bond, which I indulged in my letters home. These, of course, were opened and read by the spiritual director, no privacy nonsense when God is brooding over every shoulder. I'd bruised an ankle ligament (perhaps I was clipped by some country idiot on the road while pedaling in the rain to De La Salle) and had to see a doctor. I explained to my mother in hyperbolic terms that *really* I was *all right* despite this *appalling accident*, and that they had decided not to amputate my leg after all. When I went home on the next holiday break, my mother read me the concerned and soothing covering note or addendum Father Superior had sent her explaining that Damien had a tendency to exaggerate these matters, but truthfully, Mrs. Broderick, your son was never in serious danger, and sawing his leg off at the hip had never actually been in prospect. We laughed and laughed, you know how it is.

There was the long speculative theological letter about the status of Adam and Eve and their preternatural gifts that I'd sent to the Catholic Hour radio program at the end of 1960. I had developed the opinion that our First Parents must have had the power (and sinfully abused it) to create *ab initio,* since this was the highest capacity of the Deity Himself, and mankind was shaped in His Image, after all. This artists' credo received a rather puzzled commentary on air, but I missed it. I believe Atlantis and flying saucers played a role in this earlier-than-von Däniken theo-theoretical extravaganza.

So I'm left ambivalent: grateful for the opportunities I had there (I gained sufficient schooling to get into university, although hours a day were wasted on delusional activities and study of extraneous topics unconnected to my Leaving certificate or the enjoyment of science fiction), and infuriated that I couldn't have found some better accommodation to my family's and my own rather odd needs.

One benefit to come from my immurement in the den of God was the publication of my first magazine piece, if an appearance in a small Australian religious magazine, *The Monstrance,* can be counted. (A monstrance, as Merriam-Webster tells us, is "a vessel in which the consecrated Host is exposed for the adoration of the faithful, from the Middle English *mustraunce, monstrans* demonstration, monstrance, from Anglo-French *mustrance* show, sign, from Medieval Latin *monstrantia,* from Latin *monstrare* to show, from *monstrum,* Date: fifteenth century," and I'm glad you asked.) It was published in the June, 1960, issue, a bit more than a month after my sixteenth birthday and a couple of months after it was submitted. As the official historian of the Congregation notes, "the young writer was miffed that [the editor] had described him as 'a 16 year old student in our house of studies in Bowral' (he was only fifteen). The article matches anything written by the more experienced *Monstrance* contributors" (Damien Cash, *The Road to Emmaus: A History of the Blessed Sacrament Congregation in Australia,* published by the Congregation, 2005). Titled "The God of the Eucharist," it was a surprisingly pantheistic hymn to the glories of nature as revealed more by science than faith, and suggests the ambition of a proto-philosopher edging his way already out of belief (although that realization would not occur for another five years).

My first piece of published fiction also appeared in a small religious magazine three years later. It carried the copycat title "Walk Like a Mountain" (presumably stuck in my mind from years of reading science fiction anthologies and magazines; it had been used by US fantasist Manly Wade Wellman in 1955, and I haven't the slightest idea what his story was about). The Jesuit-edited magazine gloried in the name *The Australian Messenger of the Sacred Heart* and as I recall was a promotional tool for the multiplication of the species, especially the kind fated to be baptized in a Catholic church. My story didn't deal with conception or birth, however; like many of the other tales in this book, its focus was squarely on death and the dying. It was mawkish and rudimentary, of course (I was eighteen or nineteen when I wrote it, in my second year of university), but perhaps not entirely contemptible.

The same year, 1963, I entered two stories in a contest announced in *The Monstrance*, one in the category for students. The story I submitted under my own name got nowhere, but another, "The Journey Home" by "Keith Donovan," borrowed the identity and postal address of a Monash friend, and won first prize in the student section. Luckily Keith passed on the twenty-five pounds winnings (equal to at least $500 today, and greatly needed at the time, since I had very little income and no scholarship at that point). None of the winning stories ever appeared in the magazine, and I kept no copies of mine. I suspect from the title it was a sentimental riff on Theodore Sturgeon's story "A Way Home," and featured a troubled young man considering his future and passing a priest walking toward his family home—the priest being his future self, of course. None of this is evidence of great literary promise, heaven knows. At the age when I won that small prize, augmenting the pittance I got by serving coffee late at night to other students, Arthur Rimbaud had all but abandoned creative writing forever.

A naïve, flushed romanticism sometimes surfaced, discomfiting to recall. "The Mirrors of the Sea," the sample that follows "Walk," was published in the Monash University student literary magazine *Orpheus,* edited by Ken Mogg, in 1964. It was an angry outburst at the coarse pragmatism of the Education Department, to which I had legally bonded myself. The studentship's benefits and my fees and income were snatched away when I was temporarily suspended, after carelessly failing some exams—surely a trifle! Had they no soul? Outrageous! That I had made a solemn undertaking to study dutifully and after three years and graduation to serve as a teacher in some appalling State school seemed to slip my mind. I was meant to be a philosopher and a writer! Bah humbug! Luckily, in the end, that posturing and adolescent kicking against pricks paid off—I was finally such an unendurable pest that the Education Department showed me the door, and left me debt free. So, to earn a crust, I began turning out short fiction for Australian men's magazines (*Man, Man Junior, Squire*)—tits and bums magazines, as they used to be called in my home country, tits&ass by any other name. We'll come to those rather dismal but perhaps necessary steps in my writerly evolution all too soon. First, the baby staggers.

# WALK LIKE A MOUNTAIN
## (1963)

It is a hard thing to die.

Bram was still surprised. The air was saturated with the ripe heady scent of grass and hay, and the day was warm and bright. It did not seem to be a day for death. Through the open window, Bram could hear birds rejoicing in the approach of summer. And the breeze that touched the curtains whispered to him of glistening water and lowing cattle. Doubly hard, on such a day, to face death.

The priest had been, and there lingered still the smell of melting candle wax. He had come with his oils and holy water and purple stole and the Lord of Life in a silver pyx. Bram was not afraid for his soul. He had never been a saint, but neither was he an unrepentant sinner. His last confession had been quiet and undramatic, and now he awaited heaven with a confidence born of a lifetime's familiarity with Christ. But still, it was a hard thing to die.

They had taken away most of the pain, the doctors, with their drugs and medicines. Now there was just the throb that beat with his heart, and the catch in his throat, and the tears in his eyes.

His pillow was slightly raised, and when he opened his eyes he could see the three children solemnly sitting beside him. Anthea, the little one, she didn't know. She sat in the glow of her golden silky hair and her small soft hands played with a teddy bear. Neither did Johnny, with his cowboy hat and dancing eyes and grubby peaked nose. Noisy, boisterous, on the verge of young manhood—Bram closed his eyes against the pricking of hot tears. And Therese. Of course, she knew. She had to. Bram counted the years she had been part-time mother to the other two. Two and a half? Three? A long, long time for a girl of seventeen. It hadn't been this way with their mother, no hard painful duty of dying, just the snap of her life.

The children were looking at him now, and the smile on Therese's face was an ache between them. Here was the pain, the difficulty of dying. To have them cut loose so suddenly from the strength of their life.... Meggie would be here soon, she would explain to him this pain that had nothing to do with the burning cramp which paralyzed half his body.

How they sing, he thought, at the sound of the birds, and there was a flash of crimson as a finch chased its song across the sky. Somewhere a bellbird chimed, and with a rush of memory he saw the hot hills and wet forests and damp black soil he would never walk again.

Therese was at his arm with a glass of warm milk, and the tablet, when he heard the rumble of a car bouncing up the track. He tried to sit up, to gain a better view through the window, and the pain along his arm lanced up his neck. His great strong body tremored, and he sank back to the pillow.

And with a babble of voices outside, and a swish of robes, Meggie came into the room. The softness of her face was unchanged, and Bram regretted only that her golden hair was caught up and hidden under her nun's wimple. She came into the room with an ease and familiarity that belied the four years she had been away.

"Hello, honey," said Bram, and her face was a glimpse into the past, his wife's face. Meggie took his hand and kissed his rugged cheek and her tears were for joy and sorrow both.

"Hello, Dad," said Sister Mary Madeleine.

The dying was harder now, a terrible thing to leave such beauty alone on the earth. But she wasn't alone, was she?

"How did you get here so fast, Meggie?" It was less than a day since Bram had crashed from the tractor, doubled in pain.

"They flew me to the airfield at Leakes' station in the private Cessna, and Dr. Hill picked me up in the Land Rover. How do you feel?"

"The drugs handle most of the pain," said Bram. And then, "But I don't want to die. What'll happen to the kids? What will happen to you? I couldn't stand it if you have to leave the convent."

His daughter stood at the window, limned against the summer sun. Her face moved with the effort of the things she was trying to say, but there was no sound. When she turned he saw her mother again, the day the tiny one had died. "God's love," Ginny had explained, for there seemed no reason. And the sadness had gone from her own tears. Now Meggie's face showed the same vision and he strained to share it.

"When you stood against the rain and the sun," she said, "and beat this land into a farm, and fought the heat and the wind for the wheat, you had a need for strength and self-sufficiency. Your strength was a shield, and then when mother died, the kids depended on you and you had to be mother as well as father to them. You're a man who loves life. You enjoy fighting and winning."

Bram looked at his knotted fists, and turned them, and knew that his daughter had seen the measure of his soul. He waited in silence.

She turned from the window and took his hands again, and her voice was gentle.

"Now you're dying, and it's a hard thing to give up life, I know that. But you're not dying because you're any smaller, it's just that God's bigger than any of us. Life is His plan, for us all, and death is part of it. There is time now to let Him take the burden. If you're going to die, then it's because it is His will. Don't worry, dad, He'll look after us."

With a wheeze and the clatter, the clock in the next room chimed four, and Bram smiled at the old familiar sound.

"Thanks, Meggie," he said. "You'd better go now and see how the children are doing."

She squeezed his hand, and went out of the room.

The farmer stared at the spots on the ceiling, and the crack in the plaster that ran in a crazy line from one wall to the other, and knew that Meggie was right. You stand on your own two feet for a lifetime, and the only time you really think of God is in the droughts or the rains. You walk like a mountain and forget that God is bigger than you are. And that He looks after his own.

Bram raised himself painfully until he had his hand under his pillow, and the beads were there. He held the cross tightly, and suddenly the business of death was a lot easier.

# THE MIRRORS OF THE SEA
## (1963)

The sun is a burnished coin in a sky afire. Gentle-hinted in the west, the cool of dusk; and waters glistering in the east with a dance of flame and night. Flowers cupped and rich in perfume, long-tusked grass sighing twilight. And the minarets: lapis campaniles, turrets floating in the haze of rested fragrance.

The steed, then, black from the darkling hills to westward; his rider argent, touched with fire. Weary with the day's hard traveling, knight and beast, yet brave with the vision of the minarets. Look: the moving sun has painted Petra, the rose-red city half as old as time. And now, the sky of pale glass, and the haze a dust of powdered-blue. Xanadu, or Damascus, on the dragon-green, the luminous, the dark, the serpent-haunted sea.

Gaze on this world of dreams, of vast deeds done and told, of glimpses snatched and scarcely held; of redes unheard and shadowed forces grim, and mighty men, whose faerie blades had carven half the world. In the twilight land, the cupolas glimmering to the drowsing sun, the giant steed and silver-armored knight went tired to the sea.

From the north, as yet unnoticed by the silver knight, a man staggered in the wild meadows of grass and drowsing flowers. Unaware, he seemed, with his wild look, of the fragrances, attar and muscadine, the scents of grasses green and gold. Unlike the silver knight, this man, with his unkempt hair a white of years and an unmagical affair of lenses set before his staring eyes. The first notes of the evening birds chimed in a harmony that failed to touch him, and the cool sea breeze moved his hair without taking the sting of heat from his eyes. Strange, in his outlandish garments, unlike the weight of mail or the caress of silk and velvet.

Separate, sharing only in the common destination, mounted paladin and crazed outlander wended their ways toward the spires of the city. The knight sat easy on his gorgeous saddle, his armor chased in exotic patterns, and a crimson bundle beneath the cantle of the ornamented leather. A tall lance rested to his right, its point a flare of white metal; and his long sword, handle arabesqued in gold and orichalc, slapped against the mail of his left leg. His visor was raised, the better to see in the descending gloom, and his face was handsome with the scars of terrible battles. Iced-fire, his eyes, and set upon the flickering lights that brought the city of minarets a new enchantment in the darkness.

He fancied he could hear the slapping of the waves, and smell the fresh scent of brine on the breeze, when his huge steed muttered and tossed his head at a movement from the shadows. In a single fluid action, the knight's shield was on his arm and the lance slipped into the horizontal rest. With scarcely a motion of his corded neck, he looked into the star-flecked night. The stallion continued toward the city, toward the sea and welcome of lights, but his metaled hooves trod more lightly. In the grassy hollow, the wild man stared, huddled into himself, his eyes terror-stricken on the minaret shadows.

The knight croaked contemptuously, and slid his lance home to rest. With a touch of the tasseled reins, he stopped before the crazed man, and looked down on him. In the night, a lion howled and a multitude of small beasts scurried. The outlander wept and his eyes were torn by the city. With a mighty blow, the silver knight struck the shield on his arm with his gauntlet, and the clang echoed in a distant grove of smoke-barked trees. The small man looked up at the sound, through the faded glaze of lenses, before covering his face with tattered hands.

"What is your sorrow?" asked the giant on the midnight steed. "Why need to weep, in this land, where the strong are strong, and ferns sing by the rivers and the sea is deep for ships and salt with wonders?"

Had he possessed even the remnants of dignity, the crazed man would have drawn them about his soul. As it was, he could only stare from the knight to the glowing towers and back in a scurrying circuit.

"Horror, horror." He tore at his ears, at his hair. "Desolation and sand, burning winds all around, and an empty waste and a scarecrow tin-suited on a broken nag. Who are you, death's head, and what is this lie of beauty?" He snicked his gaze from the man, and pawed at the luxuriant grass.

Under the jutting visor, the knight's eyes were longing for the minarets, for rest after his journey. He brought his attention back grudgingly to the maniac.

"What is it you seek?" he asked. "Here, with a strong arm or a strong thought, a man is a man. Why do you snivel?"

The other man took off his lenses and smeared them on a rag he tugged from his breeches.

"Bedevil me with nonsense, damn you? I see your snaggle teeth, skull, I see your hollow sockets."

And then, on knees stained darker than the darkness with grass, "Where are the hierarchies? Who is to tell me what to do? Whom will I force to my will, if I am not forced, not told, not instructed...?"

Behind the minarets, now, the moon sailed the sea and the sky, bright in the color of the knight's apparel. On the distant waters, light swelled and moved. The man on the horse stretched the tired muscles of his shoulders, and sneered at the crazed outlander.

"See what you see, liar. Here are no deserts, save the emptiness of men who know no other way but that which others show them. Look, the city is beckoning me home from my journeys, and I go to my satisfaction."

Gently tugging the reins, he rode on the swathe of moonlit carpet toward the city. Behind him, a lost man wandered in the burning desert, parched with a thirst he had never known, and hungry even for the sight of Death who rode from him. Thick with dust, hot and dying with no man to help him, he opened his wept eyes to a glimpse of minarets and moonlight. And it was gone.

# INTRODUCTION TO
# "THE SEA'S FURTHEST END"


In a searching monograph on the sf writer James Blish, the fine British scholar, critic and novelist Brian Stableford characterizes one "subspecies of pulp SF which became popular during the Forties."

> The recipe runs as follows: an ordinary man, usually rather alienated from his social environment, is translocated by convenient literary device into another world, where he is no longer ordinary but the focal point of tremendous events. The other world is usually similar to ours in its essentials, but less advanced technologically, exotic in its barbarity. Magic usually works, though rationalized as strange powers of the mind. The hero has a vital, often messianic destiny to fulfill, but does not understand what he has to do or how. While totally bewildered, he is shuffled back and forth amid the apparatus of the plot, harassed by his enemies and aided by his allies (and sometimes *vice versa*, when the plot is sufficiently complicated for everybody to be bewildered). Eventually, in a climax involving the intuitive manipulation of awesome forces, the hero comes into his own and wraps up the entire affair. (*A Clash of Symbols*, 1979, 12-13)

Oddly enough, Stableford's chilly thumbnail catches rather exactly the plot dynamic of both my first novel, *Sorcerer's World* (1970) and my recent post-Singularity diptych *Godplayers* and *K-Machines* (2005, 2006). In many details it manifests as well the traditional engine of gaudy space opera that I borrowed to drive my first primitive science fiction novella, written when I was nineteen and published in 1964 in the first volume of British editor John Carnell's original-fiction anthology *New Writings in SF1*. Brian Hammond, reviewing Carnell's book in a British popular science magazine of the day, *Discovery*, found it "chiefly notable for Australian Damien Broderick's bizarre entry.... It is a genuine Edgar Rice Burroughs throwback, with 1920s flavoring, in which the future is dressed up in a medieval costume, with Emperors, trial by combat, slaughter on a galactic scale, and what can only be termed the ultimate in cosmic endings." Another reviewer, more acerbic, gave it the wooden spoon award, or booby prize.

This adolescent confection quickly became a source of chagrin to me, and despite its further appearances in UK and US paperback editions and translation into Spanish, I allowed it to quietly molder away for years, finally returning in the early 1990s to a heavy-duty rewrite that drew upon Hindu mythology, an attempt to redeem its patently space operatic failings. Iain M. Banks, Paul McAuley and others had meanwhile invented the New Space Opera, but I'm sure that they would have been scandalized by this story that is so ostentatiously Old Space Opera. I revive it here as a significant marker, however deplorable and prehistoric in many respects, of my evolution as a science fiction writer. Arguably it does retain a certain gusto. It might be instructive to compare this original version with the longer revision, "The Game of Stars and Souls," which can be found in my collection *Uncle Bones* (2009); it appears here with only the most minor corrections. There's a single exception. One of my characters had been given the truly ridiculous elbow-nudging eye-winking name "Milenn"; here he becomes simply Miles, whose soldierly avatar replaces, with no other facelifts, the thousand year man.

What can such a text reveal of the impulse behind science fiction reading and writing in the young? Candidly, I'm pretty sure that Stableford has it right when he says of this kind of story:

> Its purpose...is to pander to the schizoid element in the psyche of the reader, exploiting the tendency of feelings of vulnerability and alienation to be coupled with fantasies of transcendental omnipotence.... Most of the men who wrote for the pulps were assisted in their mission by their own psychological proclivities—the creation of such fantasies was sincere, and in many cases probably performed a necessary cathartic function. (14)

This homespun psychoanalytic interpretation has a condescending air, but Stableford, like me, began publishing science fiction rather young, and doubtless does not spare himself in his diagnosis. For a classic Freudian, of course, all art is a sort of evasion, a masking disguise, a means of coping with inadequacies. Easy to see, then, why artists prefer Jung, or (in the case of strenuously intellectual science fiction writers like Greg Egan) the less judgmental if somewhat insensitive tracts of cognitive science.

# THE SEA'S FURTHEST END
## (1964)

### PROEM

Earth's Golden Age of Empire had come and gone, an exotic flower in the harsh environment of the Galaxy. The age-dark maw of space had waited patiently as Earth's seed exploded across the universe at the opening of the Bright Ages, had bided time while arrogant Man bridged the stars with lines of commerce and allegiance, had reaped satisfaction when the entropy of empire brought Man's dreams crashing into the dust of a million worlds. The universe had chuckled as the heirs of mighty Earth reverted on ten hundred thousand motes in space to primitive tribal civilizations. And again it waited with eternal amusement for the Hunger that would drive men out into the hostile dark between the stars.

The Empire had died of decadence and internecine strife.

For basically, empire is an artificial system. Every planet was a self-contained unit, with its own gamut of resources. Certainly, highly organized interstellar trade made for more and cheaper luxury goods. Technique-traders enabled breakthrough discoveries on one planet to benefit the Galaxy. But peace came at the price of freedom, and the Empire fell. After the Wars of Annihilation, Man's spirit was broken and he renounced the stars in the despair common to all Dark Ages.

But the skies had cleared at last. A thousand years had given forty generations time to yearn again for the stars. And this time the groping explorers did not find an empty universe to conquer—on every habitable planet, they met their forgotten brothers, seeded there from Mother Earth twenty thousand years before.

The reavers came, and the missionaries, and the traders, and men dreamed again of Empire....

The Player laughed, and carefully moved his Queen.

# ONE

Aylan lay on his back in the hush of the garden, his lean figure another shadow in the darkness. Eyes closed, he chewed the end of a grass stem and sucked the sweet juice in his mouth. The Palace was quiet, and the only sounds were the movements of small creatures in the leaves and the long gentle swell of the sea slapping in the distance against the breakwaters. The grass beneath him was soft and smooth, buoyant like the warm sea. Aylan opened his eyes to the sky, and sobbed. Sprinkled in a great blazing halo above his head were the stars Man had once renounced, which Man had now to win back. The sign of Cain was on Man's soul, the mark of war and conquest and bloody murder, and it drove him to empire. Aylan ground his knuckles into his eyes. For those cold shining points of light were his heritage. He was Crown Prince of Loren, son of the man who was gradually making himself Emperor of the Galaxy.

Suddenly the ground seemed uncomfortable beneath him, and Aylan got to his feet. He wandered blindly in the overpowering scent of the trees to the end of the vast garden, down a sandy path to the edge of the sea. The salty acrid smell filled his nostrils and drugged his mind and he crunched across the sand to the edge of the lapping water. The sea was black, an ocean of oil, of tears, and there was no moon. Stars sank from the sky to the end of the sea, out far on the horizon, and drowned in the black salt swell. Aylan had his fur shoes off, and his robe and shirt, before he realized what he was doing, but the lure of the sea was a siren's song, not to be denied. He threw his trousers after the other clothes and walked slowly into the water. It surrounded him, wetting his long hair, carrying him drifting towards the stars on the horizon.

He licked the salt water from his lips and with powerful strokes swam to the partially submerged breakwater and clambered up on to it. The air was cool after the warm water, and it cleared his head. Above him, the stars were cold as ever, placid, condemning. There was no way of knowing, by looking at them, that men were drowning in one another's blood out there to own them.

There were wars, and rumors of wars. The pounding starships had consolidated victory on the Rim for the Loren system in the days of Aylan's great-grandfather. Now they were pressing into the Center, into territory where other monarchies and Federations were forming. There, in the more compact systems of Center where the stars were strewn so close that night was almost brighter than day the battles were waging between Loren and groups almost as power-ful.

The Prince turned his eyes from the stars, and looked back at the glowing palace. In the dark it was hard to see the wild beauty of the stone tracery that was the Imperial Palace on this pleasure world of Nara. Most of the lights were out, for even with the Court retinue present the huge palace was practically empty. Aylan sought out the light of the Emperor's room, but it was not glowing. Probably he would be.... Yes, Adriel's room was illuminated. The boy closed his eyes against the pricking of angry tears. How he hated his father! Adriel.... Violently, he shook his head against the impotent anger that raged inside him, and slid once more into the water.

☼

Veret was standing on the balustrade when Aylan reached the palace, outside the encircled cross that marked the chapel. He glanced shrewdly at the Prince as Aylan went by without acknowl-edging his presence, and ambled along beside the boy.

"Still silent, Aylan?" he commented in his quiet penetrating voice. "Our stay at Nara is almost over, you know, and your mood doesn't seem to have got any better."

Aylan stopped short, and looked with distraught eyes at the quiet brown-robed figure.

"You may be the Emperor's confessor, Father, but I scarcely see why my mood should affect you."

The priest raised one eyebrow and put his hand on Aylan's arm.

"His Majesty has been worried by your sulking and silence," he grunted as he sat on the low marble wall that edged the cloister.

The Prince did not try to hide his bitterness; he flaunted it, glo-ried in it.

"If His Majesty the Holy Emperor of Loren worried more about his own soul and less about others' the universe would be a happier place." He turned to go, but the priest's constraining hand was on his arm again.

"What is it, boy?" asked Veret, and he was all consolation and strength. "Is it Adriel?"

And suddenly the youth was on his knees, his face buried in Ve-ret's robes, his arms around the priest's legs. The old priest was not surprised at the emotional release. There was strong stuff in the boy but the Emperor had deliberately kept his son reliant on others, denied him the opportunity to stand on his own two feet. Aylan's only trouble, he thought wryly, was emotional immaturity.

In the darkness, Aylan got to his feet again, and he was calmer than he had been for weeks. And colder. In a moment, his face lost its boyish petulance and the grim set of his jaw and mouth betrayed the change his fluid personality had undergone.

"I apologize, Father," he said briskly, and strode rapidly away towards his rooms.

For a moment the old priest followed him with his eyes, startled despite himself by the boy's sudden metamorphosis of character. Then with a grunt and swish of robes he moved back to the chapel, smiling to himself. "There's one more the Emperor Malvara will have to watch out for," he muttered thoughtfully.

Aylan walked across the rich carpets without noticing the ornate beauty of the rooms around him. Here were the strivings and aspirations of men long dead, the beauty captured in straining stone and burning glass, the elegance and grace of a new renaissance. In this palace were represented the dreams and hopes of a hundred Visions, and they went unnoticed by Aylan, for there was death on his mind. He rode the grav-shaft to his floor and saw only the loveliness of Adriel of Corydon and felt only the hate no son should feel for his father.

The walls of his chambers were glowing as he came into them, and he muttered in annoyance at the cleaner who must have left them on. And a quiet voice said, "Good evening, Aylan."   .

The Prince turned, stunned, to the seat where Miles was sitting. And then the two men were in one another's arms, clapping each other on the back in happy reunion. Aylan pushed his friend to arm's length and surveyed him: Miles had changed. No longer was he the carefree debonair nobleman who had grown up with the Prince. Now his handsome face was burned black with the ultraviolet of hot suns. His right cheek was scarred with a needle-burn, and his brow was creased with responsibility. But his laugh was the same, the corners of his strong mouth lifted in happy greeting.

Miles's survey was no less thorough. He saw a man, not the boy of twenty-two he had left in the Imperial Palace at Loren a year before. The Prince was· slim as ever, but there was muscle under his patrician cloak, and new strength in his blue eyes.

They made a good pair, these two, both tall and slender, but with the resilience of sprung-steel bows. Two who held the destiny of a universe....

"When did you get back?" asked Aylan, as he punched the console for drinks. "I thought you were in Gaunilo at the Center, under the Duke of Calais."

The service console purred and deposited two smoky green glasses of a potent beverage from an obscure planet near Nara. Aylan handed one to his friend, extracted a pair of cigars from the pop-up, and sank into a seat opposite Miles.

The other man was silent for a moment as he lit his cigar, and when he spoke his voice was serious.

"Unfortunately, I'm here as official representative to the Emperor from Jon of Calais. I've just spent two hours in session with His Majesty, and he's considering returning to Loren for a Council Conference. The situation Centerside is simply this: our forces have the Central groups in check, and they're suing for peace. Calais wants to refuse terms and crush them while we have the opportunity. The Emperor is tentatively of the same opinion, and the damned Council will probably agree." He drained his glass in a hasty motion and put his left hand over his eyes against a pulsing headache.

Aylan sat in silence for a moment, wondering at his friend's upset.

"So, what's wrong with that? It seems perfectly sensible. Don't tell me your loyalties are drifting away from Loren." But he smiled as he said it.

Miles was not smiling when he looked up. He seemed upset by his friend's comment. Carefully, he put his cigar down.

"Have you forgotten so soon, Aylan?" he said gently. "Do you remember how we talked, as boys, of history and ideologies, and men's souls? You don't win a man by beating the guts out of him when he's down. These people are ready to admit that Loren is bigger than them. They're almost ready to accept Federation, if they're treated as men and not as animals. Calais will conquer them, yes, wipe out their fleets, but he'll never win their respect and loyalty. Why do you think the last Empire failed? *Because it was built on force and hatred, not affection and loyalty!* We can't let that happen again."

He was silent, and Aylan stared in wonder at this man who saw the future so definitely. And Miles was right, of course. He always was. The nights and days of their childhood together flooded Aylan's mind, and always Miles was there, guiding and helping, and always he was right.

"Is there something you want me to do?" Aylan was groping, uncertain of himself in the presence of this sure, confident man.

The sun-burnt warrior sat forward in his chair and examined his hands with elaborate thoroughness. When he spoke, his voice was strained.

"If you still believe in those old-fashioned ideals we used to dream and speak of, there is something. I want you to ask the Emperor to relieve Calais and place you in command of the forces."

The Prince was swaying on his feet, the world ringing in his ears.

"You must be mad!" In a flood, he saw the stars as they had appeared earlier that night, a blazing, cruel, contemptuous halo. He saw the burnt, pocked, blood-stained ships that limped back from the Central theaters of war. He saw his father's laughing, scorning face as he told Aylan that he was taking Adriel of Corydon as diplomatic mistress. He saw himself as a weak dreamer, and knew that he could never lead an army.

Deep in his seat, Miles sat unmoving. He was prepared for this, had known what to expect. And softly, cutting like an exquisitely sharp knife through the chaos of Aylan's mental turmoil, he spoke.

"Why? Once, you are right, I would have been mad to suggest such a thing. You were weak, for your father had made you so. But not now. Aylan, you are a man. I could tell that as soon as I saw you today. You'll be Emperor one day; you have to learn to face responsibility. And the Center *must* be saved from butchery."

Aylan was at the console again, and with a flicker of fingers he plunged the room into darkness and set up the Galactic Lens. He was a giant, standing in nothingness with the suns of the Milky Way burning and flaming around him. Spiraling in a perfect simulacrum of the Galaxy, the Lens filled the room and illuminated it with a dim radiance. The Prince saw Miles rise to his feet and come forward to the blazing luminescence of Center.

"Here is the future. A united galaxy, Aylan. Can you imagine what that would mean?" His face shone with a vision, a dedication Aylan could not deny himself. "Federation—that's the dream. Not harshly enforced Empire, but freely accepted peace. And then, who knows? There is intergalactic space, new riches, new technological achievement, perhaps mental and metaphysical evolution. But we must have peace first, and you are the vital key to it."

The whorls of light fled through the darkness, and Aylan was the colossus whose will was to form their shape. He knew, then, that he would have to accept his destiny. Always it is easier to hide in one's shell, to live in the past, to deny the future for the sake of present comforts and assurances, but he could no longer take the easy path. And Aylan felt refreshed, and strengthened.

He went to the console and flicked off the Lens. As the stars faded the walls flowed into life, and they shone in Aylan's eyes as they had shone in his friend's.

"I'll do it," he said, and gripped Miles's hand in a pact that spelled the end of a universe.

## TWO

The long carved oak table in the Royal Refectory was set for breakfast as delicately as ever, despite the fact that the Court retinue would eat only a very hasty meal preparatory to leaving the planet immediately for Loren. Aylan came to the end of the table opposite the Emperor's place, as befitted the heir to the throne, and was glad to see that Miles was sitting at his right hand. His father and his mistresses had not yet arrived, and Aylan was fidgety. He took the liberty of polarizing the great exterior wall. As the atoms aligned themselves in the field, the wall became one huge window to the gardens of the Palace. Far to the right, Nara's soft yellow sun was still surrounded with the crimson glory of the sunrise. The poet in Aylan was touched, and he was still gazing raptly at the gentle beauty of the morning when Malvara and his women came into the room.

The rough old man was clad in a synsilk crimson and gold toga that displayed his burly strength while lending him an air of respectability he would never really possess in himself. He gave his son a sardonic smile that recognized Aylan's presence, and the Prince returned the nod etiquette demanded. For him the charm of the beautiful morning was shattered and hatred was gnawing at him again. For at Malvara's right hand sat Adriel of Corydon, diplomatic mistress and sharer of the Imperial bed.

Aylan knew that Malvara was goading him. Since childhood, he had been the focus of a psychological war designed to teach him his subservient position. The Emperor needed an heir; he was afraid that an heir might not need him. So whenever the chance arose, Malvara crushed his son and topped off the lesson with the unspoken moral: *I'm on top, boy, and don't forget it!*

Adriel had been the last lesson, but Malvara had miscalculated. Aylan was not cowed. It was the last straw, and fear and self-disgust turned to cold hatred. Aylan knew that he would have to kill his father.

Adriel was the lovely daughter of the ex-Tyrant of Corydon. The scientists of that Rim system had reached their finest achievement in her, for she was genetically designed for beauty, intelligence, and...something else. Geneticists gave her a talent, a wildly improbable gift, and even they did not know what it would be.

She was an Emote.

"Chameleon-like" was the inevitable adjective, but it wasn't accurate. Adriel could control her Emoting. It was a defense-mechanism, but it was more. It was a talent, and she could use it at will.

Of course, everybody loved her. In a fraternal, helping fashion. Her subconscious knew better than to Emote in a sexually attractive manner. She had no desire to be raped by every male who came within her Emotive range. But for Aylan, the quiet son of her father's conqueror, she had felt the stirrings of love.

They had been like children, in their new discovery.

Their love was sunrise and the scent of roses and soft breath in the sheets. She drew the beginnings of manhood from the frightened adolescent who was Aylan, and their love was a burgeoning flower.

For Malvara, it was unthinkable that his son should have such a victory. So Adriel became his diplomatic mistress.

She could, of course, have used her Emotive talent to breed horror, or disgust, or terror of her in Malvara's mind, but the Emperor was not a fool and there were ten heavy cruisers in orbit around each planet in the Corydon system.

So Aylan sat at the end of a long table, his fist clenched hard on the fork at the sight of the veiled nun-like form at his father's right hand. Feed a hatred enough fuel for long enough, and hold it under pressure, and one day it will destroy either the hater or the hated. Aylan toyed with food he could not eat, and knew that he would not be the one to die.

Council was in session when the Court returned to the Imperial City at Loren. His Majesty, the Holy Emperor Malvara, Lord Master of Loren and the Galaxy, came into the vast arching monument which was the Council Chambers and took his place on the levitated throne six feet above the marble floor. The Council stood until he was seated, then found their places in silence. Malvara rarely called on the Council for advice in policy decisions.

The grizzled old man looked even more like a gorilla in his luminously white cloak. Dismissing the trivia of formalities, Malvara came straight to the point.

"My lords of Loren. In the long and bloody war we have been waging with the Central alliances, we have ever sought to bring them to allegiance with our glorious empire. Now, through the brilliant spatial and planetside command of Jon of Calais, Loren has the major powers begging for terms of peace. Calais has sent to me in the able hands of Count Miles of Danak a request for permission to reject all terms and wipe out the enemy while they are in this weakened condition. Of course, this would result in antagonism towards Loren for some generations, but the question that must be resolved today is: would this course of action best serve the interests of the Empire of Loren, or should we accept terms and run the risk of new revolt in the near future?"

His glance ranged the floor of the Chambers, and there was a moment of silence before the low hum of discussion began among the Members. These oldsters were still barbaric in their thinking, but they were shrewd enough to realize that here was a decision of overwhelming importance for the future of the Galaxy.

Malvara waited restlessly on his floating throne for ten minutes while the Members conferred hastily with one another, and then called for the first Speaker in Consultation to take the rostrum.

Even as the first Speaker came forward, there was a stir near the Family Entrance, and Aylan entered the Chambers. Garbed in the iridescent purple and white fur of the Imperial House he was a striking figure, and the maturity of purpose in the set of his jaw startled Malvara considerably. From his lofty position the Emperor watched the unprecedented entry of his son into the Council and for the first time he felt afraid.

Craning necks and furtive whispers showed that the Members of Council in Consultation were surprised too. The first Speaker took another step towards the rostrum, hesitated, and then waited for further developments, a ludicrously unhappy figure in the aisle.

The trim figure of the Prince continued straight to the limits of the Protection-field surrounding the Emperor, and made ceremonial obeisance directly before Malvara.

"I crave the pardon of the Emperor and his Council," he began, still facing Malvara, "for this intrusion, and I beg leave to take advantage of my right as Royal Family to address the topic."

There was nothing Malvara could legally do to prevent Aylan speaking, so he gave his consent as graciously as he could. As he watched his son mount the rostrum, his mind whirled in a crazy turmoil. For twenty-two years he had been pressuring Aylan, nudging, kicking, hurting, pushing him, with the express purpose of making it psychologically impossible for the Prince to take the kind of action he was taking now. The sweat of fear dribbled down Malvara's back, and it took a conscious effort to restore his normal sardonic calm.

☼

*The Player studied his Board, the billions of pieces, the vast shifting complexity of it, and saw that his King was in danger. Carefully, he shifted his Queen and sat back. The Game was nearing its end.*

☼

"Truth is more than an attitude of mind," Aylan was saying. "Federation is our goal. Empire is the means of getting there, but it is not an end in itself. We all know what happened to Man in the Galaxy last time Empire turned from a temporary tool to an encrusted system. Oh, I know it sounds like treason, and even, to some, heresy, but the Empire is only a way station to a bigger dream."

He paused, and he felt the strength of conviction running through him. The Emperor, he noticed, was stock-still in his throne, perhaps hearing his death-knell. Nowhere was there a sound or a movement; the clock of time had slowed.

"You cannot destroy a man's family and expect him to love you. This is a truism, and it isn't important when you're dealing with Empire. Love has no essential place in an Imperial world. But in a galaxy where men are free and really equal, in the Federation which I hope to God is the dream of all of us, love is *the* essential. We cannot afford to alienate the Center by brutal mass murder. For the dream is closer than we could ever have hoped. As the Emperor has told you, the Central states have sued for peace. Here is our chance for peaceful Empire, and eventually for peaceful Federation."

Blood racing at his own audacity, Aylan stepped from the rostrum and moved through the deadly silence of the Chamber until he was before his father's throne again.

"My father, Emperor Malvara. You have heard what I have said. I have spoken of theory. Now I ask you to let me put theory to the test. Transfer command of Central operations from Calais to myself. Let me go to the rulers of the Hub with peace, and I swear that the Empire will not suffer the tragedies that will inevitably befall it if Jon of Calais is allowed his bloody way."

In the vast chiaroscuro of the room, the moment of timelessness stretched on and on. The tall, slim figure of the Prince was a flare that burned to the Emperor's feet. Malvara was a cold angry statue, his lips pressed into a thin white scar, his thick black-haired hands gripped in a death lock on the ornate throne. And then the timelessness was gone, with a great croak of a laugh from the Emperor. His head went back, and the laughter rang through the hall. Mocking, amazed, angry. Aylan went limp, for he knew that he had failed and now he must do what he did not want to do.

Malvara's face was a mask of contempt and his voice was all sarcasm.

"Were you not my son, dear Aylan, you would surely die for what you have spoken. Your noble sentiments have indeed turned to treason in your addled brain. And you want the command! I would rather give it to the fool who amuses my court. My poor little boy! From the company of women and children you would venture into the domains of men?" He spat, a gout that landed at Aylan's feet. "Now go home and forget that this unfortunate incident ever happened."

He raised his eyes to the Council, the numb group of men trapped in a drama that was too big for them to understand. Without pausing, completely ignoring the Prince, he spoke to the white-haired men in the ranked levels.

"I have decided. Calais is to go ahead—the Central kings shall die, for the Empire can brook no competition."

With a flourish, Malvara wrapped his robes around himself and brought the huge throne to the floor. Aylan stood like a dummy, a clay doll, as the Emperor walked past him to the Family Entrance. As the Entrance slid open, life suddenly surged into him, and he spun round towards the Emperor.

"Wait!" His roar rang down the hall, and Malvara made an elaborate show of halting on one foot and turning slowly with a sardonic expression on his face.

"Aylan," he said, almost gently, "I have told you to go home."

But the Prince was striding forward now, and he was cold with fear for the moment of death had come.

"Malvara," cried Aylan in a voice that chilled the Members of the Council with its lack of all humanity, "as heir apparent, under the Law of Yusten the First Emperor, I plead fair cause and call you out to the Duel."

And here, thought Malvara with a sudden weariness, is my life and its meaning.

"I accept, of course," said the thick grizzled man and, turning his back on the Prince, left the Chambers.

Yusten had been a legend in his own time, and in the spreading Loren Empire his name had grown in proportion to the number of years passed since his death. His life had followed the classic pattern of a popular hero. Born amid the turmoil of the resurging empires, he had risen in the ranks of the soldiery until he had control of the Loren system. Tall and good-looking like Aylan, thickly muscled like his son Malvara, and with the profound insight given only to a few, he had been a popular hero who had made Loren into the potential Empire Malvara had inherited.

Barbaric, cultured, man of the sword, legalist, this strange and powerful figure had left behind him as his towering monument the Laws of Yusten. Prime among these were considerations concerning the internal politics of the Imperial Family. In a primitive fusion of law and blood, he had instituted the Judicial Duel. And for the first time since its legal inception, the trial by duel was to determine whether father or son should rule the Empire.

Miles sat back in the luxurious comfort of a pneumocouch and chewed his thumb worriedly. One of the paradoxes he had discovered in his odyssey was that violence is often the necessary path to peace. He watched Aylan checking his weapons for the duel, and knew that his strange destiny was coming to its fruition.

"The thing that has me worried," grunted Aylan, as he strapped his mini-load force shield under his cloak, "is the fact that my father has had live-duel experience. It could be the factor which wins him the Duel."

The automatic door keep buzzed, and a moment later a valet came into the room with a positron blaster freshly energized. With a word of thanks, Aylan took it from him, and weighed the weapon in his hand. Then, satisfied, he placed it in the jewel-encrusted holster strapped across his stomach. He looked at his watch and saw that there were only eighteen minutes left before the Duel.

"Come on," he said to his friend. "I want to test this damned thing out again in the Range before I go."

Together, they walked down the wide carpeted corridor to the Firing-range. The weight of metal in Miles's pocket bounced against his thigh, and he was in an agony of indecision as to whether he ought to take it out and give it to Aylan. It would mean deception in the Duel, but there were more important things involved than honesty with a man one was trying to kill.

The door to the Range slid open as they approached it.

Aylan went in first and walked onto the floor of the vast room, while Miles raised a heavy-power force shield around himself.

"Are you safely covered?" asked Aylan, and when Miles nodded, the Prince activated the Range. Immediately the room went pitch-black; a perfect simulacrum of the real Duel Hall. For a moment, Aylan's force-shield flared into life, a violet nimbus that illuminated him in the darkness. And with a *hish,* a long bolt of energy snapped at him. His reaction had been fast; as soon as his shield had come on, he had thrown himself to the ground and rolled feet away from where he had been. The energy bolt thrown at him by the robot Enemy hissed past, and before the Enemy had time to fire again he had snapped a shot of his own at the source of the bolt. There was no chime from the Strike-Indicator, so obviously he too had missed. His shield flickered out, and he was unprotected again.

Cautiously in the dark, as silently as he could, he crept towards the other end of the Range. Suddenly the nimbus of the Enemy's shield flickered on, and Aylan's bolt hissed towards the android. His aim was poor, and he missed by feet. And then a shot caught him with a jolt that threw him off his feet. Simultaneously, the Indicator chimed loudly, and the lights went on.

Dropping the heavy shield, Miles went out on to the Range and helped Aylan to his feet. The Prince had dropped his gun, and as he got up he picked up the weapon.

"That," he said, smiling ruefully, "would have been that, if the robot had held a real power gun. I only hope the Emperor has slowed up a bit on his reactions since he programmed for that robot."

Miles's mind was made up. When he had seen Aylan caught by the bolt, he had realized that he could afford to leave nothing to chance. Quickly, he drew a small, heavy tube of anodized metal from his pocket, and handed it to Aylan.

"Look, Aylan," he said gravely, "the Galaxy can't afford to have you killed today. We're just going to have to use a little duplicity."

The tube was cold in Aylan's hand, and he looked at it in puzzlement. It was like nothing he had ever seen before. He raised his eyes in question at Miles.

"It's an Old Empire weapon," said the Count, grimly. "It's called a stasis gun, and it was probably the most powerful weapon the Ancients ever developed. I'm not sure how it works, but I can assure you it does work most effectively. Somehow it brings everything in its range into minimal stasis, so that all the constituent atoms are brought to the one energy level. You'll have to use it if you want to come out of this duel alive."

As he spoke, he took the tube from Aylan's numb hands and inserted it skillfully under the energy pack of the positron blaster. Its weight balanced out nicely, and Miles handed the gun gingerly back to the Prince.

"Use the blaster as you ordinarily would, and for God's sake don't get shot before you have a chance to use it. The field is big enough to ensure that your enemy is destroyed even if you only have his general location."

He looked at his watch. There were three minutes left before the Duel. Aylan was still looking dumbly at the blaster.

"An Old Empire weapon?" He was shaking his head. "Where did you get it? It must be a thousand years old."

"It is, and there's a long story connected to it. But at the moment, you have a duel to win."

Candles flickered in the chapel and bathed the altar in a roseate glow. Veret finished the Mass, blessed the two combatants, and rose to give the sermon. His aged face was worn with worry, and as he spoke the tears ran unashamedly down his face. To him at least, the

Duel carried a more transcendental aspect than the future of the Empire. Today, a father would kill a son, or a son would claim his father's life.

Finally, the service was over, and the retinue moved from their pews, out of the incense-laden air to the clean freshness of the garden cloister. Somberly, the procession moved to the Dueling Range, Malvara and Aylan leading the way. For Aylan, it was like walking through thick treacle. His breath was coming hard, and his heart pounded with a frightening intensity. Death was no terror to him, not any longer. Rather it was the fear of the unnatural that gripped his limbs and tried to hold him back. His hatred for his father was gone now, in the face of parricide. Of course, he could not lose. Nothing manufactured in these barbarian days could withstand an Old Empire weapon. Sweat beaded his face, and then the retinue was in the Dueling Range.

All except Aylan and the Emperor moved behind the heavy-power shields at the side of the range, and the two were left facing one another. For a heart-choking moment Aylan wanted to cry out, to put a stop to the Duel. The old craggy face of his father swam in his eyes, and he opened his mouth and—

The lights were gone. Alone. It hadn't been like this on the robot Range. Here he could be killed. Dead. Surcease. He swallowed, and seemed to hear the dry gulp echo down the Range. He was surprised to find that he had crept noiselessly along the wall to the right. Heavy in his arms, the blaster was a reassurance. Now was the waiting game, the gamble. Whose shield would come on first? If it were his, he would dive forward, and to the left, roll forward and to the right. If it were his father's, he would fire straight at the afterimage. That is, if Miles was right. If the stasis beam was wide. What if the bloody old thing blew up? Too late to worry about that now.

And the nimbus was around him. He didn't move. Not for a split second, and that was long enough. Even as he dived, Malvara's energy stream streaked at him and caught the violet nimbus. The shock was ten times as great as the token jolt of the robot Range, and if the mini-shield hadn't been there the positron stream would have torn him apart. As it was, he was hurled backwards and he lost his grip on the blaster. It clattered away across the floor.

The neuronic blast of the feedback as the field neutralized the positron stream held him crippled. Desperately he wanted to retch, and desperately he controlled himself, for the slightest noise would invite another blast from Malvara. Shaking uncontrollably, he got to his hands and knees and searched around for the blaster. His hand touched something hard and cold, and he had the blaster in his hands again. Relief and reaction swept over him, and he sat on the floor cradling the blaster, as nerveless as a rag doll. Malvara's nimbus flickered on, and Aylan still sat on the floor hugging the weapon to himself.

As the Emperor hurled himself to one side, Aylan straightened up in the darkness and aimed his blaster. Before he could fire, the violet flame was gone. Without any thought at all, he extrapolated the direction of his father's leap, and pressed the activator of his blaster.

For a moment the room was brighter than day. A great funnel of light leapt from Aylan down the room, surrounding the fallen Malvara and bathing the back wall. Then the light was gone, but the Emperor was blazing like a torch, and a circle of the wall and floor behind him was red-hot. Slowly, his features melted into a ghastly caricature of his normal sardonic expression. With a gentle sighing sound, his body collapsed into a slag of hot liquid that mingled with the material of the floor and walls which had been caught in the field. Through the new hole in the wall, a calm breeze wafted in and carried to Aylan the scent of sweet flowers and burnt flesh. And there was no reason any more to control his retching.

### THREE

Aylan walked in a sackcloth robe down the gaunt pillared solitude of the cathedral, and he was lost in a drift of years and incense. Alone he walked, tall and strong in the century-old beauty of the vast cathedral, until he stood in the arc of the altar's great stone tracery. Here there was hope, though death and hatred had preceded it and would surely return again in the future. But there was no hatred here, only a tired age and a silent mighty blessing in stone and, somewhere waiting for him, Adriel.

Above him flamed the colors of the stained glass windows, and before him were the Archpriest and his lace robed acolytes. With measured care, Aylan stepped forward to the lowest level of the altar, and prostrated himself on the floor. The voice of the Archpriest came through a haze of unreality and the acolytes were the whole world chanting.

"Is this the man Aylan, heir-apparent, who claims the crown?"

*"Aye, this is the man."*

"Is he cleansed of the evils of pride and avarice, worthy to receive the Imperial dignity?"

*"Aye, though he is the dust of the earth, the crown must be his."*

"Then stand, Aylan, and ascend to the altar of God."

It is difficult to rise from a prostrate position with dignity, but Aylan had been trained for this moment for years. He dipped his hands into the bowl of clear oil an acolyte held, and the Archpriest carefully cleaned them again with a white cloth. Then he gently unfastened the clasps on the ugly dun robe Aylan wore. One of the priests took the robe from his shoulders, and the Prince stood, transformed, before the altar. Glistening white, flaming with precious stones, his tunic did justice to the office he was assuming.

He took his place on the great throne, and the Archpriest turned to the people.

"Here is Aylan of Loren." The crown was in his gnarled old hands, a miracle of beauty in metal and the glowing nimbus of a force shield. Slowly and majestically, he placed it on Aylan's head.

"In the name of God and the Christus, I name him Emperor. Do ye give him love and allegiance."

But, though his words were amplified through the cathedral, no one heard them. The roars and cheers of the crowd drowned everything in a spontaneous outburst of approval that sent tears coursing down Aylan's face, and he knew that he had not been wrong in accepting his destiny.

☼

The scent-drenched garden of the Imperial Palace was no less enchanting than the one Aylan had wept in at Nara. How could it be less, for there Aylan had not had Adriel beside him, laughing with her hand in his. He stopped and looked at her, drinking in the beauty of her face. In the golden afternoon, she was a rose-petal, delicate, desirable beyond words. And without words he enfolded her in his arms, savoring her lips, and their love was a soaring joy that held them wondering at the universe. They lay down on the grass, and night came in gold and red and twilight blue. There was the scent of leaves, and night came wonderfully, among the throng of dark trees.

"Can we do it?" whispered Aylan, and Adriel followed his gaze to the sprinkling sky. "Can we make a Federation from them? It seems an impossible dream, and yet—Miles has gone."

"When he comes back, we will know." She looked at his face, and kissed away his frown. "No, he does not have to come back. I know now. You can do it."

Her simple faith was touching, and contagious. Aylan's hand ruffled her hair, and he closed his eyes.

"Of course we can, dearest," he said drowsily, "of course we can...."

The sub-radio cracked viciously with the flux of the terrible energies that raged between the stars. But it carried Miles's voice, unmistakable, and he was angry.

"Calais's power has gone to his head." The Count's voice dipped and roared in the Communications room. "He refuses to hand over command, and he is already making advanced preparations to planet-bomb the two largest Central systems." His voice faded completely, and technicians twisted knobs frantically to hold the carrier wave. Subspace transmission was always a risky proposition, and Miles's ship was still almost five thousand parsecs away.

Aylan paced furiously up and down in the small room, as angry as Miles to see his dreams close to destruction because of mutiny within his own ranks.

"...only one thing to do," came Miles's voice. "Fit up the Imperial Guard force with stasis weapons and hightail it in here to Center before Jon wipes out all hope of peaceful Federation."

"But good God, man," roared Aylan, "you say you hardly know the principle of the stasis field yourself. How could we possibly implement the idea in time?"

There was a time lag of some seconds, and Miles's voice crackled back through the strange universe of sub-space.

"...my rooms in the Palace, there are blueprints of the device. Like...pire devices, it's extremely simple in design, getting its potency from total conversion of energy. You could have the projectors made in the ship's workshops on your way in here. I'll meet the Guard at Leith in two days, so you'll have to snap straight to it."

Aylan felt no resentment at the way his friend had taken control of the situation. Certainly, Miles knew more about the position Centerside, and he spoke with a new authority that the Emperor did not think to question.

"Very well." His voice travelled within seconds to the hurtling Ambassador ship. "Although I doubt whether we will be in time...."

"Good luck, Aylan." Miles's voice had softened. "You just have to get here," but he did not sound as convinced of success as Adriel had the previous night.

☼

Hanging in orbit above the Imperial planet, the Emperor's special Guard was *the* crack unit of the Loren Navy. Two heavy cruisers, mile-long monoliths whose fields could withstand a nova-bomb, and whose armament could wipe out a system, but whose relatively limited velocity made them defensive rather than tactical. More immediately valuable, the light cruisers and the two-man attack minnows. Now, five hours after Miles's dramatic message, the ships' drives were idling hot while Aylan made his last preparations in connection with the stasis projectors. Without them, such a light task force would be little use against Calais' huge war Navy, and the best engineers on Loren were gradually going crazy trying to apply millennium-old diagrams to lathe and metal. The tiny heavy projector that had won Aylan his duel was X-rayed and dissected and put together again for four hours until finally the engineers solved the diagrams. From then on, there was only the sheer mechanical work of devising efficient and rapid ways of constructing heavy-duty projectors en route to Leith.

Five hours and seventeen minutes after the message, the new Emperor was lifting in a shuttle to the flagship of the Guard. With him were three engineers, a multitude of diagrams and a good-as-new Old Empire stasis blaster.

Normally, sub-space jumping is a boring business, but the two-day trip to Leith was scarcely time enough for the machine-shops in the light cruisers to turn high tensile steel into the long innocent-looking tubes which, when coupled to heavy-power fields, would be capable of destroying an armada of ships. And would have to.

Leith was growing into a verdant globe in the viewscreen when word came to the flagship that the last of the projectors had been installed. The Guard had re-entered normal space on the rim of the Leith system and were flashing towards the rendezvous planet on solar drive. In the control room of the flagship *Ascaux,* Thony Lord Hardt lit Aylan's cigar with a steady hand, and watched in quiet amusement as his Emperor proceeded to chew the end of the cigar to shreds.

"Sit down, Excellency," he suggested. "There's at least an hour to planet-fall, and pacing up and down like a caged puma will only wear you out." He was a giant of a man, this Commander of the Emperor's Guard, and a great black beard covered most of his craggy face. He had not been unhappy to hear of Malvara's death, for he had never liked the cruel, hard Emperor, and this earnest young man appealed to him. The prospect of imminent civil war was troubling, but in the two days out to Leith Aylan had managed to transmit some of his tremendous enthusiasm for the necessity of peaceful Federation to everyone with whom he had come in contact. Lord Hardt repressed his smile and scratched the black thatch of his head instead.

Aylan released a ragged sigh and collapsed into a seat. He had lost a considerable amount of weight in the two-day trip, transmuted into the nervous energy he so liberally expended.

"Why is it, Thony, that the path of peace must run with blood?" There was agony on his finely featured face. "Why, when self-preservation is so obviously one of the primal urges in Man, must he be ever trying to commit racial suicide? Perhaps there is indeed some Original Sin that drives social man to self-slaughter."

"I'm no great philosopher, Excellency," said the bearded Commander, "but I'm sure you're wrong. Look at history. There has always been a predominant current towards peace. I think you'll find that the war-mongering element is limited to a very few malcontents, though God knows they're usually powerful enough." He stubbed out the butt of his cigar. "And there are the great mass of soldiery who, like myself, have no love for war yet fight to protect themselves and other peace lovers. Maybe 'the meek shall inherit the earth,' but unfortunately it'll only be after they've destroyed all the violent ones."

He chuckled and heaved his giant frame from the chair. "I suggest that we get on to the sub-radio and find out if Count Miles has anything new that will set your mind at ease."

Leithside, Miles knew nothing fresh, but expressed his opinion that Calais's preparation for wholesale massacre must be nearly completed. By the time the Guard ships reached the green globe of Leith, Aylan was almost physically ill with strain. Lord Hardt was visibly relieved when the tiny silver needle of the Ambassador ship intercepted with the fleet, and Miles came aboard the flagship. The presence of Aylan's tall space-burnt friend calmed the Emperor considerably, and he was able to settle down to the complex business of planning his approach to Calais.

"The rebel forces are obviously in a poor political position," mused Miles. He, Aylan, and Thony sat at the conference table in the Emperor's small luxurious stateroom. "Aylan is a popular figure at the moment, as Calais' spies must have ascertained by now. He must be banking on a *coup d'état,* so we can at least hope that he will have diverted his forces temporarily from the problem of exterminating the Central systems to the more pressing matter of removing Aylan."

"That's true." Hardt was doodling absently on a sheet of paper, but his mind was as sharply concentrated on the problem as an electronic computer. "Duke Jon may be a megalomaniac but he's no fool. He won't be expending forces in wiping out any of the Central systems if doing so leaves him at a disadvantage in facing us. If he destroys us now, cleaning up the Center will be no harder for him later than it is now. Whereas, if he wipes out the Central groups now and gets killed by our fleet as a result, his orgy of destruction will have brought him no gain."

"I think you're forgetting two things," Aylan warned him. He sat back in his seat and looked grimly at first one man and then the other. "First, Calais has a pretty vast army out there, and since he doesn't know about our secret weapon, the Guard won't appear much of a challenge to him. He has enough ships to be able to divert twice our number to deal with us while still going ahead with the general massacre."

There was a moment when the only sound was the hum of the air-purifiers; his point had struck home.

"Second, Calais is a bitter man, and as you said, Thony, a megalomaniac. If he does realize that his destruction is inevitable, he may indulge in a widespread slaughter as a kind of insane revenge."

Through the featureless dark of sub-space, the task-force sped at a fantastic multiple of the speed of light, in a race with time to cross a quarter of a galaxy. And inside the *Ascaux,* three men struggled to solve a problem on whose solution hung the destiny of a race, and though they were not aware of it, the destiny of a universe.

*The Board was a billion scintillating lights, a trillion moving pieces. Again, the King was in danger, and the Queen was in no position to help. The Player moved his Pawns. The Game was nearly over.*

☼

Across the heart of the Galaxy, the Imperial fleet of Loren hung like a fine-spun net, holding impotent the forces of the Central systems. Anani, Kiel, Ghatoos, Blucher, Menai, the proud young systems of the Hub, held under the iron hand of Jon of Calais.

In the fleet's flagship, *Loren,* the iron hand of Jon of Calais was wrapped solidly around a glass of an infamous high-proof beverage. The Duke was a hard, bitter man, and alcohol was the only weakness he permitted himself. He had reason for his basic misanthropy; in one of Nature's whimsical jests, he had been born with no legs. He had never forgiven the rest of mankind for having two more limbs than he, and it was almost inevitable that with his brilliant strategic mind he would turn to that profession where he could legally take bloody revenge on mankind *en masse.*

He sat hunched on the plastic-padded grav-plate that served him for legs, a black hawk in his form-fitting Navy overalls. The liquor burned down his throat and added fire to his hatred for the young upstart who was trying to ruin his plans. In the viewscreen that covered half the wall the stars of the Hub blazed like an inferno of jewels. Calais unconsciously licked his lips as he looked at them, and his grip tightened on the goblet.

There was a chime from the video, and its bland screen dissolved into the head and shoulders of his Chief of Staff.

"Sir, we've just received a message missile from one of your agents on Loren. The new Emperor left Loren three days ago with the Imperial Guard, with the intention of forcing you to relinquish command. The task-force with the Emperor on board should probably arrive here within a day or so."

"With the Guard, hey?" Calais looked more than ever like a great brooding bird of prey, peering down his long nose. "Now what could he expect to accomplish with such a token force against what I've got here? I've got to have time to think about this. Suspend activity on the preparations for planet-bombing for the moment; we may need those ships for a more immediate purpose. Thank you, Admiral, I'll get in touch with you." He flicked off the screen and it faded again into translucence.

Why would Aylan send such a token force indeed? Of course, the bulk of the fleet was out here at Center, but had Aylan wanted he could have brought the whole of the defense force. Hmm. The new Emperor was, of course, a moral weakling, thanks to his father's careful training. Did he then expect the forces to be handed over to him just because of a personal appearance? It seemed hardly possible, but the milk-sop Aylan was naive in the ways of real men.

The Duke made his decision, and flicked on the video again.

"Admiral, hold developments here as they are at the moment. I think I'll take a small task-force vessel to deal with our impetuous young Emperor."

Jon of Calais smiled to himself. Events were turning out better than he could ever have hoped. Rid himself of Aylan now, beat the Central fools to their knees, and then....

The stars blazing in the viewscreen were a song of worship to his name.

☼

All Aylan's questions were resolved ten hours later when, still in sub-space, the ship's detectors revealed a fleet of unknown size approaching from the direction of Calais's base of operations. Thony advised against sub-radio communication with the other fleet until they broke radio silence first.

"If Calais is with them," said Miles, as the three men stared in semi-darkness at the green traces on the detector screens, "and knowing his power complex he's sure to want to be in on the kill, we can try negotiations first, and if he isn't interested we'll have to use the stasis fields."

Lord Hardt's practiced eye studied the screen intently for a moment, and he voiced his opinion that the other fleet was only two or three times as big as the Guard.

"Then probably the rest of the war-force is maintaining the *status-quo* Centerside." Aylan looked across to Miles. "If we destroy Calais, will the rest of the fleet come back under Imperial command?"

His friend gave a short snort that could have been a chuckle, but there was no humor in it.

"Most of them are unaware of their rebel status. It is the high-ranking officers who have fallen under Jon's spell that we must watch. But I think that with Calais gone they will lick your feet as though nothing ever happened."

A speaker squawked, and an adjutant's voice informed the Emperor that the approaching ships had made sub-radio contact with the Guard.

The communications-room was humming with the static of deep space when the trio arrived to take the message from Calais's ship. Lights flickered from banks of meters as the ship's cryotronic computer struggled to hold the carrier wave that was propagating across the strange not-world of sub-space. Five hours and over three thousand light-years apart, the two fleets were connected by a magic not understood properly even by those who used it.

For the first time since his adolescence, Aylan heard the deep handsome voice of Duke Jon of Calais. Torn and distorted though it was by the static of sub-space, the compelling voice conjured up pictures of a clear-eyed golden haired god, a cord-muscled, beneficent pagan deity. Here, thought Aylan, is the secret of his power over men, and it was incredibly hard to substitute the image of a hawk-faced maniac for that of the glowing god.

"You realize, of course," the golden voice was saying, "that I cannot accept you as Emperor. I have had no word from the Council, and I am left with the inevitable conclusion that you have murdered your royal father and seized the reins of power illegally."

Aylan glanced helplessly at Miles, and the Count took the microphone.

"Listen, Calais," he grated. "I came to you as authorized legate of both your Emperor Aylan of the line of Yusten, and the Council, and I left with you documents that ordered you to relinquish your command at the Center to the new Emperor. If you continue in this insane mutiny you can expect only execution, and dishonor to your name. If, even at this late hour, you acquiesce in the Emperor's orders your name will be cleared as acting in good faith. Make up your mind; the time has passed for childish lies."

The handsome voice was cold now, with a hard, cruel edge, like a god admonishing his creatures.

"True enough," it said, "the time is past for games. I have with me a force three times as large as your own, and behind me I have the whole Imperial offence-force. I intend to rule the Galaxy, *Emperor*, and unless you turn and run home like the scared mouse you are, I'm afraid I will have to kill you myself."

White and shaking with anger, Aylan snatched the microphone from Miles's hand and roared his fury across the light-years.

"I return your ultimatum to you, carrion, and formally remove from you your command, your Imperial rank and privileges, and your right to life. Come, rebel, and discover what death is like at first hand." There was a loud click as he broke contact with the oncoming ships in one violent sweep of his hand.

☼

Five hours and eleven minutes later the two fleets intercepted, and after the hours of tension the battle was almost terrifyingly anti-climactic. The Guard flipped out into real space in a half-moon formation, the horns towards Galactic Center. They were near the center of a globular cluster, and the stars hung coldly about them like a million teardrops, a million celestial diamonds. Seconds later the larger task-force from Center precipitated into space in a sphere formation. Jon's ship hung in the middle of the sphere, a heavily-armed cruiser sitting in the safest position.

Aylan's flagship sat on one of the horns and inside her control-room three men sat watching the other fleet, hoping against all reason that there would be no need to use the stasis fields. A green flare silently flashed from the rebel fleet, and engulfed one of the Guard ships in a titanic incandescence of energy. The ship's lights dimmed as the force-shield struggled to neutralize the flare, the momentarily under-powered stabilizers tossed the ship crazily, and then the lights came on again. The shield had held. In the control-room of the *Ascaux*, Aylan realized that the fleet could not withstand such a one-sided battle for long. Reluctantly, he gave the order to activate the stasis projectors.

Space was a vast white glare, a ghastly effulgence of death. For an eternal instant. Then there was only the star filled darkness, and sixty pink glowing drops of molten metal, plastic, flesh....

The whole encounter had taken less than twenty seconds.

## FOUR

Of all the Ancients' wondrous works, the most awesome and permanent was Prima. The Old Imperial planet, a world—to look at it—dedicated to loveliness, where the grandeur of Nature under the restraining guidance of Man sang an everlasting hymn of praise to beauty. Lifted in an unimaginable engineering feat from a cold dark sun that had held it trapped in the death of night for eons, it had been placed in orbit around the barren white sun which stood like a virgin Queen in the center of the Galaxy. And under the inspiring genius of the hand of Man, Prima had flowered, her oceans had foamed again, her mountains had learned anew to cry at a living sun.

A monument to beauty, to Man. But this was as nothing compared with the reality that lay beneath the skin of the planet. For twenty, thirty miles beneath the surface, Prima was honey-combed with the nests of men. Here had been the administrative Center of the Galactic Empire. Here was the Imperial Palace, in the planet that men had placed at the center of the Galaxy. And here, in tiers of metal and superfluid helium, was the Computer that girdled the circumference of Prima.

But now the Computer was dead, the cryotronic dance of its memory stilled a millennium before in the shock of the civil war that had shaken the Galaxy back to barbarism. Most of the vast area of office- and living-space, where once had teemed a planetary population of bureaucrats, had crashed and fallen in that cataclysmic war, but the Old Council Hall had been miraculously untouched, and the king of the new Monarchy of Kiel had made it his own. And relinquished it to his conquerors from Loren.

Miles felt a heart-clutching sense of foreboding as he stood beside his Emperor and Empress in the garden of Nature that stretched to the horizon in waves of green and yellow. In a few short minutes, they would descend the grav-shaft to the Council Hall, and if everything went well, the Galaxy would see for the first time— Federation! The wild elation that was obviously gripping Aylan had completely left Miles, and he was swamped with a nightmare conviction of unreality. It was as though the blackness before his eyes were really there, the singing in his ears, the head-pounding blood....

"Aylan," he cried, in a terror that was almost childlike.

For a moment the world spun around him, and then he was leaning on the solid assurance of his friend's arm.

"Aylan," he said with a tired weariness, "I have a story to tell you."

Once, the universe must have been young, an emptiness filled with fiery gases and slowly-spinning newborn suns. And even then, the Player must have been preparing the Board for his game.

Miles first saw the light of day on a smoking, roaring world of shaggy beast-men and thudding hairy animals. It was a world on the Rim of the Galaxy, with a feeble yellow star and a single pockmarked moon.

It was the only world that ever produced sentient life, and its children were destined to seed the Galaxy.

For the Game. For the Player's inscrutable purpose. Miles, the shaggy beast-man, possessed no more than the limited awareness of his fellows. Later, though, they called him Prometheus. He did not discover fire, but as elder of his tribe he saved from death the man who did. He caused a priesthood to be set up, and his tribe worshipped fire, and conquered their world.

And he was punished with eternal life, to come again and again as a child and to remember and to die and to come again.... Of course, he learned. Memories of his previous life returned to him at puberty, and each life wrote new wonders on the tablet of experience. For a time he rebelled. He refused to be the Player's instrument, refused to pass his knowledge on. And there was no retribution, save in his soul. He could not live with the sloughing beasts he was born among. Frantically, he tried the life of the hermit, and he was driven back by loneliness to human companionship.

So, finally, he became the Civilizer.

He was Gilgamesh, Odin, Ra, Indra, Zeus, Tonacatecuhtli, Moses, Gandhi, Holden-Smith, Porter, and Andreas. In the mud of the Nile he trod water and straw; his statue was carried before the tallow candles in Tenochtitlan; he advised the Great One in Tibet while the wind whistled against his thin bones; he thundered in the Terran Planetary Parliament; he labored on alien worlds, muscles twisting to hammer wood and steel into homes for his fellows. And everywhere, he remembered. Peace was his goal, for no man can go through a million years' odyssey without learning compassion and humanity.

"I lived as legal counsel to your grandfather Yusten," Miles said quietly, "as an adviser to the Monarch of Kiel, as a singer of ballads in the halls of Blucher, and now I am your friend—and you are about to bring about the widespread peace I have labored eons to achieve. And I am afraid of the Player."

In the great garden that was Prima, the birds continued their singing unconcernedly, and a gentle breeze tossed the leaves and grasses as it had done for centuries, but the breath of age was strong now, an age greater than the ancient Council Hall below, greater than the dreams of men. Miles stood with his friends in the quiet afternoon, strong, young, and his mind encompassed a universe of history.

Aylan's eyes were focused on a horizon beyond the azure sky of Prima, and when he turned to Miles his face was shining with a great vision. He took Adriel's hand, and said in a strange forced voice, "Come. We have destiny to meet."

The grav-tube was waiting, and the three floated down towards the Council Hall.

☼

In the vast hall sat the rulers and representatives of the Galaxy. They were restless, waiting to hear the terms desired by the young Emperor whose father had conquered them. Aylan looked at their faces and there was resentment and bitterness everywhere. These were men beaten by virtue of Loren's technological strength—there was no lack of spirit among them. The Emperor was glad, for he wanted strong men, capable men with the vision to see beyond their own pettiness.

The three were the last to enter the Hall. Bitter the conquered leaders might be, but they had no wish to antagonize their new master. Aylan squeezed Adriel's cool lovely hand, and when he rose to speak there was silence throughout the hall.

"My friends," he began. There was a discernible brightening of some of the faces-a hostile dictator would hardly call his victims *friends*. "Although you are unaware of the fact, the capital planets of your systems were almost nova-bombed by my forces less than a week ago."

He paused, and glanced sideways at Adriel. Her eyes were closed, and he could feel the waves of apprehension she was directing out into the audience before him.

"My commander of forces mutinied against Loren and was endeavoring to set himself up as Emperor. At personal danger to myself, I took a fleet out and destroyed him and sixty of my own naval vessels."

Puzzlement, dawning awareness. Aylan's head was held high, and his words were intense, his eyes bright.

"I did this because I had your interests at heart. I could easily have been killed, but I considered the risk worth taking if I could in this way convince you that I am not seeking my own aggrandizement." A wave of relief, and a warmth towards the young man before them. Adriel did not have to engender the emotion; she merely intensified it.

Aylan's speech had been semantically designed to elicit the desired emotional response from the audience. Beside him, the beautiful Emote sent wave after nuanced wave of complementary emotion out into the Hall, judging, balancing, dancing in an emotional control that was practically instinctive. They were on the edges of their chairs now, breathing the glory of the vision Aylan was painting. Memories fled through Aylan's mind: childhood days, talking to Miles, nights of anguished mental conflict, the evening at Nara with the Galactic Lens burning around him and Miles's words setting his mind on fire with a towering hope for the future. And now, in the huge ancient Hall, the leaders of the Galaxy were sharing this dream, guided by his words and the Emotive control of a slim lovely girl.

Finally, Aylan was silent, and Adriel played a last crescendo of trust, enthusiasm, and accord. Without prompting, the audience who half an hour before had stared with bitter, angry eyes at the young Emperor rose to their feet in wild applause. Their shout was a mighty *Fiat* to peace, a cry that rocked the walls....

Literally. Miles came to his feet, and the terror was black on him again. In numb horror he saw the walls of the Council Hall fold in like a freckled banana skin, and the roof gaped wide as the whole planet seemed to peel open. Around him, the other figures of the Game screamed and ran amok, tearing, howling like animals. The noise somehow faded away, and the ruined planet bubbled with spurting boiling magma that ran around Miles but could not touch him. He realized that he was screaming too, for the stars were whirling in a mad kaleidoscope of light and they were falling on him, globes of roaring fire, tiny marbles of cold luminescence, a spraying spiral of light. He was huge beyond belief, the pinpoints of light were stars, galaxies, and the universe was fading, eddying, insubstantial, and he was screaming at the Player why, why, why...?

☼

*Alone. Darkness, bodiless, infinite. All the questions answered and the tears wept. The Immortal wondered at the memory, and knew the reason. There was no Player. There was only himself, alone, eternally lonely. Infinity is a quiet place, eternity a lonely time. The Immortal remembered himself as Miles, and forever the memory satisfied him. But forever is a short while, and memory is no cure for loneliness. Only participation, and forgetfulness.*

*The Tasks had been a good idea, but they had ended. The problem he had set himself: a universe, a race of naturally belligerent sapients, a goal of peace, freely accepted by them. And three times he had succeeded. Planetary government, Galactic empire, Galactic Federation. Himself eternal, not knowing the reason, only aware of the compulsion.*

*An Immortal Child grows lonely in the dark of eternity, and he knew that there was forgetfulness in the Game. So again in the deep of himself he uttered the Words.*

*"Let there be light!"*
*And, yet again, there was light.*

# INTERVIEW WITH DAMIEN BRODERICK, PART ONE

## QUESTIONS BY RUSSELL BLACKFORD

I have broken this interview (from almost three decades ago, at the start of my career as a novelist rather than short fiction and magazine journalist) into three mostly chronological parts. In places it touches on matters already sketched above, but I hope the redundancy is less irritating than illuminating. I also hope that a certain merry humor comes across. Dr. Dr. Russell Blackford—yes, he holds two doctorates and a swag of other degrees besides—and his wife Jenny, are two of my oldest friends in the Australian sf community. One of the few downsides of my move to America has been the great and increasingly expensive distance between the two countries. This long conversation from 1981 took place just as I was starting to break out of my bad habits of commercial writing and taking on more ambitious work; I had published a short story collection, an anthology and two novels at the time, and a third novel, *The Judas Mandala,* was due the following year.

**Blackford:**

*"Never trust the artist—trust the tale," says D.H. Lawrence. But is there anything we should know about your experience or your general intentions* as *a writer?*

**Broderick:**

Like so many middle-aged people named Damien, I was raised a Catholic. I was raised so fervently in that manner, in fact, that I sped off at fifteen to the Junior Seminary of the Blessed Sacrament Fathers in Bowral, New South Wales, an event fraught with mysterious possibilities. It's worth noting that sociobiology has demonstrated, quite convincingly in my view, that religion was a primordial substitute for science fiction. Throughout the ages, men and women have lifted their eyes to the stars, driven by a powerful yet indistinct urge, a craving embedded in their genes. Only with the advent—indeed, the epiphany—of *Modern Electronics,* the *Electrical Experimenter, Amazing Stories*, and *Thrills Incorporated* was this galvanic thirst earthed and quenched.

**Blackford:**

*I think I missed the experiments in this case. Anyway, tell us more about the theory.*

**Broderick:**

Proof, if proof is called for, can be found as close to hand as Australian sf fandom. Many were called but few were collared. John Bangsund, Bruce Gillespie, and John Alderson were every man jack of them victims of a fundamentalist confession known in the United States, unless I miss my mark, as the Three Seed in the Spirit Evocational Wailers. Bangsund, who was later to turn to drink after his faith in sf followed its precursor into desuetude, actually studied for holy orders in this heterodox rite. John Foyster's father was a minister in a somewhat more bourgeois faith, and though John was later to cross the line he was doubtless raised to toe it. I must leave Irwin Hirsh to speak for himself. All told, it's a pretty tally. And though one can enumerate more than a single case where religion was abandoned in favor of sf, you'd be hard pressed to find an instance of the reverse.

Bowral, as everyone knows, is the seat of the great cricketer Sir Donald Bradman. It was the font also of John Baxter, the notorious filmographer. When I arrived at Eymard College on a chilly summer's day in 1960, three inches below my terminal growth spurt, Baxter was an urbane, world-weary, apple-cheeked man of twenty-one, and his parents' modest Bowral home was the hub of a high tensile network of fannish activity. American fanzines like *Shaggy* and *Yandro*, the stuff of fable, lobbed every day upon his mum's doorstep, and it was easy for the prescient to see at once that Baxter would soon take that short but giant step into professional story-flogging. Less prescient than most, I went through my daily devotions for many months before news of Baxter's presence in the same dot on the map (pop. 5,000) electrified me from my dogmatic slumbers and sent me racing for the phone (after obtaining Father Superior's permission, you understand). An urbane, world-weary voice answered me, and learned that even in Bowral in 1961 (for by now it was a year after my arrival, and my growth had begun its incessant spurting) it was possible to touch the soul of another warm meaningful human being by having your guest editorial published in *New Worlds* in Greater London, U.K.

Well, from that point on the genes had their way. On my bicycle (chosen from the monastic pool) as often as possible, I'd pedal to Baxter's family hearth and bore the shit out of the poor bastard, glutting my incredulous and imprint-primed eyes upon his fanzine trove, borrowing wicked books from his unrivalled sf collection, arguing the toss about the existence of God, meeting the strikingly Peter Sellers-like Foyster and suffering the slings and arrows of the two fans' scornful japes, jests, and cynically world-weary gibes and jeers, and so on until finally I returned a wiser and better-educated man to the World, the Devil, and (eventually) the Flesh.

It was not Baxter's fault, of course. How could I have seen his name in *New Worlds,* locked as I was in the bowels of a seminary, unless I was already a helpless sf junkie?

I'd started long before with comics: Brick Bradford in the newspapers, *Strange Adventures* and *Superman* in the second-hand swap shops. That led to Franklin's Book Exchange, a large second-hand store in Melbourne's central business district, and various small suburban library-cum-exchange shops run by little old ladies; these dealt in Vargo Statten thrillers, *Science Fantasy* (far and away my favorite magazine at the time), and old copies of *Galaxy* and *Astounding.* Municipal libraries had kiddie-sf (Mary Patchett: *Adam Troy, Astroman,* 1954, *Lost on Venus*, the same year; Patrick Moore; others), and Bleiler and Dikty anthologies in the adult section if you could gouge the bloody things out of them at the age of eleven or twelve. (Foyster also used the Preston library during roughly the same period, before going on to Proust, Lie groups, and brain surgery at the age of fourteen, so our eyetracks scored the same volumes; could the need for sf be a communicable virus, despite the sociobiologists?)

Through *Astounding,* I learned of pioneer parapsychologist Dr. J. B. Rhine and my mind was ruined. Certain psi experiments I conducted at thirteen or fourteen so staggered me (and still do) that I never shook off a desire to crack the secret of getting psi to work reliably. I abandoned that interest for years at a time, but kept nudging back to it. A lot of my time in the 1970s went into excruciatingly tedious ESP studies. It sidetracked me from writing sf, but it also saved me from a boring life as a Public Service Clerk.

Although I saw very little motion-picture sf, radio was a powerful medium for fantasy. The "Argonauts" show of the Australian Broadcasting Commission (the national broadcaster) ran superb kid-height serials, on a par with Arthur C. Clarke's early space-boosting books. Commercial radio offered higher peaks. 3DB ran a mind-croggling serial called *Captain Miracle,* which began with the eponymous officer and his youthful chum or charge locating a ditched mini spaceship in the vicinity of Woomera (the famous rocket testing site in the desert), fighting an Earth-menacing Star Beast, hurtling at the moment of victory into the sun...and out the other side of hyperspace after an encounter with a gloriously chord-evoked Divinity (there's our theme again, folks) Who was to pop up at vital crunches; the captain traded in his vessel for a...wait for it...goddamn, it blew my *brain* away...a genuine mile-long starship!!! With force-fields and artificial gravity and for all I know ravening bolts of pure energy. Oh woe is me that I didn't fall upon Doc Smith in those innocent tone-deaf style-blind days. After about sixteen it was impossible; lost, that great city! What was *not* lost, by God, was the greatest of all star-cities—Diaspar. I found *The City and the Stars* when I was fourteen, and then *Childhood's End,* and I suppose it became definite on some floor in my mind's high-rise that I was doomed to write sf.

I'd been scribbling it earlier than that, of course. My first published story was typed and duplicated by a school friend's luckless parent, or at least his secretary, when I was in, I think, sixth grade, aged eleven. The kid lugged about fifty copies in with him and we stood at the gate at day's end distributing the thing. My only fanzine. The following year my Jesuit primary school teachers and my parents decided that I lacked the intellectual capacity to sustain a full secondary education, and I was shunted to a Christian Brothers' technical school in the then slum suburb Abbotsford, where, it was hoped, my more menial aptitudes might blossom. This failed to happen.

I sidestepped the problem by discovering an overwhelming vocation to the priesthood. That got me out of the house, into the rest of my education, and satisfied my profound but not-then fully understood craving for science fiction, which of course I mistook for an interest in the divine.

You'd be surprised, though, how useful soldering is when you come to renovate your home.

And the same principles of architectonics apply to structuring novels as one learned in those woodwork and solid geometry classes. The world is a wonderful unity, isn't it? All one thing. Nothing is ever lost. Except your life. Except your life. Except your life.

Before you drench your hankies, I should hasten to add that there are far more heart-rending tales in the annals of Australian sf. Consider the harrowing path trodden by Lee Harding, boy drop-out.

**Blackford:**

*A number of your early stories were originally published in places like* Man Junior. *In fact, there's a legend that when you were involved in editing the Monash University students' newspaper,* Lot's Wife, *you once had to dodge a thrust about turning the paper into a girlie magazine....*

**Broderick:**

Someone's pulling your leg. We were strenuously serious, dedicated to keeping sport on the back page and high-brow think pieces (pilfered without acknowledgement from John W. Campbell Jr. and Isaac Asimov; I mean *high-brow*, cobber) on the front. We once ran a story by Pete Steedman explaining that Norman Banks, a prominent smooth-tongued radio commentator, possessed and promoted views which would not have got him thrown out of Hitler's bunker. Years later, I learned that lawyers had spoken long and hard to my parents about this. I was not a fully-accredited adult at the time, but it's a far cry from putting anti-Vietnam protestors in the dock, as happened in Australia a little later.

*Lot's Wife* came into existence as such with Vol. 4, No. 7 of *Chaos*, as the Monash students' newspaper was then known. June 24, 1964. I'd been involved in *Chaos* from my first weeks on campus, in 1962. Monash had been open for only a year, the place was glutinous with mud and baby intellectuals unseasoned by dreaming red-brick spires erected in the 1920s. In the fullness of time, my cronies and I seized control of the rag and changed the name, on very similar principles to those that apply after the liberation of a Third-World nation, but with considerably less justification. The name is my responsibility. It is, of course, pure Dada, and has no further metonymy.

Our great innovation was the shift from letterpress hot-metal printing to Web Offset. This genuine breakthrough was nosed out by Tony Schauble, a co-editor, later one of the founders and beneficiaries of *Go-Set*, arguably the world's first teenybopper newspaper. Offset opened the floodgates to filth, corruption, fun, energy, last-minute paste-ups to fool the censors.... I'm not certain if we were first with offset design, and I doubt we truly grasped the wonderful possibilities for silliness and delight and provocation it opened. Our idea of a great night out was to mimic the austere, impeccably clean layout of the German newspaper *Der Neue Welt.*

Our finest moment was publishing John Romeril's first demented outburst of lyrical pain. April 22, 1965 (my twenty-first birthday!). We spelled his name wrong, though.

**Blackford:**

*You were a prominent "character" on the Monash campus, I gather.*

**Broderick:**

So it seems. I was probably half-mad at the time. I didn't *really* start to fly until my fourth year at Monash, when I was part of a proto urban commune/ collective sex 'n' speed 'n' hard-philosophisin' household down the road from the Uni. Two couples, me alone, women in and out as residents, tutors known to drop in and employ the place as a venue for the debauchment of themselves and their academic charges. We accidentally set fire to it midway into 1965 and had no kitchen or living room thereafter; this immensely enhanced our mutual dependency and closeness, as cooking in random bedrooms will do. It's all mindcrushingly banal now, of course, but back then it produced some agitation among our mentors. The Vice Chancellor, we learned later, wanted to close us down, for our own ethical, health, and educational good. Finally our lavatory stopped working (that was the health consideration). Dear old Lot 4. Tractors came later and leveled, mounded, contoured the land for factories. We went back there on a windy, cold, sunny day and danced silently, our scarves flying all melancholy. Secret Seven Go To Uni.

Because I was extremely poor (cleaned the kitchen in a pub miles away, acres of post-lunch grease but free lukewarm munchies; they paid contemptuously, and I left with a curse), my clothes wore out. This made me a strange figure to behold. Elbows sticking out, buggered shoes. I wore a baggy old dressing gown for a while, inherited from my grandfather; the winter weather was bitterly cold, had to do something. For a year I secreted myself within a room we built inside a campus office; slept most luxuriously on four Fleur chairs abreast, drank coffee with strange nightwatchmen. I had a vast box of John Foyster's sf magazines, fetched by me on a trip from Sydney; they'd come from the States, fantastic bargain, via John Baxter. As the months went by, visitors to my small furtive kingdom pilfered the goddamn magazines. I was so ashamed of the diminished hoard that for years I held off returning the rather small remnant box to John. (Later, being a good-hearted man, he let me off the hook with the news that a few years later his house, library, and effects were firestormed to cinders anyway....)

## AFTERWORD 2010

Since my first sale was in the premier issue of a moderately prestigious original-fiction series in Britain (reprinted the following year in the USA, true home of category science fiction), why didn't I persist with submissions overseas? The money might be better than the rates available from any magazine open to sf in backwater, provincial Australia in the 1960s. Certainly my older genre colleagues were taking that overseas path: for years, motoring journalist Wynne Whiteford had been published in the US and UK, Lee Harding and John Baxter were not only fanzine writers and reviewers but had already broken into Carnell's magazines *New Worlds*, *Science Fiction Adventures*, and *Science Fantasy* in their twenties, soon followed by David Boutland and Stephen Cook. I might have done the same—certainly I was envious of their frequent appearances alongside J. G. Ballard and Brian W. Aldiss in these magazines I'd doted on in later childhood and adolescence—but the sorry truth was that I needed money for food, and *now*!

Unluckily, I had the customary epiphany of many beginning writers in those days, leafing through magazines aimed at general audiences, that surely I could write as well as *this*, and get paid quickly, no need for weeks-long, expensive sea mail to and from Britain or the US, and costly bank conversions of alien currencies. In late 1963 I happened upon several moldering copies of *Man*, once a respectable if faintly saucy journal for Australian men at war but by the 1960s a feeble imitation of *Playboy* and its less expensive emulators (mostly banned in pure, heavily-censored Australia), and found in its pages some rudimentary sf by no-name writers. Good god, I thought, and sat down at once to bash out a story of glacial simplicity. Off it went, and within days I got back from editor Fred C. Folkard a kindly and enthusiastic acceptance and check. Not a large check, but it paid my way for several weeks, and that's what I needed, holed up in my digs, eating beans and sausage out of cans, drinking fake coffee with sweetened condensed milk. In the event, "A Man Returned" appeared in June 1964, its ending rewritten and dumbed-down by Fred. Annoying, but it was pay dirt. Of course I hadn't kept a carbon copy of the original, so the butchered and watered-down version was used in my first collection, under the same title, sold when I was twenty and published not long after I turned twenty-one.

For the rest of the decade, I wrote quite a lot of this derivative, simplified genre product, cautiously pushing the perimeters of what the magazines would permit, and eventually graduated to writing think-pieces on topics such as guerilla warfare and its likely technological future (a topic of some urgency, given the Vietnam conflict), flying saucers, radical psycho-political thinkers such as Herbert Marcuse and R. D. Laing, sex, drugs, everything but rock 'n' roll, which I would cover elsewhere for the music magazine *Go-Set*. Most of the decade's fiction was later given a sanitary scrubbing and incorporated into novels, eventually making its way beyond the shores of Australia. One especially awful piece, "The Disposal Man," was taken by Fred Pohl for the premier number of his doomed magazine *International SF*; even that one, though, was much later the spark that kindled two ambitious novels.

My style, alas, was badly corrupted by catering at top speed, without much revision, to this tawdry milieu. The narrative voice was usually hysterically overwritten. ("Childhood nightmares flared and echoed in the vault of his mind. Slowly, silently, dreadfully, the door opened. The tattered twisted man stood there gasping in maniacal exultation...'Death, death, death,' the specter shrilled.") And the stories were unthinkingly sexist to a sleazy extent not really visible to me in those bad old unreconstructed pre-feminist days. (Women were always "girls," breasts and legs received a lot of ogling emphasis, this sort of thing: "Absinthe curled up on his lap, her saffron hair swinging like a fluid bell, and her gorgeous breasts settled out of free-fall to point at the roof. Gower could have sworn her nipples stood up as she settled against Yarrick's chest.... His long fingers caressed the air indecently close to Absinthe's right breast. He resisted temptation....") In the several items that follow, representative of that period, I have stoically trimmed back some of the overgrowth without entirely sanitizing the originals. Neither "Exorcism," "Murder is in the Eye of the Beholder" nor "Incubation" is strictly science fictional; they are scarcely so, but each seems to me rather like the kind of story Rod Serling might have used for an episode of *Twilight Zone*. Having no TV set in those days, I don't think I'd ever seen that classic show, nor any of its competitors, except perhaps briefly in a store window or when I visited my widowed grandfather. That admission will surely seem to anyone younger than I like a note of horror in a *Twilight Zone* episode....

On the other hand, "Murder is in the Eye" was first written as a TV script submitted to an Australian television production company in the mid-1960s. They rejected it in part because of the legal and other absurdities in the plot. I'll return to these in an afterword, with some discussion of ways in which such a story might be salvaged by an editor, but be warned: if you know anything about legal protocol (I didn't in those days) you will be outraged at the writer's ignorance and sloppiness. Hey, I was a kid, okay?

These stories are, after all, a sort of time machine back into the mental horizons of forty or more years ago. In "Exorcism" I felt it necessary to include a short explanation of this strange new substance, LSD, and its effects. In 1966, the hallucinogen was generally unknown. Wikipedia notes: "LSD became a headline item in early 1967." The Beatles and other fabulously visible bands drew media attention to acid, and the hippie subculture went on to make it a sort of sacrament. I'd first heard of it only a few years earlier in a science fantasy story by the British sf writer John Brunner, and it seemed a neat idea to add a nightmarish touch to a fiction about a sort of behaviorist mind-treatment. I didn't know that the CIA had been trying just such "treatments" on luckless subjects. Speaking of which, in 1965 I wrote a rather sardonic story, no doubt influenced by Kurt Vonnegut, for a current affairs magazine, *The Bulletin,* impelled by the Vietnam War. I imagined a near future battlefield where the soldiers were all clinically insane: probably psychotic to start with (who'd miss them?) and made more so with psychoactive drugs and conditioning. The story was rejected; if it was returned I never got it, and that was the only copy.

"Incubation" (first published as "Incubation of the End") was a collaboration with my friend and sometime housemate John Romeril, later a notable award-winning dramaturg, playwright and screen writer (*The Floating World*, etc). I can't remember anything at all about how we confected it, although I can pick which were probably my portions and which his; I provided the final rewrite. It has appeared under each of our names separately and under both together. Apparently it did neither of us any permanent harm, although little luster was cast upon us; much later we each received lucrative two-year senior fellowships from the Literature Board of the Australia Council to work on major projects, so I guess we were forgiven such youthful indiscretions.

# EXORCISM
## (1966)

"Blood," muttered Yarrick, inscrutably. He sprawled in a grotesquely overpadded couch, and gazed placidly out into the pale winter's afternoon. "Blut ist ein ganz besonderer Saft," he added.

"Wup?" said Dr Jack Gower, rather inanely. Iago Yarrick always left him some three steps behind. It's in the nature of the man, Gower mused. Boy wonder. Professional genius. He makes no attempt, decided the doctor wryly, to hide the fact. It's his living.

Yarrick was probably the only consultant philosopher in the world.

"Sorry," Yarrick grinned, not at all sorry. "That's a remark Goethe put into the mouth of Mephistopheles. 'Blood is quite a special fluid'."

"Without doubt," Gower agreed amiably.

He didn't say anything else. Yarrick was about his profession, thinking. He came lithely to his feet and strolled at random about the room, picking up books from untidy heaps where they lay on the floor and putting them down in untidy heaps on his book shelves.

Gower watched him lope around the floor. Yarrick wore bright blue cords and a black polo-necked sweater. It made his lanky frame look thinner than ever. This was business-hours. In his leisure time he wore an old green track-suit and bare feet. Or a dinner jacket. Or a tiger skin. A genius, but nuts.

The office door slid open and Yarrick's secretary slid in, her saffron hair swinging like a fluid bell. Gower, the compleat physician, kept his eyes on Absinthe and counted his own pulse with one finger. The woman was nearly as tall as Iago, with a shape like a shiver of joy and the walk of a lynx. Gower's pulse leapt up the spectrum.

Yarrick was standing at the window, face buried in his hands. His was an odd face, big ears, dark depressions under his eyes. Absinthe found nothing odd in it. She gazed at him with bright-eyed attention. He snorted.

"Blood," came a sepulcher tone from Yarrick, dragging Gower's mind back to unpleasant business, "that knits up the raveled sleave of care, the death of each day's life, sore labor's bath, balm of hurt minds, great nature's second course, chief nourisher in life's feast."

The doctor was chilled and puzzled, but he knew a misquotation when he heard one. "Shakespeare was not talking about blood. That was mentioned in favor of sleep." He felt he had scored an obscure victory. "From *Macbeth*."

Yarrick let that pass, quoting something else Gower recognized. From Thackeray. "'Nothing like blood, sir'," he grinned, "'in hosses, dawgs and men.'"

He avoided the doctor's eye, bounced back to his mutilated Shakespeare quote like a yo-yo.

"Yeah. The Bard was talking about sleep." His grin shifted wryly to the left. "We're talking about blood." Gower felt suddenly very queasy.

"You surely don't mean...."

"Mm," nodded Yarrick blithely, rubbing his long nose. "It looks to me suspiciously as if we have a vampire in the city."

*Blood,* Yarrick had misquoted, *chief nourisher in life's feast.* The suggestion was incredible. But then, the crime was unheard of. Gower, physician in charge of the Blood Bank at City Hospital, had been shaken and then stunned at the gradual disappearance over several months of many pints of stored blood.

Despite the meticulous records of the huge hospital, the thefts went unnoticed for months. Once security measures were stepped up, the theft stopped. As was to be expected. But Gower didn't dare let it happen again. Road accidents, and the demand for transfusion, often exceeded the Bank's supply. The maniac responsible for the theft had to be grabbed, and instanter.

The police had got nowhere. The crime was beyond their experience and, Gower acidly suspected, beyond their imaginations. In time, the fuss blew over. Security lagged. The blood started going again.

Out of his mind, Gower presented the grisly business to Iago Yarrick. Four years earlier, with a PhD at 20, that young man had set up office with the gold letters *Consultant Philosopher* on the door. He was the only all-purpose genius for hire in the country. Grinning at Absinthe, he had set an exorbitant fee and then listened to Gower's tale.

☼

Shadows were lengthening outside the window, and the lights glowed on automatically inside Yarrick's office. That was one of the cute gadgets he had devised under the prodding of his appalling laziness. Wherever he went Yarrick strewed his path with strange devices, spawned by his errant genius for the sole purpose of conserving his energy.

Indolent as he was, though (his mental activity running on like a stream, seemingly costing him no effort), when the time was ripe and the need sufficiently urgent all that conserved energy was expended in prodigious, if efficient, fashion.

Absinthe had returned to her typewriter. Her employer propped himself up in his luxurious chair and drew a lighted cigar from an armrest, raised an eyebrow. Gower nodded, and he repeated the legerdemain, producing another lighted cigar from the same unlikely source.

"Much as it pains me to converse while smoking," he growled, "you're paying by the hour."

"Quite," agreed the doctor. "And you've got a lot of talking. Justify your vampire theory."

"I can't," Yarrick said breezily. "It's a hunch. Look, you say the blood stolen is not consistent in type. A, B, AB, O, even Rh neg. It's not being used to transfuse one person."

"Thank you for the obvious," said Gower testily. "And it isn't a doctor who took it—he could get it straightforwardly enough. And it isn't someone who wants to paint the bathroom a daring color. Blood flakes off when it dries."

"Yeah." The philosopher tapped a button sunk into the desk. After a moment, Absinthe walked in with two tequila sours. Gower felt suitably put in his place.

"You say it's a maniac," Yarrick rapped accusingly. "How could a full-blown maniac get into the Blood Bank time and again? This neurosis is integrated so well no trace of it shows. The word for that is 'vampire'."

"Oh." Gower was relieved. "You *don't* mean the thief actually, ah, consumes the blood, then?"

"Don't jump to conclusions." Yarrick peered moodily into his glass and worked his way through the intricate procedure for devouring a tequila sour. Gower tossed his back like a philistine, coughed monstrously, and earned a sneer from the younger man.

Abruptly, the philosopher stood up and walked to the door. It slid open, and he stood there with his hand extended. Confused, the doctor leaped to his feet and shook his hand.

"The vampire's one of your nurses, Doctor," stated Yarrick as he ushered Gower out of his office. "I'll have her for you in three days. Good afternoon." The door closed and Gower was alone in the hall.

Flabbergasted, he shrugged his shoulders and headed back for the hospital.

Attired in cutaway Beatles jacket, tight pants and stomping boots, a transistor radio hugged to his chest, Yarrick prowled on the following morning around City hospital. He looked through the smiles of three pretty nurses, and dated the first dowdy one he found. In the evening, dressed the same way, he escorted her to a discotheque and spent four excruciating and profitable hours. The woman had a gratifying evening discussing all the other inmates of the Nurses' Home, and Yarrick earned her immediate hatred and everlasting gratitude by advising her to wear a bra, a girdle, modest lipstick and her hair up.

In the next two days, four possible leads panned out and Yarrick was reduced to a single suspect. On foot, he followed her into the city. A brisk wind whipped up late in the afternoon and spattered some drops of rain into the cold streets, but Yarrick continued his pilgrimage.

The woman disappeared into a small newsreel theatre. Curious, Yarrick followed her in. Exultation welled up in him when he saw what was being billed.

"Of course," he muttered to himself. Even a well-integrated neurosis required some fantasy outlet. Coins clattered behind a grille, and he went into the horror movie.

For three hours, he suffered that ghastly naive movie twice in patience, observing the woman. She was stock-still, eyes fixed on the screen, only her hands moving. Fingers tremoring, she grasped the seat in front of her. Finally, obviously exhausted, she left her seat. Casually he followed her out.

Yarrick noticed her shiver slightly as she stepped out into the cold darkness of the evening, and he slipped on his own jacket. She hesitated at the footpath, and Yarrick gazed at her in interest. Her face, like her body, was thin yet not unattractive. Her nose was snub, her hair darker than brown but not quite black. Her stance, as she hesitated at the edge of the night, indicated that she was quite oblivious of Yarrick behind her. She turned, then, quite consciously, and looked directly into his eyes.

Yarrick experienced a moment of fright. In the pale face with its dark halo, her eyes were full only of night.

She glanced away just as consciously, and they were green eyes. Yarrick licked salt from his upper lip, and drew a woman's handkerchief from his pocket.

"Pardon me." He cleared his throat and followed her out from the narrow foyer.

She turned again. "Yes?"

"Perhaps this is yours." Yarrick proffered the crumpled handkerchief.

"Thank you, you're mistaken." She looked at him curiously. "That isn't mine—Oh!"

Yarrick drew back his hand, and put the blood-stained handkerchief back inside his coat.

"You see," he explained gently, "I know you."

"No," said the woman with empty eyes, "no, you don't know me. You only know what I am." She shook her head sadly in the cold breeze, and laughed a tinsel laugh. "I'm Valerie."

She slipped her arm into Yarrick's.

☼

Valerie unlocked her apartment door and ushered him in. Unlike most of the nurses, she had a private residence. Ubiquitous of design, the apartment had about it an added pervading essence of— what? Grief? Weariness? Ennui? Yarrick felt it in his flesh: the impression of the woman's personality.

A wistful, tearing sympathy had grown between them. As they walked in the cold night, it had bonded and strengthened itself on their silence. And yet, somewhere deep in Yarrick's bowels, an age-forgotten primeval fear clenched tight. He fought it bitterly, and the welling sympathy smothered it for all but the single moment of distress that twisted him when she smiled. The sharp, the long, the canine teeth had glanced bright ivory....

Edgy, he sat in a chair while she poured claret into two glasses. Their unlikely rapport became a sudden barrier, a synthetic hostility to mask the lack of genuine antipathy. Valerie brought him the glass and sat opposite, brittle, nervous. Her knees were pressed tight together, a line of tension that carried to her rigid shoulders.

Abruptly, Yarrick sprawled back in his chair.

"Nobody's declared a war," he said wryly, "so it's difficult to call a truce."

She relaxed in a fluid tremor, a tension broken. When she smiled, this time the sharp canines did not bother Yarrick. Her lips stained red as she sipped the claret. Yarrick thought of blood, and sorrow washed through him.

"I've been running since I was a child," Valerie said. There was no self-pity, only weariness. "You're the first person to guess what I am."

The young man lifted his glass, gazed at the fluorescent strip through the rich warmth, then drained the claret. Carefully, he set the glass down and stood up.

"People are scared of blood," he said, moving restlessly about the room. The young woman sat unmoving, following him with her eyes. "They scream at wounds. They faint at accidents. What's the traditional mark of the savage, the barbarian? Bloodthirstiness." He made a short bitter sound: a growl, a laugh. "Our literature fairly reeks with the smell of blood. Blood is horror. It smokes from the madman's blade."

The woman's eyes were on him, following the jerky angry movement of his frame. The contact was there, growing on his anger, growing with her wonder at his anger. He spun about, saw her watching him, collapsed back into the chair.

"You can see why. Bleed too seriously, die." Fingers together, his hands assumed a posture of prayer. "True, but wrong. Like fearing life, because one must come to the end of life. Food, air, light, blood—life." He shook his head. "All of *them* must eat, must consume the flesh and fruit of other life to live themselves. When they bleed too terribly, their loss is made up from the common store. They live because of the transfusions of others. Are they monsters? Do they think themselves monsters? But you—" Yarrick's voice broke.

Tears were welling in the woman's eyes, and he reached to take her hand. It was cold. It grew warmer as he held it in his own.

"So we must come to you," he said briskly. "You are a nurse at City Hospital." Her eyes grew wide in astonishment; dumbly she nodded. "You have an—incapacity. As one must share the life of others in words, you must live through the blood of healthier bodies. And you find yourself ashamed, fearful, because they would call you a monster, a loathsome thing to hate and kill."

The tears were full now, and fell from her eyes. Again, dumbly, she nodded, grasping his hand. And then, shaking the tears away she violently shook her head.

"More than that," she whispered, "there's more than that. You're trying to help me, but I was beyond help the day I was born. There's death in me, death and horror." She sniffed, and Yarrick opened his mouth. "No," she interrupted, "let me speak.

"I have an urge to rend and kill. To destroy and live in destruction. Why do you think you found me in that movie? I have to watch them, to bleed the death and slaughter out of me."

Yarrick knew this already. He nodded in compassion.

"There *is* a monster in me, clawing to get out." Her head dropped to his hand, and he felt her tears. He could scarcely hear her voice. "I can't even kill myself."

That hurt. He shuddered with her torment. Gently, he lifted her to her feet and cradled her shaking body against his. She sobbed, and his body ached for her misery. She clung to him and he lifted her swollen face and kissed her.

He felt the fear pass out of her. Her kiss was clumsy, as though she had held back all her life, trapped in her loneliness by the fear of the thing inside her. His fingers touched her face, pushed back her long loose hair, and he kissed her again. Her lips lingered against his, slipped along the line of his jaw and nuzzled his neck.

Shockingly, her mouth opened and her teeth clamped against his throat. Yarrick threw her hands from him and hurled her away with a spasm of revulsion. There was no thought in it, just a sharp pain and the woman lay white and shaking across the room.

Yarrick felt his throat in cold amazement, then looked aghast at what he had done. Valerie lay crumpled on the floor, shuddering, chalk-white.

"God," he groaned. "My God. I'm sorry." He moved toward her, and she blindly scuttled away from him. He stopped, and looked down on her. Christ, he thought, this is how it's been for her. Never able to trust herself, always the *thing* inside her....

"There are doctors who can help you," he said. The woman cowered from him in a corner, afraid of herself. Yarrick's perceptions were cold and sharp and clear, his senses trilling a thousand messages to his mind. The green pastels of ceiling and walls, the floral design of the carpet, the shards of light from bric-a-brac about the room. The sounds of his own breathing, the ragged gasps from the woman huddled in the corner. The frozen stillness of the night, the chill and the silence. The tiny trickle of sticky warmth at his neck.

He stood, bones and flesh and sinews hanging loose as the straw body of a scarecrow, and sadness crowded about him.

"Valerie, I'm not afraid of you. I do not hate you. What happened then was my body reacting, not my mind. And there *are* doctors who can help you. You can stop running, Valerie."

He reached down, lifted her, cradled her in his arms like a child. That way, stumbling, he carried her all the way to his own apartment.

Breathing deeply and slowly, looking frail as a child in Yarrick's huge quilted bed, Valerie slept. Gower, eyes puffy with tiredness, felt confused emotions as he looked down at her.

"I injected ¾ cc. of sodium thiomorphate intravenously." Yarrick was quietly brisk. "She was in an advanced state of compound shock, anxiety, and lack of sleep."

He yawned himself, and smiled wanly at the doctor.

"Once again, I must apologize for getting you out of bed so early in the morning—"

Gower twirked his lips mirthlessly, his mouth momentarily a scar. "Don't be ridiculous, Iago." He glanced again at the white face in the bed, framed by its dark hair. "If this is the woman responsible, I'd want to see her if it meant spending my holidays in hell."

The younger man rubbed his hand briefly across his eyes.

"That might be what it means. She's the one, Gower. But I don't want you to take her in. Least of all call in the police."

Gower shot him a sharp glance. "Professionally, I can't see how—"

"Professionally," came Yarrick's cool voice, "is precisely why. The Hippocratic Oath, I needn't remind you, concerns itself with the patient's health, not his legal standing. In this case, it is more important to heal than to condemn."

"Naturally." The doctor's tone was taut, aggrieved. "I'm listening."

"Thanks." Relieved, Yarrick sighed. He fiddled with a whisky decanter, poured a couple of shots, handed a glass to Gower. Brooding over his own, he sat on the edge of the bed. He told Gower the whole story.

"God." The physician was badly shaken. "'I've never heard of anything like it. What could have caused it? Something in her childhood, some awful thing she's repressed."

Yarrick stroked the sleeping woman's forehead very gently, and nodded. The strain was catching up with him. He looked haggard and exhausted.

"Doctor," he said carefully, "I believe I can cure her. I believe I can find her ghost, confront her with it, and drive it out."

"That's possible, of course," said Gower. "A psychiatrist could do it in about three years of therapy."

"I can do it in three hours," Yarrick said bluntly. "There's a bio-feedback apparatus I've developed that can strip her mind bare. It can expose the fibers of her unconscious to the glaring light."

Gower stared. "The hell you say!"

"The very hell indeed." Yarrick met his gaze evenly. ''The process requires the use of psychoactive drugs, and for that reason the presence of a doctor."

"Has it been tested?"

"On myself, yes." The young man's face was rigid. "It isn't pleasant but it's very revealing."

The doctor looked at him incredulously, and his estimation of Yarrick soared even higher. "It's a big responsibility to take," he said.

"Yes."

"I'm prepared to take it."

Valerie lay on a white operating slab, head cushioned, limbs restrained by cushioned straps. A net of electrodes covered her body.

"I'm going to inject 100 micrograms of lysergic acid diethylamide," explained Yarrick. "You know the drug, I presume?"

Gower nodded his head.

LSD-25 was an incredible substance used not in thousandths but in millionths of a gram. It produced vivid hallucinations, sometimes schizoidal states. Users might regress to childhood, experiencing again in full the terrors of infancy.

"As well as the LSD, Valerie's nervous system will be stimulated through the electrode net. I'll plague her with demons. She'll have every nightmare she ever ran away from, and she won't be able to wake up."

The doctor looked at the sleeping woman. He shuddered.

Yarrick said, "She will know herself. And she will be cured."

Abruptly, he took up a syringe and sent the drug into her bloodstream. After a time, he covered her with a blanket and went to a keyboard. Swallowing hard he sent his hands dancing across the keys.

☼

*She was swept into a blazing, gobbling, shrieking, hurtling hell.* She ran howling down dark and clammy corridors, pursued by shapes she dared not look at. Hands fluttered about her, touching her in cold and terrifying flicks. Voices whistled, old evil, mocking, laughing into echoes....

Flames leapt out of darkness, roaring incandescence, and she was falling into them, sliding into burning horror, powerless to stop....

Water sucked at her body, dragged her paralyzed exhausted near-corpse into choking damnation. Salt burned her eyes, pounding ceaseless waves battered her, crushed her, drowned her. She opened her raw throat to scream, and gushing torrents choked her....

She clawed her way up out of death agony, and found herself in darkness. Terrified, she lashed out her arms and struck wooden planks. Above, on either side, wood. The air was stale, heavy with the stench of decay. Claustrophobia strangled her. Suddenly, she knew where she was. *She was in a coffin, buried under six feet of wet and heavy soil....*

She screamed and writhed, and *his* face was above her, looming, contorted. The kitchen knife glinted. He scowled in fury.

"Do it. Let me do it to you. Damn you, I'll cut your heart out."

"No," she screamed, "no, *no,* NO!"

He leaped after her when she ran from the house, through the undergrowth, through the tangled midnight thorns and shattered bottles.

His face was bloated, pimpled, sweating.

"I'll kill you," he roared. *"I'll make you drink your own blood!"*

She ran, limbs jerking under her cotton dress, heart shrieking with pain. His hand caught her, and she stumbled, and he tripped over her, and his knife spun crazily in the starlight and he fell on it and he screamed and screamed and screamed.

Like a trapped animal, she lay under his weight and his warm sticky blood poured out of his wound. He thrashed in his death agony, crushing her small body in his mindless spasms. The blood pulsed out of him, running over her face, mixing with her tears, *running into her mouth....*

And then it was gone, gone into the past with the other nightmares, gone with its power over her, gone with all its horror. The darkness came up, clean and warm and cleansing, and she slept.

☼

Weak dawn light filtered into the room when Yarrick turned off the overhead lights. The electrodes had been removed, and he carried the limp body of the woman into his bedroom. Gower stumbled after him, mentally stunned by the experience of the last three hours.

After they had covered her sleeping form, Yarrick and the doctor went quietly out of the room. Sipping coffee, they let the tension drain out of them.

"I'm astounded, Yarrick," whispered the physician, "astounded."

"We're full of wonders, all of us," agreed the younger man, gravely. "And full of horrors." He bowed his face into the steam from the coffee and, closed his eyes for a moment in weariness. He drained the cup and got unsteadily to his feet.

"I'll phone you a cab," he said.

After Gower had gone, driven back to his home through the early morning brilliance of a glorious day, Yarrick went back into the bedroom. He stood for a moment in the semi-darkness, looking at the sweet, childlike face of the sleeping woman. The horrors she had carried, deep and rotting within her mind, were gone. When she awoke, she would hardly remember them. He bent, kissed her closed eyes. She smiled in her sleep.

# MURDER IS IN THE
# EYE OF THE BEHOLDER
## (1966—HERE SLIGHTLY REVISED)

The front door, down the hall, had snicked open. That was all. Chris Hazlitt was terrified. The skin tightened on his face. The text-book slipped from his hands and thumped on the floor.

From a great distance, through the singing in his head, Chris heard footsteps. He breathed, fast and shallow, felt his hands knot on the arms of the lounge chair.

His eyes slid from the closed dark-polished door to the rifle above the fire-place. He was swaying, trembling on the border of madness. The uneven steps halted, as he knew they must, outside the door. The crystal doorknob turned.

Childhood nightmares echoed in the vault of his mind. Slowly, silently, dreadfully, the door opened. The tattered, twisted man stood there, gasping in exultation. Light glinted from the bloody knife in his gnarled fist.

Chris edged out of the chair, close to vomiting. The leprous face followed him blindly. Its lips parted. The knife rose, dripping dark stains on the thick white carpet.

"I am going to kill you slowly," the specter told him. "I will hack the flesh from your bones."

The boy growled, an animal fusion of fear and inarticulate warning. The air swam before him. Hoarsely, he said, "Don't come any closer. Stay where you are."

His fingers clamped convulsively on the rifle. It was loaded, as he knew it must be.

"You will die, boy." The creature came toward him, dragging one leg, its rotted face twitching. "You will die in agony."

"Get back," Chris shouted, his voice high and hysterical. "Any closer, I swear I'll kill you."

The intruder capered, shrieking curses and laughter. Its arms reached out in a loathsome embrace. Chris screamed, and thunder filled the room.

Carefully, he placed the rifle against the wall. Averting his eyes, nostrils full of the stink of fear, he stepped around the bleeding corpse to the telephone.

For a moment, he held his face in his hands, then deliberately dialed.

"Homicide, please...." The phone burred, then the connection was made. "My name is Christopher Hazlitt, of 14 Dolin Drive, Toorak. I have just shot a man."

For a moment, his gaze flickered to the body soaking in its own blood.

"Yes," he said. "An intruder. He threatened to kill me with a knife. I had to shoot him."

Numbly, Chris hung up and went back to his chair. He was still sitting there, body slack, eyes blank, when the police arrived.

"Don't ask *me* to explain it!" Walter Landor paced in angry agitation before the psychiatrist's desk. "I'm just a humble attorney. *You're* the expert in impossible happenings, doctor."

Gordon Frere was the Court psychiatrist, a thin man in his early fifties, cerebral, cool, sardonic. His lips twirked in irritation at the older white haired man before him.

"This is what I've got." Frere waved a thin sheaf of papers from his desk. "Homicide, Forensic and Ballistics reports. A copy of the boy's statement. You're the young man's lawyer, Mr. Landor. Do you dispute these as facts?"

Wearily, Landor collapsed into the seat opposite Frere. "They're the only ones on paper, doctor."

"Quite." Frere riffled the papers into a neat pile. "I'm not the jury, Mr. Landor. I simply have to determine the state of Hazlitt's mind at the time of his mother's death."

Urgently, Landor leaned forward and struck his hand twice on his knee in emphasis. "That boy would not kill his mother. And he is not insane. God damn! I knew Chris's parents for more than thirty years, and I've known Chris all his life. That means more to me than all the so-called 'facts' the Police Department have produced."

The psychiatrist raised one eyebrow and leafed through the papers.

"Let's see.... The bullet which killed Mrs. Hazlitt was fired by the rifle found in the lounge room of her home." His tone was unemphatic but deliberate. "The only recent fingerprints on the rifle were those of her son, Chris. But there were traces of earlier prints by his father. Right?"

"Yes."

Inexorably, Frere pressed on. "So, since his father's death nearly a year ago, Chris is the only person to have touched it. Yes?"

"That," said Landor, annoyed, "is obvious."

"Oh?" Frere expressed surprise. "A moment ago you were quite certain Chris had not shot his mother."

Vehemently, Landor cried, "I still am!" Then, confused, "That is, damn it, I know the boy. He couldn't have killed his own mother unless he was out of his mind."

"Perhaps." Frere smiled thinly.

Desperately, Landor declared: "But the boy is one of the most stable young men I have ever known. I tell you, I *know* Chris!"

"Yet the boy rang Russell Street and reported he had shot an intruder. A *male* intruder, Counselor. A man who threatened him with a knife. That is what his statement says."

Wearily, Landor agreed. "And he's telling the truth. I've been a lawyer long enough to know when someone is lying. And Chris is *not* lying!"

Frere leaned back in his seat and thoughtfully rubbed his eyes. "And that, of course, is why the Court ordered me to give him a psychiatric examination." He leaned earnestly across the desk. "Let me assure you, Landor, that I am not taking sides. Not yet. All I want is the truth."

Chris Hazlitt lay on the couch in the stark, functional psychiatrist's office. Quietly, Landor murmured: "I'd like to stay, doctor. If not as defense counsel, at least as Chris's friend."

"All right," said Frere.

"I saw him, doctor," the boy said in a high, taut voice. "They say I shot my mother, but I...." He choked with tears, struggled with his voice: "...I couldn't have...I *saw* that man. I wouldn't kill my mother. She was all I had left...I *loved* her...." He broke into racking sobs, face curved to his chest, hands wet with tears.

Frere's voice was soothing. "Nobody's blaming you at the moment. Tell me exactly what you can remember about that night."

As Chris regained his control with difficulty, the psychiatrist's voice was aseptically impersonal. "Just lie back, now."

Landor's own eyes closed as Chris's voice slid into the now familiar, dreadful grooves of the story. And beyond the words he saw the people he had known and loved for so many years—Chris since infancy, his mother, his tragically-dead father. And in imagination, the monstrous image of the intruder Chris believed he shot.

"Everything seemed very clear, and cold, and distant. Then the police came in, and said I had shot my mother—"

The monotony of his account swirled, collapsed again into emotional turmoil. "—I pointed at the man's body; but they wouldn't believe me. They wouldn't believe me...."

"That's, fine, Chris," Frere said soothingly. "Tell me a few things about your mother and father."

"I—I'd rather not talk about my mother, doctor."

"I'm sorry, son, but that's what we are here for."

"Look, Frere—" Landor began.

"Excuse me, Mr. Landor," Frere said icily, "but, as you agreed, you're here as the young man's friend and not as his lawyer. You will kindly sit quiet without interrupting."

Landor sucked in air and exhaled raggedly. "I just don't want to see the boy hurt."

"Naturally, Counselor. Let me assure you that I have only the truth and the boy's welfare as my concern."

Chris's gray face, not quite adult, managed a ravaged smile. "It's okay, Walter. Let the doctor ask what he wants. I'll do what I can. What do you want to know about my father?"

"He was a wealthy man, I believe."

"Yes. Very wealthy. When he was young, Dad inherited control of my grandfather's shipping line."

"And he hoped you would take over, I imagine?"

"Yes, I suppose those were his plans."

"Did you get on well with your father?"

There was a moment's hesitation.

"Yes."

"Did you like him," Frere pressed.

"It's hard to put into words. If I wanted to be melodramatic, I suppose I'd say I idolized him."

The psychiatrist put aside his brisk manner. "It's a funny thing," he said reflectively, "but in my experience people never get very close to their idols. Is that right, Chris?"

Distantly, the boy said, "I guess so, doctor."

"You can worship an idol," Frere went on, almost to himself, "you can glory in your idol, but it's hard to be intimate with one. They're too high above you."

"Too high and too perfect and too distant," affirmed Chris, with unselfconscious passion. "Do you know, doctor, I never could believe in God?"

"Why is that?"

"I don't know." Chris looked puzzled for a moment. "It's just that...if there's a God, He'd be too big to care about us up in that Heaven of His, running the Universe!"

Very gently, Frere asked, "How often did you see your father?"

"I saw him in his coffin." The flat bitterness shocked Landor. "And three days before that he had dinner with us. I think the time before that was three months before his death."

"Was he away from Australia very often?"

"He was home just often enough to justify his citizenship."

"How do you remember him?"

"Big, Doctor Frere." Chris splayed out his hands, shook his head in wonder. "Big like those idols you were talking about. And he strode about, my God. Mum was always singing this song from some show, over and over: 'Love makes the world go round.' Finally I couldn't stand it anymore, and I cried out, 'It's not true. Daddy makes the world go round. *Daddy* does.'"

Abruptly, Landor laughed. In surprise, the other two looked at him.

"I'd forgotten all about that," he exclaimed. "You were about four. That's what you said." The lawyer's heavy face creased in smile. "I told him about that when he got back from London, and he didn't dispute it, either."

"Yeah," said Chris, embarrassed. He blinked. "I just couldn't believe it when he died. It must be like that for a Christian who suddenly sees that his God is a myth. That Jesus didn't rise on the third day."

"How did your father die?" asked the psychiatrist.

"In a plane crash," Chris barked, "a stupid, idiot plane-crash. He'd got back from Japan three days before and stayed the night at home. Then he flew up to Sydney in the company plane. He should have been there for a week. Only he came home early and the plane crashed."

"Why did he come home early?"

"Mother sent him a panic telegram. She thought there was something wrong with her." He snorted, a mixture of anger and derision. "There's never been anything physically wrong with her in her entire life!" Then, in horror, he realized what he had said. "I shouldn't talk that way about her when she's dead. But I didn't shoot her. I shot a great hulking fiend with a knife. I didn't kill Mother!"

Hysteria raged through his frail barriers of self-control. Frere shook him by the shoulders. "Stop it, Chris! Stop thinking about that. Your friend Walter Landor believes you, and I believe you."

Incredulous, the boy lifted wet blue eyes to the doctor. "You believe me? But you're supposed to think I'm a homicidal maniac."

"Don't be absurd," snapped Frere. "I repeat—I don't believe you willfully murdered your mother."

"Then why...?"

Carefully, Frere explained: "I believe that you shot her, Chris. The evidence is unassailable. But I don't think you deliberately killed her in cold blood."

"But if—"

"Something happened in your mind, before and after your mother's death." Frere spread his hands. "You are completely sane at the moment. But your memories of that night are...inaccurate." The psychiatrist nodded in the direction of Landor, hunched in his chair. "Your friend the attorney will have to plead temporary insanity. You killed your mother, but you don't want to remember doing it. Your 'memories' are an hallucination, an unconscious camouflage to hide your action from yourself."

Unbelieving, uncomprehending, Chris shook his head. "No. No. If that's true, why did I murder my own mother?"

Frere said, "Let's go back to your parents. How do you remember your mother?"

Chris sighed. "She was nearly always with me in the long months when my father was overseas."

"Did you love her?"

His eyes shot with anger. "Of course I loved her!"

"Didn't you ever feel irritated with her—annoyed, hurt?"

"Well, yes. Particularly in the last couple of years. But I guess that's pretty inevitable when you get to my age."

"How's that?"

"You know. Independence, self-assertion, that kind of thing. What people refer to when they say about a teenager, 'Oh, he's just going through a phase.'"

"You're being remarkably objective about it."

"It doesn't mean I like it. Look. I'm not a fool. I know that people of my age act irrationally. Sure, we're going through a phase. A necessary phase."

"So you resented your mother."

Chris shook his head, rubbed his chin. "Not in the usual sense. For the tacit restraints." The boy frowned. "The unspoken complaints. The web of circumstances that bound me to her. Damn! I'm getting this all confused. I loved her, and I did what I could to please her. But she demanded too much, sometimes, without saying anything. And most of all, she thought of me as a child."

"Did she ever compare you in your presence with your father?"

Surprised, Chris glanced up. "You're astute, aren't you? No, she *never* said anything. But she was doing it all the time. And I just wasn't big enough to hold up to the comparison."

"Was there anything specific that annoyed you?"

"I suppose her hypochondria. She never complained, but she always thought she was sick."

"Did she tell you this often? Did she say what she thought was wrong with her?"

"No." Chris rubbed his forehead thoughtfully. "It was just the way she got around sometimes. As though she had the weight of the world on her shoulders. And she was always running off to some doctor."

"How do you know if she never spoke of her illness?"

Angrily, the boy rapped, "I used to see his bills in the mail. The swine probably lives like a king from the money of neurotics like my mother."

Landor felt his heart tighten with compassion and puzzlement. Something was very strange here. He opened his mouth; Frere shot him a quick, guarded glance of warning.

"Did you ever wonder whether your mother really was ill?" he asked.

"Oh, at first. But I've read enough psychology to know how women of her age get neurotic about their health."

Despite Frere's warning look, Landor broke in, "Chris, I think there's something you—"

"*Mr. Landor,*" the psychiatrist said with controlled intensity, "you must not interrupt!" He turned back to the youth. "Our session is nearly over for today. When you come in tomorrow I want to help your memory along with hypnosis."

"You think you can get rid of this—hallucination, these false memories?" Chris searched his face with pathetic hope.

"I feel sure we can."

A police sergeant entered the room while Chris shook hands with the thin doctor. Landor watched him leave, the lawyer's eyes bruised and heavy with sympathy.

He turned in ponderous confusion to the now-seated psychiatrist. "I can't understand it." His white-maned, leonine head turned from side to side in a perplexed negative. "'Hypochondriac'! 'Neurotic woman'! I thought he knew: I naturally assumed that his mother would have told him. Anyway, the autopsy report was read in Court when he was bound over for trial."

"He was in severe shock then. Nothing would have penetrated."

Landor stared at the cool psychiatrist. "But that was one of the reasons I was sure he was innocent. The simple fact that his mother was dying of cancer!"

☼

Next morning, Landor drove in the bright spring sunlight to Frere's office. The burgeoning colors mocked and stunned him, the warm breeze, the subtle flowering everywhere of life. As he came into Frere's office, he felt old and shaken.

When Chris was ushered in, the lawyer went straight to him, shook his hand.

"Hello, son. How are you feeling today?"

"Frightened, Walter."

"An honest reply," acknowledged the doctor.

The boy smiled. He let Frere lead him to the couch. "I've found a remarkable capacity for honesty in myself, the last few days. I suppose that's what the threat of death does to you."

Landor's head shot up.

"You won't die, son."

"And if I don't? What then? Locked in an insane asylum for the rest of my life? That's just a more terrifying kind of death."

Frere allowed a calculated measure of sarcasm into his tone. "Asylums are places to get well—not prisons."

"Don't treat me like a child," Chris snapped. "It's not the mental hospitals I'm afraid of. It's my own mind. If I can't trust my own memories now, what comes next?"

"You're not insane, Chris. I do think that you were mentally unbalanced at the time of your mother's death. That's what we'll find out about today."

"Under hypnosis?"

"'That's right. And with a bit of luck, and some work by us both, I'll get your memories untangled for you."

Nervously, wiping salt from his lip, Chris said, "I—I'm not sure I want to remember *that*. If I did kill Mother, I'd rather it remained buried in my mind."

"You can't, Chris. You have to confront it."

Shuddering, the boy covered his eyes. "All right, then. Let's get it over with."

At the doctor's injunction, he loosened his clothes and lay back on the couch. Frere drew the curtains.

"I want you to relax," he intoned, his voice settling into a drone. "Your whole body is limp, your arms, your shoulders, your face...."

In the darkened room, Chris moved uneasily. "I can't relax. Everything's boiling around inside me."

"It isn't easy at first," explained Frere. He was used to this; he was practiced at taking his time. "There's nothing to be frightened of. Hypnosis isn't black magic."

"I know that, doctor. I know it with my mind. But my body won't relax."

"That's not surprising." Frere's tone grew brisker. "Don't get upset about it. We'll try another method."

The psychiatrist set up a metronome and a black device with an inward-spiraling face. In the dimness of the room, the spiral's illuminated orange spinning had an obsessive fascination. Landor had to jerk away his own gaze.

Frere set the metronome ticking slowly. "I'll explain what I'm going to do. The heart normally beats between sixty and seventy-two pulses a minute. By some unexplained sympathy, it slows down if a metronome is ticking more slowly. I've regulated this one at forty beats per minute. Now just try to relax, Chris, and let your eyes follow the spiral...."

His voice settled into a fluid, ululating, persuasive pattern. Landor felt his eyes drifting back to the spiral, felt himself falling into it, felt the weariness seep warm and clean through him....

"NO!" Chris's scream was shattering. He was hunched, hell-lit, angular, racked.

Frere leaped to his feet. The office lights came on.

"No," moaned Chris, hands pressed into his white face, "no, no, no—"

"What is it son?" whispered Frere. "What happened then?"

"I don't know, I don't know." The rigor slowly left Chris's limbs, the cyanotic blue faded from his lips. "Something terrible, something I don't want to remember. Words, words, I don't know...."

"It's over now, Chris. There's nothing to frighten you now." Frere swung around to the old lion-headed man. "Landor, I'll have to use sodium pentothal. You're his lawyer. You'll have to give me permission."

Landor still saw the tortured figure in the orange hell-light from the spiral. "My God." His lips framed dry rustling words. "The poor kid." His heavy head turned to the psychiatrist. "Will it help him?"

"It's the only way."

"All right. Go ahead."

Frere opened a drawer, took out a syringe, filled it from a vial. Carefully, he held it to the light, squeezed out the air bubbles. "Now, Chris, I'm going to give you an injection. It'll put you to sleep for a while. When you wake up, you'll feel a lot better."

He slid the needle into the boy's slack arm. Again, he dimmed the lights.

In a low voice, he told Landor, "Pentothal acts on the reticular formation of the brain. It depresses the higher centers, and releases the lower ones."

"And?"

"It will make it easier for me to hypnotize Chris. Something is hidden in the lower centers of his brain, in his unconscious. Whatever it is, his conscious mind doesn't want to recognize it, it censors the memory, so to speak."

"And pentothal paralyses the censor?"

"More or less. It makes it possible for Chris to confront whatever he's running away from."

"Perhaps," said Landor slowly, "he shouldn't face it. Perhaps his subconscious is right in hiding it from him."

"No, Landor. The unconscious is very much like a child. It runs away from what it doesn't like."

"But what is it that Chris is running from?"

The doctor spread his hands. "Responsibility. The same thing we all try to run away from. That's a pretty good definition of maturity, Counselor: facing the responsibilities and the joys of adult life instead of fleeing from them."

"You think it's the responsibility he has for his mother's death that Chris is running away from?"

"Not precisely. What he won't face is the reason why he killed her. His motive for murdering her."

Landor swung his tormented face toward the psychiatrist. "What reason could a boy like Chris have for slaying his own mother?"

"He gave us the reason himself." Frere looked at the now-sleeping boy on the couch. "Revenge."

The lawyer gave a harsh corrosive bark. "Revenge? You're out of your mind! Because she sometimes treated him like a child? All mothers do that."

"Not his own revenge. His father's. He killed her because she caused his father's death."

Abruptly, Landor's composure collapsed. He closed his eyes, swallowed thickly.

"Oh God!" he breathed. "She did cause his death, by making him fly home early."

"That's the way his unconscious mind would have seen it."

"But she thought she was dying! The doctors only gave her a week to live!"

"Chris didn't know that, Counselor." Frere was merciless. "As far as he was concerned, she was just a selfish, foolish, neurotic hypochondriac."

"And because of her, Chris's idol died. Why didn't she tell him about her illness, doctor?"

"I imagine she didn't want to upset him. His father was away for long periods while he was alive, and she must have seen how that distressed her son. She didn't want to add extra worries."

"She was a wonderful woman. She didn't even tell me until months after her husband's death." Landor lay back, haggard, remembering. "It was at a party, Chris's twentieth birthday party. She took me into a room with her brother-in-law, Edward Hazlitt, and told us both then."

"Did anybody else know?"

Landor shook his head. "I assumed she had told Chris. No, only Ted and myself."

Behind his desk, Frere stood and stretched. "That's what he's afraid to face, Counselor. It must have been seething under the surface for months, waiting to explode. And when he killed her, his fixation was gone."

"You must be right," Despite himself, Landor nodded. "It explains that hallucination." Then he shook his head angrily. "But I still can't accept it. There's something wrong with your idea...."

"I'm afraid not." Frere's face was grave in the gloom. "But he won't hang. He was deranged, mentally unbalanced. He's been a very sick lad."

He turned, sat at the couch behind the quiescent form of the boy. "Chris, you can hear me, and you'll be able to talk to me when I tell you to. Your whole body is limp and loose, your mind is free and ready to follow my words. Is that right, Chris?"

Completely relaxed, but in normal voice, Chris said, "Yes, doctor."

"That's fine. You're floating in time, now. Your memory can move freely back into the past. Nothing will frighten you, you will simply follow my voice and tell me what you see."

"Sure."

Frere took a deep breath.

"I want you to go back to the evening of June 17. You are sitting in the lounge, reading. Are you there, Chris?"

Distantly, yet with bewildering normality, Chris answered. "Yes. I'm taking notes on my Economics lecture for tomorrow morning."

"Tell me what happens next."

"Someone is coming in the door. It must be mother, she's been shopping. Yes, it's mother. But there's something horrible happening."

"What is it, Chris?"

His voice became tense.

"Somebody seems to be talking. I feel scared."

"What is your mother doing?"

"She's come into the room. She's got a little parcel, and she's undoing it. But I can hear that voice. She bought a pearl necklace. I can't understand this. The voice says it's not her. It says she's a murderer. That's not a string of pearls, it's a knife." He uttered an appalled, terrified cry. "Oh Jesus, he's going to kill me. He's going to kill me—"

Landor, his hands gripped together in the darkness, felt cold sweat dribbling over his body. His mouth was dry with horror.

"Stop, Chris," ordered Frere. "Stop. Go back and look very carefully. There's nobody there but your mother."

"I know. She wants to know what I think of the necklace. What am I doing? I've got the rifle from the wall. I'm pointing it at mother." Even under the restraining drug, Chris's voice rose. "Why am I doing that? Oh God, oh God, I've shot her! But it's not mother. Don't lie to me, doctor. The voice says it's not mother. Mother,

mother, where are you? A man tried to kill me, mother. I had to shoot him. Mother, why are you lying there on the carpet? Did the bastard kill you, mother? Mother! Christ, I've killed her! Mother...."

Chill spasms harrowed Landor's frame at that hysterical crescendo. Frere, calm in the midst of horror, gently pushed down Chris's threshing arms. His voice cut through the boy's animal screams, "It hasn't happened, Chris. You're floating quietly in dark space. You're calm and relaxed."

Chris relaxed immediately.

His voice came, unperturbed. "I'm floating, doctor. I can't feel my fingers anymore."

"That's right. Now, I want you to tell me about that other voice. What is the voice saying?"

"What, when it started?"

"Yes."

"It says, 'When your mother comes into the room you'll see a hideous intruder.' It says, 'He'll try and kill you. You'll have to shoot him or he'll cut your heart out.'"

"Where is the voice coming from?"

Chris faltered. "I don't know. It—it's coming from my head. It's in my head. 'Kill the murderer,' that's what the voice says, doctor."

"Thank you, Chris. Good boy." In the darkened room, Landor was somehow relieved to see Frere wipe his forehead with a handkerchief. "Forget the voice now. The only thing you're aware of is *my* voice, and won't even hear that for a while. You just float there until I say 'Attention.'"

The psychiatrist got up, an edge of light on his face showing Landor a kind of fatigued exaltation. Frere sat back behind the desk.

"You see?" he asked the lawyer quietly. "He wasn't killing his mother. Even his unconscious couldn't allow him to do that. He was avenging a murder."

Again Landor was forced to agree. "Avenging his father's murder. What did he say? 'It must be like that for a religious believer who finds out that his God is a myth.'"

"As you say, Landor," the doctor said. "But this was more than a boy avenging his father's accidental death. It was a worshipper taking revenge for the death of his idol."

The lawyer prowled among the words, worried the ideas, gnawed at the near-perfect fabric of the psychiatrist's theory. "There's still something wrong, Frere. Something.... What is it? That

voice he spoke of.... What does it remind me of? Wait a minute."
Landor rose with a look of amazed, sudden comprehension.

"What is it, Counselor?" Frere was thrown off balance by the
lawyer's grin.

"You accused me of being too close to the problem to see the
significant features," said Landor. "But this time you're the one
who's too close."

"What are you talking about?"

"That voice. That wasn't his subconscious mind talking to itself."

The psychiatrist's voice was gritty with pique. "You are out of
your specialty, Mr. Landor. And out of your depth."

The lawyer brushed the words away with a wave, muttering almost to himself. "And the way he rejected your first two attempts to
hypnotize him. That's got to be it! Look, Frere, ask him about hypnosis. Ask him why he was afraid of your hypnotizing him."

"Tell me what you have in mind."

Excitedly, Landor shook his head. "No, no, you ask him."

Frere shrugged. "I don't know what you're playing at." He
turned back to Chris. "'Attention,' son; you can hear me now."

"I hear you, doctor."

"I want you to think back, Chris. I want you to remember something special, if you can. I want you to think about hypnosis."

There was a long silence. Landor went sick with hope lost.

Then, "He told me not to."

In a great tremor, Landor relaxed. Frere, startled, asked. "Who,
Chris? You can tell me."

"Uncle Ted."

"Your father's brother?"

"Yes. He told me I would never be able to be hypnotized by anyone except him."

"When did he tell you that?"

"Both times," said Chris. "Mainly the second time."

"Tell me," suggested Frere, "about the first time."

*Chris's twentieth birthday party. Edward Hazlitt, returning
grave faced with his sister-in-law and Landor from a private conference, had soon regained his good cheer and amused the group by
hypnotizing everybody in sight. His pranks, the traditional tricks of*

*the amateur Mandrake, had kept the party in riotous laughter for hours.*

*In the midst of these escapades, he implanted a post-hypnotic key in the mind of his nephew, Chris Hazlitt.*

*When the time was ripe, if he had the wish, that keyword had trigger Chris into hypnotic trance.*

☼

"You mentioned another time," said Frere carefully. "When was that?"

Even in trance, Chris showed signs of agitation. "Do I really have to say? He said not to. He said I was to forget all about it."

"Ignore what he said," ordered the psychiatrist.

Chris said, "It was a couple of weeks later...."

☼

*Ted Hazlitt had dropped in to Chris's home. By carefully planned coincidence, Chris's mother was out for the afternoon.*

*Within minutes, prey to a post-hypnotic trigger, Chris was deep in trance.*

*"Anything I tell you now," his uncle told him in a commanding tone, "will be forgotten when you wake, up. You won't even remember you were hypnotized. You will forget that I was here. Do you follow me?"*

*Deep in thrall, Chris had agreed.*

*"Very good. This is what I want you to do. In two months time, on June seventeenth, you will go down to the living room and load the rifle over the fireplace. The next time you will see your mother, you will not recognize her. Instead of seeing your mother, you will see a hideous intruder...."*

*In appalling, explicit detail, Ted Hazlitt had laid a trap, an hallucination, a murder, deep in the unprotected folds of his nephew's unconscious. .And, when the time came, that trap had sprung, that murder had come to fruition.*

☼

Doctor and lawyer stared at each other when the boy's calm recitation had droned to a stop.

"Monstrous," said Landor, finally. "Fantastic, incredible and monstrous."

"I always knew it was possible in principle, with the right subject and the right unconscious motivation," whispered Frere. "But I don't think it's ever happened before."

The old lion groaned. "That poor, poor boy. Used like a robot."

Frere was plainly struggling to fit together what he had heard. "You say that his uncle knew about the mother's cancer?"

"Yes. He was Chris's only surviving relative. In the event of Chris's death...."

"The Hazlitt fortune would revert to him."

"Yes."

"But if he knew about Mrs. Hazlitt's cancer, why didn't simply he kill Chris?"

Landor smiled mirthlessly.

"Too obvious. Edward was the only one who could have gained from Chris's death. More risky anyway."

"Yes. This way, Mrs. Hazlitt dies, Chris is convicted of the murder, and the money passes neatly to Edward."

They both looked at the sleeping boy, stunned by the enormity of the scheme.

"I can't understand," cried Landor, "how he hoped to get away with it. He must have had a madman's conviction in the invincible power of his own post-hypnotic spell...."

Frere jumped at the words. "I would phrase that a little more rigorously, but yes. And besides, he nearly did get away with it! I was trapped by the neatness of my own psychological theory. If it hadn't been for your unscientific belief in the boy's innocence, the real killer might have escaped."

Landor was standing at the window, opening the curtains. Midday sun streamed into the room and the fresh scent of blooming flowers billowed in. He stopped; his stomach cramped. Hand trembling, still clutched to curtain, he turned and stared at the psychiatrist.

"Frere," and his voice was cold and lost, *"we can't touch him, anyway.* We have no proof, no possibility of proof. At the time of the murder, Edward Hazlitt must have been hundreds of miles away.

"All we have to go on are this boy's memories under hypnosis."

"And, Frere, *that is not admissible in court!*"

Caressed by the sweet spring zephyr, warmed by the promise of summer, the two men regarded each other with impotent dismay.

# AFTERWORD 2010

Because this story began as a TV script at a time and place when the budgets for sets and actors were minimal, I deliberately chose to ignore some quite obvious absurdities. No court-appointed psychiatrist would permit the lawyer of the accused to attend such a session, of course (leaving aside the whole matter of medical confidentiality), nor would they exchange information about the case outside of a formal discovery procedure. It might be possible to recast the story so that Dr. Frere has been retained by Chris's counsel, rather than the court, but even then Landor would not be permitted to witness the examination and hypnosis.

One point that might seem ridiculously incorrect, however, is right: until 1968 or so, several years after the story was written and published, evidence obtained under hypnosis was not admissible in court. Today, I gather, it is still treated with understandable caution, because we know now that memories are *constructs* rather than perfect downloads, and that they can be tampered with quite readily in a suggestible state.

Is the plot entirely preposterous anyway? We are often assured that nobody can be hypnotized into acting contrary to their moral principles, but that doesn't mean deception can't take advantage of one's self-protective instincts. Since the wicked uncle is making use of deep unconscious animosities, and disguising the nature of the act from his victim-perpetrator, this kind of murder by proxy might indeed occur. Indeed, it's now a cliché of thrillers—but forty-five or so years ago it wasn't.

The next story, though, is a skein of plot holes, quick talking and hand-waving. I won't try to justify it. The original version published in *Man* magazine was worse; this text was cleaned up a little for subsequent use in the Australian-UK magazine *Vision of Tomorrow*, and later an anthology. It's an index of how little viable local science fiction existed in Australia in the 1960s. For all that, I still think this little *Twilight Zone* look-alike tale retains a certain weird tingle.

# INCUBATION
## (1967)

## WITH JOHN ROMERIL

He strode like a hero in the teeth of a gale, big, relaxed, his grin wide and brilliant. He walked as though the street were there for him alone. At a corner newsstand he bought a morning paper.

He wended his way to the park, relaxed on a favorite wrought-iron bench under the serrated shade of an elm, flicked through the paper. The glaring headline was barely worth a glance: GIANT NU-CLEAR TEST TIPPED. Christ, he thought, the money they squander on ways to kill themselves. He growled in uninterested disgust, turned to the Personal Columns and the business of making a living.

Four lines leapt up for attention. *Rogel,* he read, *Situation finally under control, but we must go. Meet midday, Kings X library. Silver.*

Soame passed his tongue over dry lips, felt the old excitement flutter through his body. This one was perfect. A woman, surely, and Silver certainly was not her surname. He knew this was perfect, without knowing why it was, or how he knew it. It was his gift.

He reached the library with thirty minutes to spare. A discreet display advertised an exhibition of the works of Patrick White, with a blown-up reproduction of Sidney Nolan's marvelous cover for *Riders in the Chariot.* He went in. Practically deserted as the place was, he knew already that their eyes were caressing him. A plump spinster peered from her pimpled face between the catalogues. And—ah! the youngest of them stared from the desk with an un-ashamed innocence that fluted in his blood. She was no more than seventeen. As one would approach a doe, gently, he crossed to her. There was plenty of time to indulge his taste, in part at least, before the fated Silver arrived.

*You lucky girl,* thought Clive Hymes Soame, holding her eyes as he approached, *you beautiful young thing.*

He touched the desk, bent slightly to her. A fine-veined throat, delicate copper, inspired the connoisseur in him. She swallowed prettily.

"Yes, sir?"—her soft startled voice. "Can I help you?"

"I hope so," and the growl was deep from use, a warmth that enfolded her. "I'm anxious to see some of Patrick White's novels. You see, I've not been here long, yesterday in fact, from Paris." He let his voice stroke the city's name, evoke the voluptuous mad-wild Paris that hardly exists in reality. A wisp of illusion caught in her sigh.

Soame smiled engagingly. "I heard nothing but praise for his work in New York. It seems a nice way to fill out my new experience of Australia, by looking at some of your best literature."

"Of course," she managed, still trapped in the net of his brilliant smile. She glanced nervously behind her; the old spinster was not watching them. "Well," she said, slipping out from behind the desk, "I think I can offer you a special surprise." A door marked *Private* opened for her and he followed, aglow with the old satisfaction.

They came into a dim inlet bay of books, a small hidden atoll of jutting shelves and covered tables.

"The library is preparing a public exhibition of Mr. White's work," she whispered. "Here, in fact, we have all his original manuscripts...." Her voice trailed away.

With the air of a world-weary expert, Soame let his eyes drift from books to manuscripts to photographs and tapes. The girl's fresh, animal body pervaded his nostrils with the scent of lust. Vulnerable as a puppet, she waited for firm direction from the strings.

"Fascinating," he said, casually replacing a first-edition of *The Aunt's Story.* "Of course, the insight literature can offer is ultimately less significant than that which one gains through people, the immediate relationships, the role of chance." He trailed off, as if reflecting on the thread woven by fate through jet-setting travels. And, after all, there was a thread. With him, crowding his mind, were all the women of his past, the Silver of his future, and this delightful creature of the moment.

"Yes," she breathed. "Ah, um, here's an unbound copy of Mr. White's new novel...." She reached up towards the volume, slender arm shaping the light fawn of her sweater. Soame watched her breasts shift and hungered for them. With a trembling hand she offered him the book. He took it, brushing her hand.

"Can I, uh, anything else'?" Her breath came in short stabs.

"Thank you, dear," he murmured, "no, this has been excellent."

But he did not move. Close to her face, he held strings of suspense. He slipped down to her alluring mouth, lifting her face. Full, warm, fired, he structured their lips in a damp unison, an erotic geometry. Angles, tensions tugged her into the whirlpool. His hand lured her arm, smothered her young breast. A shiver rippled her dress. It pleased him. He had made her alive, everywhere alive, everywhere his. Through her scent, a dewy freshness shook him into an echo of memories.

"My dear," he said, bending to her face, "you must have dinner with me some—" But her eyes had skittered away from him, stared in near-terror into the cool reprimand of the plump spinster who stood at the opened door.

"I—I hope this has helped you," the girl stammered, not daring to meet his gaze. "I'd best, better go." And she scurried off with burning cheeks.

It did not really upset Soame. He glanced at his watch, moved smoothly back into the body of the library. Still, he would have enjoyed playing the little drama out. The old prude waddled past, and Soame regarded her with cold contempt. She dropped her wrinkled eyes to her wrinkled breast, and he laughed silently, cruelly. She winced, hating his beautiful body, and fled behind the catalogues.

Lunch-hour borrowers had begun to file into the library. Casually, he made his way among them, searching the faces. The woman, his instinct told him, had not yet arrived. His was a precarious game, he reflected idly; against time rather than the two other abstract personalities involved. If Silver were late his scheme was lost, blown, just as it would be if the oddly-named Rogel were to come early.

As the clock sliced seconds from the hour, tension paced like a beast he knew and respected. He savored his controlled fear, tasted it, let the honed edge of habit cut away all superfluous thought.

And she was there.

From the corner of his eye, he saw the woman enter, captured and analyzed without conscious effort the minute keys of stance and attitude which identified her. He breathed evenly, coiled the tension back on itself and closed it away. A clear flexible mind was the prime necessity of this moment; he needed to sum up her character, attune himself to her. He slid unobtrusively forward. Before anything else, he had to gauge her financial status.

Yet even his experienced clarity had not been prepared for her. The beauty of the woman brought him up short. Stupid fingers reached for a cigarette. A library, fool, he snarled at himself, dismayed at the near-blunder. Gingerly, struggling for lost composure, he approached her.

"Silver," he murmured softly. Rogel's emissary, urged the posture of his body, the angle of his arm, the carefully-weighed values of his tone. The role was merging with his own instincts and memories, a sense of conviction that came straight from sinew and bone.

"Yes?" she said, voice hushed, puzzled. Somewhere in her tone, anxiety raced. But in the half-gloom a radiance remained in her pale features, an ultimate firm confidence. "Where is Rogel? There is not time to alter the arrangements."

An assignation? A return to a husband? A business matter? The possibilities gridded themselves like a chessboard. Somehow he would have to get the details, or he was lost.

"Regrettably," Soame said, projecting calm capability, "there has arisen the need for a small change of plan. I'm here to—" He swept his eyes around the library, lowered his voice still more. "Look, we can't really talk here. Best we go and talk over coffee. I'll give you a full account then."

She nodded reluctantly. "We'll go to my apartment." An odd smile touched her lips as she glanced about her. At what? The people, the books? Her enunciation had been too perfect. Her face, too, was perfect, a faultless masterpiece of femininity that defied classification. Where is she from? demanded his disciplined mind. There was so much he needed to know.

Gently, he took her arm and guided her to the door. They stepped outside into a cool wind, and drifting leaves lapped their feet. Almost sluggishly, his stunned mind tried to reckon her wealth. Never had there been less cause for worry on that count. Silver passed his test of affluence easily. Better still, in the lack of ostentation about her deep topaz brooch, couched in simple exquisite silverwork, there was nothing of the suspicious, flashy nouveau riche. Her plain tweed jacket impressed Soame—not the material, nor the way it tastefully pronounced firm breasts; the cut spoke eloquently of high-priced fashion. There was the same classic purity in the woolen dress which fell, in the current mode, just above her knees. Playful wind tossed at her hair, and she pushed back an errant lock. Her hand—jeweled with a single sparkling diamond—her arm, in its wide half-length sleeve, her graceful body inflamed his imagination. Here was the opportunity of a lifetime: money, beauty, grace. Quickly, hand barely at her elbow, Soame guided her to a taxi. Determinedly, he slammed the cab door, settled into the upholstery.

They sat for five minutes in silence while the cab threaded through snarling traffic. A rustle of nyloned knees, a twist of tweed, brought her around to face him. Aesthetic appraisal, appreciation moved her face. With a touch of real pleasure, Soame watched the slight smile curve her lips. We're two of the same breed, he thought: the beautiful people.

"What are you calling yourself?" she asked, her voice a song. And it was there again, Soame noted. He could not place the foreign quality.

"I'm Clive," he said. "Clive Hymes Soame, from the old world, newly of Australia." Always, even with a woman seemingly as beyond pretension as this lovely Silver, it paid to get Europe into the picture.

She laughed, a tinkle of joyful melody. "Such a complicated name." Then, soberly: "What of the others? Are they all safely under field?"

Soame was lost and sinking. He had not the slightest idea what she was talking about.

"They are, my dear," he said, holding her gaze, no smallest trace of hesitation in his voice. An open snare, his mind waited ready to snap down on anything which might be a key to this strange, entrancing, rich woman.

"Naturally," she laughed, and shook her head in self-mockery. "If they were not, we would not be here, would we?" Gravely, Soame agreed. "And what of Rogel?" she pressed.

Abruptly, Soame knew what to say. *We must go*, her notice in the Personal Column had said, and she was obviously still anxious about something. Adding to her indefinably foreign beauty, her curiously perfect articulation, it was clear that she and Rogel and "the others" were preparing to leave the country. Christ, I'll have to pounce, and pounce fast.

"As you appreciate," he said carefully, "the situation is precarious. Rogel felt that he ought to attend personally to final preparations." In the pupils of her eyes curved the calm, urbane features Soame presented her.

"There is a great deal of urgency," she quietly agreed. "Now that I've located the Egg, we must get it away before the weapon test disrupts my control."

Ignorance sucked at him. Soame felt dismay. A single wrong word would blow the whole goddam scene. He'd waited years for such a victim. His grasping soul itched for her wealth, his jaded senses lusted for her body. And he could feel the prize slipping out of his hands. Sharply, he grabbed for self-control.

"Let's not talk about it for the time being." Soame indicated the cabbie, alert, efficient, listening. Again she nodded, turned away to view the passing streets. He relaxed, fought the varieties of tension in him. Still, he couldn't resist her profile, the piquant blossoming lips that had lapsed into silence, the brow curving uncreased into ash-white hair. The sun, cooler now in a concrete sky, burned copper into the cascade of that hair. Soame's eyes slipped back to her unblemished cheeks, smooth as satin, her fine high cheekbones that lent fragility to her spirited jaw.

A cool sweat of desire pricked out on his palms. A long lifeline there, he had been told once. At this rate he would die within the hour. He forced himself back to business. "l left Rogel at the airport making final arrangements."

That seemed safe enough. It was in all likelihood damnably close to the truth. If Silver was preparing to leave the country, even the carefully prepared tale about poor Rogel's "unfortunate accident" wouldn't hold her for long....

She was looking at him with amazed disbelief. He had said something dreadfully wrong. His stomach butterflied, knotted.

After an intolerable silence, she laughed richly. "Of course, dear," she smiled, taking his hand, "the natives. You seem to have assimilated the local humor. The quaint gigantic lying." Her eyes shone when she laughed, bright and reassuring. Soame laughed with her, he who had laughed long and loud at the painful wit of old, horrible, redeemingly-rich widows, and he wondered what they were laughing at.

Natives. That was the key. And her foreign aura. And the library. People do not meet in a library, even the cultivated. The answer was gnawing for attention. Christ, yes. A scholar! No wonder he had taken so long—this beautiful, wealthy creature a scholar? Perhaps, Soame sketched in his mind, she's a member of some ancient landed aristocracy, secure still in their prosperity despite the encroachments of the welfare state. The scholar-gentry. An anthropologist, perhaps, or a sociologist.

The taxi turned against traffic, stopped before an expensive apartment block.

The apartment confirmed his evaluation of Silver, rich, rich Silver. Soame, you lucky devil, he congratulated himself, handle this right and you've got it made. Wide latticed windows gave on to a magnificent view of Sydney Harbour and the arching Bridge with its antlike traffic. Expertly, he cased the flat: two bedrooms, kitchen, the living room where Silver busied herself at the mahogany bar. Her tweed coat was slung lazily on a low tonal purple divan. His mind kept flickering with the image she'd made against the window, slipping out of the coat as he held it: smoothing down her skirt, her head thrown back, so that swirling strands had sent fire through him. Hawk was dangerously close to becoming prey. She turned and sang a melody of gay gibberish. Mental snares snapped tight, held for Soame the knowledge that these were words in a language he had never heard before. In the frozen moment of panic, he raised his eyebrows in mock reproach.

"Let us use the local language," he scolded, and the touch of whimsy in his reproof was staggeringly adroit. "It has its own amusing charm." Dear God, did I really say that, without hesitation, with only my reflexes to guide me?

Her lips quirked in acknowledgement. "Will whiskey do?" she asked. "For a laugh, as they say. It's growing cool."

"Fine with me." Soame watched her shoulders move beneath the violet blouse. "Anything." A brown-gold carpet met deep oak walls of vertical boards to a gold and ivory wallpaper. The high ceiling was a soft, almost translucent gray. Subdued lighting touched the room with rose light that mellowed rather than dispelling the dimness. Here, he decided, under the Edwardian ceiling, amid the faded leather of old books, before the colorless seasons of Turner and Constable, he would take her.

She brought whiskey, and captivated him. Her breasts in the rose light were beautiful as she bent with glass in hand as though offering her body in some delicate exotic ritual.

"It is quaint enough, is it not?" She swirled her glass, watched red-gold fire dance.

Lost in a different intoxication, he almost caught the incredible import of her words. Quaint? Scotch, *quaint*? Nobody can be *that* foreign. But he was awash with her, and criminal artifice was lost in the darkness of his captivity....

"It took a little while to adapt," she was saying. "Still, we are an adaptable race, are we not?"

Soame nodded, clutching at the social gambit.

"Astonishing thing, the survival instinct," he agreed. She was his gold-spoon girl of the year—of his life. If he played the right cards he could score magnificently.

☼

The flicker of candles threw long shadows against the wall. They danced, music sweeping soft and tantalizing. Soame was at ease. He had dined superbly, managed to fend off Silver's anxious questions, and now she spun before him in a chiffon twirl. It floated about her, shifting over perfect limbs. Thin wreathes of blue smoke drifted in the air from a Sobranie left burning in the ashtray. He followed the wreathes through slitted eyes: the smoke symbolized his future, the same soft lazy drift, pregnant with a poignant odor of wealth.

"Mmm," she sighed from his chest, nuzzling his jacket. "The sound-tape has stopped. What will we do?"

"Nothing," growled Soame, "nothing, my sweet, just—" Long fingers unbuttoned his jacket, a slender white arm slipped along his side. He brushed with his lips the translucent glow of her arm as she traced the muscled flesh of his shoulders. "You are lovely," he whispered into her ash-blonde hair, "you prepare a wonderful meal, you dance like a sylph, you're more than a human being deserves to be in this vile world."

Incredulous, she swept back her head. The pale arch of her neck ravished him even as the wonder in her gaze sent a strange fear through him. And—

"Of course!" Then her laugh, sweet as water over pebbles. "Ah, darling, a local saying! Your humor has bite." Again she nestled against him, brushing his thigh. Bewilderment misted Soame's eyes. Once more he had floundered beyond his depth. He cringed internally before the enigma she presented. What was his joke? His simple, silly words—trite banalities, utterances without significance—were suddenly yawning chasms, dangerous deeps for which he could make no preparation. Desperate, he sought the country of the mute. Her fingers were a hot pressure, and he drew her to the divan.

Every vestige of control slipped from Soame in that moment. He was lost; for the first time in his adult life he was not the manipulator. The shock was extraordinary. He reeled toward an abyss of unknowledge, a vertigo of jumbled raw sensation. A wonderful sigh swelled in Silver's throat, flowed soundlessly through him. The pain of touch was a rainbow eruption....

Stopped. The room froze.

"No," she cried. It was, in the terrible silence, almost at scream. It wrapped itself like concrete about his abdomen. "What are we doing'? The fields, the Egg!" Her brilliant eyes, as she shuddered, filled with real terror, and she thrust Soame away from her.

Bewildered, shocked even beyond the sentimentality that had carried him near the edge of remorse, he stood gaping. Furious pressures raged inside him, as if he were a bomb held at the moment of explosion.

Her breathing slowed. "Not yet," she said, with surprising softness. "Tomorrow night, when we are gone." Her face held the sadness of happiness recalled in sorrow. "You're too beautiful," she moaned. "It hurts. I'll have to turn you off."

And her eyes seemed to glow, fierce and troubled. Soame felt a new pressure, a tiny tearing agony, like some obscene torture. An icy, psychic wave grew, raced dripping wet through his blood.

Silver's cool tones, sharp and clear, echoed in the colder vault of his raped soul.

"That was dangerous, my sweet." Smooth as marble, her beautiful features were raised to him. Somewhere, beyond the room, there was a dull ticking.

"My God," Soame shrilled, barbs in his throat. "Baby, what happened?"

She passed a hand wearily across her brow, and her mood changed to irritation. "You've really been an observant boy, haven't you?" she snapped, not looking at him. Her lips were pale where the muscles caught light. "But please, I've had enough of the indigenes tonight. I'm too lonely and too vulnerable. I want home and I want you. So please—"

He didn't understand. He could not. What the hell was he doing standing here if she was so lonely, vulnerable? Soame eyed her, feeling no arousal, could not deny the psychic castration she had somehow worked on him. And the anger grew, anger out of impotence and ignorance and the pain of humiliation. Blood pounded in his ears, and beyond that was the ticking, the shuddering grinding metronome that hadn't been in the room before that appalling instant.

Silver's scream, when it did come, was a piercing thing of grief and the very taste of blood as it tore her throat. Her face leapt before him.

She was gone; and stood in front of him.

Blanched, she held out a black ovoid. It riveted his eyes. It seemed to suck light from the room. It thundered in his mind with a terrible beat. He was cold and put his fingers in his mouth, and was very afraid. She held the thing, the muscles of her arms starkly taut and they were not what held it, and the shuddering beat died away, was contained.

"What we nearly did!" Her chill voice came shaken to him. "I ought not to have lost control, even for a moment. But I had expected to be out of this planet by now. We should have already had it under the null-field." She turned distraught eyes on Soame. "We must go to the ship immediately. I have lost face with the Egg; I doubt that I am capable of containing it much longer without field-force assistance. And we have to get it out anyway, before the mega-bomb finally triggers its memory."

The words fled over Soame's mind. In terror, he pointed at the black thing she seemed to be calling the Egg. "What is it?" he screamed. "Christ, what *is* it?"

The woman stumbled back from him. "No," she said, and he was lashed by an impact greater than the words of her mouth, "no, you're so beautiful," as though a rent had opened in her soul, and the furious incredulity of her very thoughts was a hurricane in his mind, "no human could be so—"

Like a badly-matched stereo, Soame saw himself against the image of Silver's face, saw, through the torrent of strangeness that poured from her opening soul into his, the transfixed stupidity in his face, his stance, caught the incomprehensible truth that smashed at her in that blurry blinding moment. "Human!" she screamed.

Her hand hung before him, ripped down, furrowed, raked his flesh. He stood bleeding and dumb like a whipped mule.

"Where is Rogel?" she cried. It singed the edges of his consciousness, fried him until he seemed aflame in her fury. The drumming, humming beat grew again, pounded as her control slipped. "What have you done with Rogel?" The name clanged in his head and meant nothing, made no connection in the broken dynamo of his skull. He whimpered, and the angry beat said Rogel, Rogel, Rogel in neat bars.

"I don't know him, I never saw him, never met, never saw, never—"

Silver screamed through the thunder of the Egg, an alien hysteria that brought vomit to his mouth. Soames saw the rage in her beautiful eyes despite the wild astigmatism in his own clotted sight. It was more than fury, more than fear, wonderful, vast, a stature of Lear and Oedipus in those eyes, a ground-quaking, venomous, magnificent, futile torment.

"This is death," she said. She thrust the black crystalloid form at him. It hummed and glowed jet as coal. "Death, human, in cupped hands."

The man's eyes were trapped in its blackness, his sight rup-
tured, for the dark thing was still and silent in her arching hand for
all that it beat a crashing smashing, booming tombing convulsion
that should have leapt like a heart in her naked grasp. And the edges
of her soul were leaking out again, cutting through the fibers and
fabric of his ravaged parts:

> She looked across the street-light jewels of the
> city which enslaved her. Too late for Rogel to reach
> her. And how could he find her, now that they had
> missed their rendezvous? For the essence of their
> mission denied them the use of parasensory contact,
> demanded that she work alone in her cocoon of deso-
> lation until the Egg be found and restrained. And
> now, indeed, it was too late to bind the Egg those
> several days required to renew contact with Rogel
> and the ship, wherever in the city it was.

Golden tears hung in her eyes, tears for herself and the end of
immortality, tears of stupid, primitive, doomed humankind. The
flaming mosaic of her awareness fused against the fragments of Soame's shattering personality, welded them to the shape of her an-
guish, a resonating fork, the paradox strangeness of her reality, the
sharp poignancy of her resolve. He rang her dirge:

> Perhaps there would be time to warn Rogel, time
> to have the spacecraft wrap emergency protective en-
> ergies about itself. She would lay herself bare, open
> out her mind in one last moment of mental unity with
> her people. And, in the doing of it, she would per-
> force loosen her last tenuous psionic restraint on the
> Egg, permit the end of its incubation. For it would
> hatch at any moment. Already the megaton flare was
> igniting beyond the horizon, already those barbaric
> scientists were sending their unwitting final instruc-
> tion to the Egg's pseudogenetic core, already was it
> beyond her endurance to contain it for any longer
> than mere minutes more. At least she could warn her
> companions.

In her hands, death hummed and glowed black as coal, and still
Soame cowered in the dementia of his terror without understanding

the magnitude of his final betrayal. The superhuman, poignantly-mortal creature standing above him looked down in something that was nearly pity.

"You don't realize, do you, my poor human?" Her voice was distantly calm. "This piece of hell, this crystal Egg, this fragment of destruction from the black depths between the universes—it has lain harmless on the face of your planet for three thousand years."

Soame whimpered, crawling in the jaws of death.

"Your bombs," she said, "began its incubation. We have been seeking it for twenty years on your planet, to bind it, for unconstrained it gorges on energy. It will suck your world dry, it will blacken the hot core of your green Earth. It will eat your sun."

His voice, rough as rope: "Who are you?"

"We are the Seekers, the Binders." Silver's eyes filled again with remembered pain. "Our star is far away in space and time, a twisted ember. Your world will die like ours, for I cannot hold the Egg much longer. Its nuclear enzymes have called it from sleep to a furious reawakening. "

Like a bounding, bouncing echo her voice fell into the chill eternity of frozen portraits from her soul. Soame looked as she looked at the ruined mindless animal at her feet. "You were too perfect," she whispered, "too much like us to doubt you. And I dared not touch your mind for fear of disturbing the Egg." The goddess made a harsh bark lost in the thunder of the hatching doom she held. "I thought you were one of the young ones born on the ship while I roamed this world seeking the Egg.

"But I will warn the others." Her eyes flared, her lips twisted like shrapnel.

Intense, shattering an instant of time, her mind speared a darkness deep as the darkness of the Egg. She found Rogel and her people (the clear tinkling minds of the newborn panged, and she knew a flooding joy in her sacrifice); they waited, puzzled and tense, in the ship. "Go, go," Silver cried, and felt a last moment of warm, sorrowing union before crashing energies locked the starship into safety.

There was a roaring in the room, a leaping incandescence as the Egg sucked light into itself.

And there were no human beings, there was no Earth, to see the sun give itself up.

# INTRODUCTION TO THE
# FICTION OF THE EARLY 1970S

In 1971, a decade after my first appearance in print, I added editing to magazine writing. Years of freelance fiction and nonfiction for *Man* persuaded me to apply for the position of editor, despite having very meager credentials (I had worked for six months or so in the magazine department of a major metropolitan newspaper, and my first novel had appeared from Signet books the year before, but I had the long hair and beard of a folk singer, not quite the recommendation required for such an establishment job). Somehow I talked these hard-bitten journalists into hiring me at what was called an A-grade salary; its inflation-adjusted equivalent these days is perhaps $80,000 or $100,000 a year. I had very little idea of what I was up to, except that I was tired of living on the dole, supplemented by occasional writing gigs, so relocating to bright, zingy, sexy Sydney sound like a very fine change. Somehow I managed to keep the job for almost six months, trying desperately month after month to turn *Man* into *Penthouse* or *Triquarterly,* but the censors remained fearfully vigilant in the face of the threat to public (and pubic) morality and order represented by the so-called youth rebellion. It couldn't last; it didn't. I was fired, yet oddly enough the company's magazines continued to take fiction and think-pieces from me for several more years before we became entirely unendurable to each other.

I had moved on a temporary basis into a beautiful Balmain Harbour-side urban commune run by a relocated Monash university friend, and stayed there, rather like The Man Who Came To Dinner. The golden sandstone house resounded to Janis Joplin and blues guitars, suffused with the aroma of marijuana (but very rarely on my lips, I never liked the stuff) and endless flagons of wine. Shamefully, I enticed my pal's girlfriend away from him; it ruined our friendship, as such crimes do, but Dianne and I ended up living together for 16 years, longer than most of the married couples we knew. A few years after I was fired, short of work again, I took a cut in journalistic pay and status to become assistant editor on the famous Australian travel magazine *Walkabout*, and a new men's magazine, *Club*. That didn't last long either—both magazines expired—but a lot of my energy and attention in the 1970s became devoted to researching parapsychology (yes, I Was a Victim of John W. Campbell's *Astounding*, As Were We All). One of my *Man* stories from the early 1970s became the seed for my first award-winning novel, *The Dreaming Dragons*. The resentful sibling rivalry rage of the younger brother toward the older in this version still seems somehow valid to me, if overdrawn—although, as an eldest child, I have no personal experience of this particular unhappy variety. Perhaps my perfidy in the sandstone house is folded somehow into the story....

# SYMBOL OF THE SERPENT
# (1972)

Max felt the pressure of his girlfriend's thigh as she shifted uncomfortably in the seat. He kept staring out through the Land Rover's grimy window into the endless desert, painfully aware of the baffled hostility that grew inside him. He was acutely conscious that Valma's taut body was pressing against Alf as well, and that Alf didn't mind one little bit.

It didn't help at all to remember that his brother was a married man. Mary was a thousand miles behind them, putting out lunch for the kids at this moment no doubt. It didn't help, either, that Valma was supposed to be Max's girlfriend. The whole trip was becoming a disaster, a nightmare. He'd been mad to bring her. Trying to show off, prove his masculinity. All he'd done was provide an arena in which to demonstrate Alf's tough competence and his own ineffectualness.

The horizon seemed to dance, splitting and rippling and merging again.

Directly overhead, the sun seared the barren land. A broad band of darkness hung at the earth's western edge. Max moved his cramped arm, tugged at his shirt where it stuck to his chest and back.

"Looks like a dust storm, Alf. Pretty soon we won't be able to see where we're going."

His brother, behind the wheel of the bouncing vehicle, glanced at the dashboard.

"We should reach the caves in an hour, Max. The dust won't bother us."

Max reached for the map, found the inked-in location of the caves. He squinted into the hazy distance. The entire region was so desolate, so abraded by an eternity of sun and wind, that there were no useful landmarks.

"How were the Aborigines able to find their way around?" Valma asked, glancing at the map. "Everything looks just like everything else."

"It wouldn't if you'd lived here all your life." Alf sat easily behind the wheel, a wiry, sunburnt man of thirty. "We're used to a city environment, that's all. Still, I know what you mean. Anyone who thinks Aboriginal society is primitive needs to come out here. You can see just how subtle they had to be to survive in country like this."

Max gritted his teeth, told himself he was being paranoid. Alf had made no explicit move in Valma's direction. She and Max had shared a double sleeping-bag every night, and if her response was increasingly cool perhaps that was because, as she explained, she felt inhibited with someone else sleeping nearby. In this place Alf was king, Max a bumbling intruder; and Valma had always been the sort of woman who shifted effortlessly to where the action was.

The distant mass of whirling red dust marched toward them as the Land Rover battled across the stony desert. At first it was no more than a darker haze in the limitless landscape. Quickly, it seemed to darken and solidify, become a brooding presence replacing both sky and earth to their left.

The dark, earth-hugging bones of ancient hills came into view far in the distance. The Beast's jolting progress was a thudding vibration in Max's bones. And then, with incredible suddenness, the dust was all around them.

Visibility shrank to three feet in as many seconds. Alf grunted, went down through the gears as rapidly as he could, edged the vehicle into a hissing universe of dust. Gusts and eddies swept ochre waves across the windscreen. Trickles of dust leaked into The Beast past the edges of the tightly wound windows, through the various gaps age had opened in the bodywork.

Valma drew a choked breath. There was no real danger, yet Max shared that sudden suffocating terror. The bumps and buffets of the heavy wheels made it seem they would overturn at any moment. Alf shot the girl a reassuring glance.

"Don't worry, babe. I've been through this before. As long as we keep the windows up and the doors sealed the cabin's pressurized. The dust stays out. More or less. Poor visibility's the only risk, but there's not much to bump into out here."

"Except," Max observed sourly, "the odd tree or two. Or cliff."

"The Beast's a tough old girl, she can handle saltbush. And the cliffs were a long way off last time I looked." He continued to creep forward at ten miles an hour.

Valma stirred restlessly. "Bloody awful place," she said peevishly. "I still can't understand how you expect to find a Bunyip in the middle of the desert."

Max felt a flash of anger. *Maybe sarcasm's her way of telling herself she's not frightened,* he thought. But he couldn't avoid the feeling that she was baiting him.

"Bunyip's a bastard term," he said. "The Aborigines called it the Rainbow Serpent, and you know as well as I do that this desert used to be a huge inland sea a hundred million years ago."

Valma lapsed into silence. The Beast crawled in the midst of a red gale. Max brooded on the legend of the Rainbow Serpent. He'd done enough anthropology at university, following in Alf's footsteps, to know that in one Aboriginal tribe after another the myth of the Serpent stood out as singular and inexplicable. Of all the *tjukurapa* figures, the cosmic beings of the Dreamtime which had formed the world into its present shape, the Serpent was the only one the Aborigines did not propitiate with religious ceremony. It was a myth so sacred and fearful that they went out of their way not to devise rites in its name.

Alf had found old records that described a long-dead tribe from this region, a tribe with a cult that centered on the Rainbow Serpent. If the records were right, it was the only one of its kind. It was Alf's guess that caves in the area contained a well-preserved dinosaur fossil, the remains of a giant lizard from those ancient days of the inland sea. If they found such a fossil, and cave paintings nearby, they would have the key to the anthropologists' puzzle.

*Fame and glory,* thought Max. Unless there was a showdown pretty soon, Alf would have all that and Valma as well for a bonus prize.

The red sleet was abruptly whipped away, as suddenly and totally as it had struck. And the caves were a quarter mile away, dead ahead.

A forbidding jumble of stone and boulders reached a hundred feet into the bright sky. Apart from patches of gray lichen and a few hardy, stunted trees, no living thing relieved the stark landscape. It was easy to see why no white man had ever bothered exploring the place.

Max helped Valma out of the Land Rover, stretched his cramped limbs. Heat struck from every side. He went to the back, pulled out a rucksack and heaved it onto his shoulders. Alf was scrutinizing the .22 they'd needed a special license to carry.

"You think there might be dingoes up there?" Valma asked.

"Probably not," Alf said. "Snakes are the main thing to keep your eyes open for. And not just Rainbow Serpents."

The three of them stood for a moment gazing up at the ancient cliff. Max felt a faint shiver of apprehension.

The silence was total, except for the vague rush of dry wind from the desert and the slight movements of stone expanding and shifting under the sun's baking heat. Yet that total silence was itself a kind of sound: a vast, distant hum that filled the head without touching the ear, a presence of solitude such as he had never known. He began to understand why even the Aborigines to whom this land was home had found the place sacred and terrible.

"It's—sort of eerie," he said. He glanced at his brother.

Alf's eyes were hidden behind sunglasses, but he nodded. "Come on, kids, let's get going before we spook each other."

A sudden exhilaration filled Max. He seized Valma's hand, and started clambering eagerly up the dusty slope of the rock face.

The first four openings they found led nowhere. Wind had scoured shallow indentations, shifting pressures had split stone, but there were none of the deep caverns hinted at in the old foragers' diaries. They climbed in silence, stopping to investigate various crannies in the rock walls.

Dust gradually caked into a messy paste on their sweaty skin. Max started to forge ahead, as Alf carefully examined signs of ancient Aboriginal activity Max failed to recognize. Valma did not keep pace with him. He heard her utter a small cry, stopped to peer down. She had stumbled, and now leaned against Alf's arm as she rubbed her ankle. Her breasts pressed briefly against his brother's body, and the two of them clung together for a moment longer than was necessary. Then they moved forward again, her arm on Alf's.

Max growled, clenched his fists, began to climb once more.

In his fury, he almost missed the opening into the cavern. Then he spun back, stared into the dark hole. It was almost hidden by two great slabs of rock. Disguised as natural formations, they'd evidently been positioned ages before to block off the entrance. Time had caused one of the slabs to slip aside.

"Christ," he muttered. The darkness beyond the gap was forbidding after the glare of desert sunlight. He pulled a flashlight out of his rucksack, thrust its beam ahead of him like a spear.

The light glimmered faintly on the far wall of the cavern, picking out etched shapes, in red, white, yellow, black. Aboriginal paintings.

He moved into the cavern cautiously, testing his footing with each step. He reached the far wall, bent to examine the paintings. They were an anticlimax. Even his meager knowledge of Aboriginal artwork told him that they were a couple of hundred years old at the most. There were no references to the Rainbow Serpent. He directed his beam around the cavern. It was large but completely closed, apart from the gap to the outside. No fossil bones.

Max shrugged, leaned his back against the cold rock and closed his eyes. He could hear Valma and Alf outside, chattering in excitement as they discovered the entrance themselves. *There's nothing I can do about it,* he told himself. *If she prefers him, that's it. She's got a mind of her own. But I'll never talk to the bastard again in my life.*

Torchlight flashed at the edge of the gap as they squeezed into the cavern. Max pushed himself wearily away from the wall...and felt the blood drain from his face. The rock wall had trembled behind him, as if a great door had begun to open slightly.

"Max!" Alf had seen him now. "Why didn't you let us know about these paintings?"

Max said nothing. He was pushing against the edge of the vertical fault line with all the strength he could muster. Abruptly, he lost his footing. The solid stone swung inward with massive grinding force, pivoted at top and bottom. Behind it, a tunnel sloped gently upward into the darkness. A taint of stale air wafted into Max's nostrils as he climbed to his feet.

Alf and Valma were beside him now, staring into the tunnel.

"God," his brother said, "you're a genius. This is it. Look at those engravings." His beam was directed at the section of rock ten feet up the tunnel. "It's the symbol of the Rainbow Serpent. I think it's a warning to anyone except the highest initiates to proceed no further. The dinosaur fossil must be in there."

Valma was staring at the perfectly balanced slab that had blocked the tunnel. "Alf, that's incredible. How could Aborigines without power tools place that doorway there?"

"Dedication," Alf ventured. He rubbed at stubble on his chin, "Or fear. The Rainbow Serpent was said to be a ferocious creature.

They believed it would appear literally in the form of a rainbow and kill anyone who ventured into its realm. It's the sort of myth, in fact, that's perfectly tailored to keep the initiates in control."

"Are you going to talk all day," Max said in a surly tone, "or are we going in to look for the fossil?"

Alf looked at him sharply. "I think you and Valma had better stay here. The tunnel may be weakened by strata shifts—"

"Bugger that!" Max snapped. "If you're scared the tunnel's going to cave in, *you* stay here with Valma." He shouldered his way past his brother and started striding along the ancient watercourse.

"You stupid bastard...." Alf yelled. Max heard echoing footsteps behind him, knew the others had followed. He ignored them, moving recklessly up into the rocky belly of the hill. The air was musty but breathable. The tunnel turned abruptly, and he stepped into a large grotto. And stopped, his eyes wide.

Alf's hand seized him by the shoulder, jarred him out of his shock. "What the hell do you think you're—" And then his brother's voice faded.

"I don't believe it," Valma said faintly. "Tell me I got sunstroke. Tell me I'm sleeping in the Land Rover."

Max stared at the rectangular metal framework that stood before them in the closed-off watercourse. Violet light pulsated like a living membrane within the burnished metal bars. It was totally unlike anything he'd ever seen in his life.

It grew stranger as he watched. The violet light brightened and changed to electric blue, to green, to brilliant yellow. It was something from a science fiction movie set. But this was no movie set. He was hundreds of feet into a sun-scorched hill in central Australia, scores of miles from the nearest human community.

He walked stiffly to Valma, took her hand. Her flesh felt cold and damp. "Baby," he breathed, "you're not the only one. I don't believe it either."

Alf blew his nose noisily. "Well, kids, unless we've stumbled into the middle of a secret missile tracking station, or Dr. No's headquarters, I can think of only one explanation. It's unbelievable, but it's the only one."

"There must be someone here," Max said tightly. "They turned it on after I came round the corner."

"Max, I don't believe there's anyone here. This thing's connected with the Rainbow serpent myth, and that myth goes back deep into the Dreamtime. I think we're looking at a machine left here by alien visitors from the stars, thousands of years ago. I think it's automatic, that we triggered it by coming here."

"Von Däniken's Chariots of the Gods?" Valma laughed shakily. "But what does it *do*?"

Heart thudding, Max moved closer to the thing. A low hum began, and the yellow light rippled a curious hypnotic pattern. Abruptly it turned pure white—and then, somehow, they were looking *through* the grid.

What they saw was not the smooth wall behind the metal bars, where the tunnel had been closed off. They were looking at a series of steps that started on the same level as the cavern floor and rose up out of sight. The image was perfectly three-dimensional. It was impossible to believe that the steps were not actually there.

"Why the hell would it show us a hologram image of *steps*, for God's sake?"

"Maybe it wants you to climb them, Alf," Valma said. A breeze was ruffling Max's hair. He suddenly felt very frightened. "Alf," he said. "There's a draft. It must be blowing in from the desert. But this end of the tunnel's closed off. *The draft's going out through that thing!* You *can* climb the steps!"

"You're crazy." Alf stepped back, stared about the walls, looking for an opening.

"No." Max went closer to the grid. "It's a teleportation gate, a direct link with some other place. The next logical step after spacecraft. Jesus, maybe those steps are on Mars or something. Or whatever the aliens came from."

"Garbage. You've been watching too many late show horror movies. Teleportation's scientifically impossible."

Max felt anger flare anew. The bastard was always putting him down. He looked at Valma, and there was an uncertain grin on her face. Without thinking, he wrenched a box of matches from his pocket, hurled it at the grid.

It sailed through the bars, struck the third step, bounced. Lay there.

Nobody said anything for a while. Finally, Alf said, "That was a bloody foolish risk to take. But I guess it proves you were right. And this is as far as our little expedition goes, folks. We'll have a meal in The Beast, rest up a little, then high-tail it back to civilization."

Max stared at him incredulously. "Go back now? When we're on the verge of a discovery bigger than atomic energy?"

"We don't have the competence to take it any further, Max. It's going to require experts from a list of disciplines as long as your arm to make sense of this thing." He turned, made for the tunnel entrance. Valma started to follow him, hesitated, waited for Max to join them.

"Just one goddam minute," Max shouted. He was suddenly almost blind with rage. The jealous rivalry with his brother that Valma's shift of interest had brought into shocking focus overwhelmed his fear. Alf might have led them to this cavern, but the tunnel and the teleport grid was *his* discovery, by God, and he wasn't going to give it up this easily. "We're not going to hand this over to some bloody committee without finding out first where those steps go. You two can piss off if you want, but I'm staying here. I'm going through the grid, Alf."

His brother had tensed, white-lipped. Valma took several steps towards Max.

"Alf's right, honey," she said. "I mean, you said yourself the steps might be on Mars for all we know. The air on the other side might 'be poisoned. It might be a vacuum."

"Use your head, Valma. If the atmosphere was poisoned we'd be dead by now. The air pressure in there is slightly lower than here but not much—otherwise there'd be a gale rushing through instead of a draft." He gave Alf a glare. "I'm going in. You can do what you like."

Alf had been in combat; he moved with trained speed as Max spun and began walking stiffly toward the grid. His arms came down around his young brother's shoulders, pinned his arms against his chest and jerked him back off his feet. They both fell heavily on to the dusty rock a yard in front of the grid.

"You'll do what I say, you pig-headed little bastard," Alf growled in his ear, pulling him to his feet, one hand clamped on his neck. The rest of his words choked into an angry gurgle as Max dropped to one knee, seizing the arm behind him, and hurled his brother over his shoulder in an instinctive judo throw.

It was the first time in two years of club training he'd ever used judo in a real fight, but the reflexes spasmed his muscles with automatic efficiency. Even as the body hurtled over his shoulder, he told himself: *Christ, I've been wanting to do that for years.* A sense of illumination filled him, glowed in his blood as he rose to meet Alf hand to hand and thrash him or be thrashed, and Valma's scream cut through it, obliterated glow and hostility both in one moment of freezing dread, and he saw Alf crash onto the stairs beyond the grid.

His hair was on fire.

Max was paralyzed by the sight. Valma's scream went on and on, high and shrill and driven by horror. Alf must have been screaming too, as the skin bubbled and charred on his face and hands, crisping like baked pork, but no sound penetrated the grid. Max stared, nauseated, as his brother staggered down the steps, beat in frantic silence against the one-way barrier of the teleportation gate. Then Alf fell, limbs twitching, his clothes igniting at last from the heat of his burning body. Thick oily smoke billowed up and failed to hide the blackened, disintegrating corpse, for the draft through the gate caught it up in eddies and streamers and carried it away as Alf fell into glowing ash.

"Jesus," Max wept. His mind was numb, and he was only distantly aware that Valma was holding him back, yelling at him as he tried uselessly to go to his dead brother's aid. He fell against her, then, pulled her tightly against him for comfort in his guilt and shock, and there was no victory anywhere for him as her breasts pressed against him.

They stumbled together, finally, to the tunnel, the inhuman thing behind them fading as they went to a violet shimmer trapped in burnished bars of metal. There were no words he could find to say.

# INTERVIEW WITH DAMIEN BRODERICK, PART TWO

## QUESTIONS BY RUSSELL BLACKFORD

**Blackford:**

*Many of the stories in your* [1965] *collection,* A Man Returned, *are black jokes, often irreverent towards religious ideas. Yet at least this critic is prepared to argue that the finest piece in the collection—I'm thinking of "There Was a Star"—is also the very one that treats Christianity affirmatively. Do we have to insist—a sad prospect—that "There Was a Star" is a cynical exercise, or is there some other reason for this discrepancy?*

**Broderick:**

Hmm. I liked that one myself. So much so that I've massively re-written it under the title "The Magi"; it's probably going to appear in an American anthology devoted to sf/religion. It was one of the first stories I wrote for publication, in my second year at Monash, tapped out in the back room of Brian Ferrari's Formal Wear hiring shop where I lived surrounded by naked tailor's dummies. It was meant as a tribute/retort to Clarke and Blish ("The Star" and *Case of Conscience).* I was then a ferocious advocate for the Newman society on campus, and spent my spare time reading Etienne Gilson, Teilhard de Chardin, Jacques Maritain, Jean Danielou, and Ayn Rand. I attended church and the sacraments religiously, or at least to the degree consistent with my sins of solitary lust. The opportunity had not yet arisen (well, only a few times) for me to be tempted by mutual lust, though there were moments when I wished with all my might.

Despite this, my better instincts emerged in fiction. I've always been an ironist, a sly jester, a remote punster; "It wouldn't kill you to smile," said the famous Australian broadcaster Phillip Adams the second time we met, but he was wrong. I *hate* smiling. This had led Lee Harding to declare me, as often and as publicly as possible, to be without any trace of humor. Naturally I deny this with the stiffest conceivable quivering lip.

Ahem, my black jokes. You tend to forget that Kingsley Amis, in those good old days, was being chided by C. P. Snow for his "cheek"; *Catch-22* was virtually overlooked (thank God I was put onto it by a tutor); who'd heard of Barth, Vonnegut? (Not my American literature tutor in 1965; and she thought my epigraph from Marcuse had been naughtily invented!) Robert Sheckley was an early stylistic influence, though perhaps it isn't obvious. Sheckley was not notable for his reverence.

**Blackford:**

*All the early stories are remarkable for their extreme tightness of plotting. You were turning out a rapid succession of "well-made" tales when you were still very young. Did literary craftsmanship come easily to you?*

**Broderick:**

Every now and then someone with years of academic reading and writing shows me some of his or her awful creative work and I fall down aghast. Surely the rules of grammar, plot, basic character definition, verbal dexterity (of whatever mean order) are assimilated by osmosis as we read, as we rave to each other over the all-night flagon, as we knock out our essays or letters home to Mum. No, not so. Well, it was like that with me, mate. Natural sense of rhythm. Constricted no doubt by years of reading pulp diction into a "natural" sense of hack. One drew in through the finger-pores the shibboleths and formats of Campbell, Gold, Boucher. I never re-wrote, because typing was so damned laborious (I never learned to touch-type). This shows, of course. It was a stupid, wicked way to learn to write. If I see anyone else doing that I'll give 'em thirty whacks.

**Blackford:**

*Maybe your religious background has been a pervasive influence on your work. Even in* Sorcerer's World—*and in a lot of the shorter pieces—you combine science and religion or at least science and magic. Is this some conscious program?*

**Broderick:**

John Foyster is scrupulous in checking with me on the Dominican point of view, whenever a major science fiction breakthrough is achieved.

Actually, I am also prepared to comment on behalf of Jesuit and Franciscan postures.

I can do spots from an Orthodox or Hassidic stance, but I'm still rusty on Shi'ite Islamic. My Scientology is so-so, and I can tell you a bit more about Aboriginal concepts than Keith Antill, who thought that the Moon is a female.

**Blackford:**

*May I ask you about the story called "Growing Up"? It seems very cerebral; let's say it's not quite the most accessible of Damien Broderick's stories. Is there a message in it? Or don't you like to talk about messages?*

**Broderick:**

"Growing Up" is essentially a bleeding lump from *The Judas Mandala.* Its main thrust is that deep in the future, when people are in the custody of transcendentally intelligent machines, our thought processes will be wonderfully ornate, deft, quick and allusive. Hyperion to a satyr.

Even kids of thirty-five, hormone-halted, will be capable of multileveled on-the-spot structural analyses before breakfast: six impossible things. That being the case, my attempt to convey this mise-en-scène could not fail to be pretty inaccessible. There's nothing that can't be dug out, though, and it's not (intentionally, or to my knowledge) van Vogtian bullshit.

The question which then arises is why I write like that all the rest of the time as well.

Swallered a dictionary, have ya?

I'll try to get all that under control. I really will.

Part of the problem is that, to an enormous and mysterious extent, I don't intuitively know what words are common knowledge. Yes, there's Basic English; but I crave to sport in words as Aldiss does, or Burgess, so the risk's always there that most people will be deaf to some of your lexicon, or unprepared to clamber through complex syntax. This is Delany's problem. I've just about given him up for lost. It's a nasty warning to those of us (John Clute's a prime candidate) who enjoy playing funny buggers with language.

Messages? With all you critical swine lying in wait to expose, foully to view, the unforeseen sub-text? I've recently been involved in a lacerating correspondence with a powerful feminist writer who loathed my novella *The Ballad of Bowsprit Bear's Stead.* Vilely sexist, she maintains. Not so, say Ursula K. Le Guin and Virginia Kidd (editors), and I. Quite the reverse, if *I'm* to be believed, but not because of the insertion of a "message," more due to the subversive tensions demolishing the unreliable narrator and all those he engages with. Message? piss off and mind your own business.

**Blackford:**

*"Growing Up" appears in the anthology you edited,* The Zeitgeist Machine, *which is the book many people would have automatically associated with your name until recently. Do you ever worry that the anthology obscured your reputation as a creative writer?*

**Broderick:**

Many are the strange cautionary tales hanging on that book. It had its conception in a spur-of-the-moment phone call I made to the Sydney publishers Angus and Robertson in October 1973. Their editor, Patrick Cook, the peculiar cartoonist, thought the notion a good one. My first letter tied the project to the forthcoming World Science Fiction Convention in 1975; Melbourne had just won the bid.

Then a few things happened. The bone in my typing arm flew into a thousand pieces one day when it came between me and a concrete step, and stayed on the mend for three months. Contracts lapsed and story line-ups altered. By April 15, 1975, I was writing to Lee Harding: "In effect, my editorial prerogatives have evaporated. Walsh [the publisher, of *Oz* magazine fame] can reject any story I suggest, and (if he has a mind to, which is quite on the cards) postpone publication forever."

For all the delay, curious judgments were made under pressure. In the same letter: "Basically, I just want to get the bugger out in time, so I'm suggesting Glaskin's (to me, incredibly boring) sheep to Walsh." ["The Inheritors," in which rampant sheep overrun Australia.] That story had been sent as a gift (sort of Trojan lambington) by Harding after he'd snatched Morphett's sf novella away from me [for *Beyond Tomorrow* (1976)].

On 7 July 1977, Angus and Robertson sent me an advance copy of *The Zeitgeist Machine*. It hit the stands in September. Just under four years. Nifty work, team.

**Blackford:**

*Another fairly recent story I'd like to ask you about is "A Passage in Earth," which appears in both Lee Harding's anthology* Rooms of Paradise, *and Van Ikin's* Australian Science Fiction. *You're known to be proud of the story, and it strikes me as completely successful in its fusion of serious modernist materials with ironic, almost light-hearted tone. Would you like to comment? Where did the idea come from? Zelazny, by the way, has compared you with Cordwainer Smith, whom I know you admire. That must be gratifying.*

**Broderick:**

Not "proud." Pleased, satisfied. I'm certainly delighted by what you say, however: the story worked for you the way I hoped it would. There was some soothing gratification in reading Zelazny's remarks, under the constraints that (1) he was after all boosting for a representative of the country which had just shown him a good time—and he's a gentleman—and (2) Roger thinks well of some pretty awful schlock. Have you seen his comments endorsing *The Snow Queen?* (It grieves me to dun Joan Vinge, too, because Vinge has said nice things about *Dreaming Dragons....*) Even so, a comparison with Cordwainer Smith, no slacker at the mythopoeic stakes, is not rendered lightly, and *that* I'm proud of, if you see the distinction....

**Blackford:**

*"A Passage in Earth" obviously has* Finnegans Wake *behind it as one source of ideas. What did you have in mind in reworking James Joyce? Have I missed a broader Joycean influence? And what other writers have had an influence on your work?*

**Broderick:**

The voice in "Passage in Earth" is surely derived from Zelazny himself (though I hear snorts and chortles from Nabokov and Burgess), whose project is precisely that fusion you specify, rather than Smith's sentimentality.

I think I'm at the *sentimentalische* end of the *naive und—* spectrum posited by Friedrich Schiller in 1795, where the German word, counter-intuitively, means "sophisticated, trained in thinking, self-conscious" (I quote Martin Seymour-Smith). The source of the story is not Joyce, who provided its post-mythic frame. It's ripped off from Friedrich Durrenmatt's play *An Angel Comes to Babylon,* as *Bowsprit Bear's Stead* is stolen from the same playwright's *Romulus the Great.* I prefer to rob Germans: my first published novella, *The Sea's Furthest End,* was a contorted version of Schiller's own *Don Carlos.*

In general I am poorly read, so hunting for "influences" is risky. This can be directly attributed to cortical damage done by an early infestation of sf. I waxed indignant on this score, preposterously so, at the 1968 convention; Bruce Gillespie wrote down my lament and keeps reminding me. "Neurons flaking away in great scabby bits," that sort of rhetoric.

Here are some writers I know hardly at all, if at all: Auden, Baldwin, Bellow, Berryman, Brennan, Burrows, Cary, Conrad, Dos Passos, Douglas, Dreiser, Durrell, Eliot, Faulkner, Fitzgerald, Ford, Forster, Frost.... It worries me, and these are just the English-speaking twentieth century writers. A few crumbs from Joyce; second hand Marx, Freud, Piaget; undigested lumps of Popper; half-remembered Fortran; a thousand pecks at bland *Britannica* entries....

**Blackford:**

*What about sf writers? Who do you like to read?*

**Broderick:**

Here I am, tugging at my constricted collar. What about sf writers, eh? Should be easier....

Back in 1973, whacking out the draft introduction to *Zeitgeist,* I nominated Cordwainer Smith, Thomas M. Disch, Ursula K. Le Guin, "and perhaps Samuel Delany and Joanna Russ." Still a pretty interesting list. Smith declining after seasonal adjustment, reservations about Delany and Russ, deepening with their replacements of heavy ideology for supple invention; Disch leading, Le Guin in the doldrums but well buttressed by previous laurels (that metaphor came from my food processor); Gene Wolfe, Brian Aldiss, Algis Budrys, Greg Benford (sometimes), Phil Dick (well...), Ian Watson (stunning, but at risk), Wilhelm, Tiptree (maybe), Zelazny (against my better judgment), and of course John Varley (a surprise entry? but look, he's got fun, energy, tricks, but is getting duller), and even Larry Niven, good ole positivist cartoon-cowboy Larry. M. John Harrison *(The Centauri Device* was wonderful). A few of Chris Priest's short stories. M. A. Foster's early sagas. Some Cowper yarns. Great looming oneiric van Vogt, middle Bester (Gully Foyle being still the greatest invention in all sf), the cold salt sea swells of Blish, the melancholy wistfulness of Clarke, old Mother Heinlein's chaw.

Of all the writers I read as a child, the one I strove most gruesomely to emulate was purple, sentiment-besotted Sturgeon. I hated Bradbury. John Carnell, buying my first long story when I was nineteen, told me I reminded him of Bradbury. Aw, shit.

**Blackford:**

*By contrast with your earlier stories, those you published in the seventies have been more ambitious and intellectual. What's your attitude now to the early work and the "old" Broderick?*

**Broderick:**

How can you be embarrassed by the pratfalls of a child? Still... adolescents make me squirm....

Knowing I was so very adolescent makes it worse. I remained a sub-adult rather longer than most people, which showed whenever I wrote from the heart rather than from my recurrent need to earn instant money. Once, in 1965, I was driven to Sydney with some friends, including my beautiful first true love. The engine broke down just as we arrived. We crashed at the commune of a semi-friend. Everyone slept on the floor, in bags. I didn't; I sat up, stoked with coffee by interested parties, writing a short story. It was funny, about a kid with a new love and a tied tongue; solved in Cyrano de Bergerac fashion. I sold it in the morning and we got the car repaired. Harlan Ellison does it all the time, but I don't think I can any more. The story was professional and doesn't embarrass me. My poetry from that period does. What also makes me squirm is the waste, the failure to push out into riskier, better satisfying areas. I did that later, of course, and discovered the joys of not selling any more....

## AFTERWORD 2010

The next story is a case in point, although I make no claims for its worth as literature. I wrote most of it on my pound-the-keys office typewriter (no computers in 1969 and 1970, not even affordable electric typewriters, and newspapers used small slips of coarse paper just the right size for single sentence paragraphs—the olden days' equivalent of writing on screen, since one could juggle the pars in a sort of paleo-cut&paste), probably in a protracted fit of rage at the meaninglessness of my journalistic tasks and the fact that I was being paid well enough that I couldn't bear to chuck the job in. Eventually the magazine department was closed down, and I escaped back to poverty and writing what I wanted to write.

I don't have much in common with Herman Belling, you'll be relieved to learn (although I would say that, wouldn't I?). Barry Malzberg directed my attention to an eerily similar hate-filled plaint in L. Sprague de Camp's August 1955 *Astounding* story "Judgment Day." See if you can find this brittle portrait of a man tormented, hazed, mocked and brutalized by a quite ordinary schooling among children stronger and significantly less intelligent than he. "The one genuine emotion I have left is hatred. I hate mankind in general in a mild, moderate way; I hate the male half of mankind more intensely, and the class of boys most bitterly of all. I should love to see the severed heads of all the boys in the world stuck on spikes" (72). Barry is of the view that Sprague's tale of terminal resentment against the world, a sort of hideous analogic diagnosis of the nuclear arms race that even then was threatening all life on the planet, is driven by the character's sexual pathology and denial. I disagree, although I see the point. Nor do I think sexual denial, per se, is the root of my narrator Herman's despair (or that of the real Dr. Strangeloves of the 1950s' world), although that was what I made the visible engine of the story. After all, Attila the Hun was exceptionally beastly without suffering any noticeable sexual frustration (he left more genomic tracers in the world than any other identifiable male). I suspect the root is an absence of love and existential worth given and received, as my world-killer seems to be confessing even as he rants about schoolgirls and frottage on escalators.

# DROWNING IN FIRE
## (1970)

Pick a hand, any hand. Very fucking funny. Right thumb button and 5,000 amps takes me out. Kentucky fried. Black contact under my left thumb, ah, my left thumb, the whole world goes with me. By God, a sweet sweaty choice. All mine.

Listen, assholes. If anyone's playing this tape you know already. I've spared you. Bastards. Like God—that's how I feel. Destroy or reprieve. Have I made the noble decision? Not yet I haven't, not here as I sit in my wired chair. If you're hearing it you better be weeping. With remorse. And gratitude. You won't, will you, you pigs? Oh, the smug smirks and nods, yes, the nasty little fat man was obviously insane. Jesus, I should jab that—

Not just yet. Feels too good, just sitting here holding the smooth cylinder in my left hand, stropping the button with my thumb. I'll push it, don't worry. But not just yet. Christ, it must be like this. Not that I'd know, fuck. Building and building, pressure in the back of your throat, tight in your crotch, all warm and climbing and peaking, the magazines...fire. Explosions. Well.

Anyhow, that's how it'll be, fire in the earth, night shadows, daylight, purging and groaning and slobbering all your stinking bones clean. Ash. But I won't push it yet. Maybe I won't push it at all. Maybe you're not even worth that. You're listening to me now on the tape.

And I'm scorched meat in my metal chair.

It's not every man can simplify his choices to suicide versus the...obliteration...of the whole goddamn world. Of course you all have that fantasy, don't you, you cruel maniacs? But you can't bring it off. You're not Herman Belling, though. You're not, let's face it, the world's greatest scientific genius. No false modesty at this point.

And you don't have the guts. You pretend it takes cowardice to kill yourself, cut the snail trail through the dreary grayness of you all. Listen, you're the pathetic pricks who try it on the sly, smearing your lives out in road accidents, accident be God-damned, you want to die, all of you, look at the fucking military budgets in this morning's paper, I could hardly believe it, they could have had this for practically nothing.... You're disgusting. You can't even face up to your useless triviality. Scared shitless of nothing, which is all you are now, but you won't even...expunge yourselves. Poisoning the air. Gray cancer in every breath.

I can do it, though. To myself. To all of you. One tiny spasm of my left thumb and you've gone. Do you think the universe will mourn? No, Freda, this old Earth will shake herself and give her rind a lick like a bitch with vermin. Cleansed in one wash of flame. My choice. One push and whoosh.

I can't help laughing. You must admit there's a funny side to it. Your pretensions. Your stinking pomposity. None of you wants to know me, touch me, speak to me, act with the merest trace of human compassion when I'm screaming out to you. Contempt and coldness. Well, I can give that back as good as you can pay it out. It's really amusing. I can't make up my mind which option is the more suitably, justly, contemptuous. Should I wipe you out with one Olympian gesture, or let you breed and slaughter yourselves into your own polluted oblivion? The leading philosophers never worked out a final calculus of death and justice. Pardon me if I laugh.

It's such a little thing to blow the world up with, sitting on the bench. It's not even very pretty. Just a square lump of metal with wires welded here and there, and the control cable snaking off the edge of the bench and up the leg of the chair to its black contact in my left hand.

The main power transformer I've coupled to the chair is much more impressive, and that's just to take out one life. If I make that choice. I don't think I will. The Quark Catalyst is so much more elegant. A single short sequence of subatomic exchanges inside that little box and the Earth shatters itself into blazing fragments. And you all die. An apocalypse of judgment.

You want me to justify myself? Too late for that sort of shit. My life is the justification. You have turned your face against me. I will take my price. Your deaths for my living hell.

I know what the smartass psychiatrists would say. Self-pity. Only they'd phrase it in high-flown garbage full of German and Greek. I've read a book or two. Self-pity, Jesus. They try to make it sound like a crime. It's the only possible response. Christ, if any other one single human being had ever shared that pity, had ever reached out his hand...her hand, let's be honest...it would've been different. But no one did. You smug bastards. My only regret is that you won't have time to feel the flames eating your gray slimy guts out.

Anyway, I do not have to justify myself. I've got a gun against the head of the world. Remember Orwell? A boot stamping into the face of humanity forever. I'll do it more neatly than that. Less than a second, and the skin of the Earth will peel off and blow into space. I have the power. No one ever has before. But I've got it. I could do with a cup of coffee. And I've run out of bloody cigarettes, too. Damn. It's getting dark in here, the lights are all off now that I've hooked the power into the chair. Grubby little window. The sky's gone purple. Will it be like that when I die? When we all die. Despite the fire. God, the last smash. No pain, though. I abhor pain. Either way, there won't be any pain, just the white fire and then nothing.

I'm going to make my decision pretty soon now. I don't want to be still sitting here in the dark. You'd think I'd be used to sitting alone by now, dear God it's my whole life, stranded in emptiness with the noise of traffic up from the street and laughing voices and me alone screaming with loneliness. I don't want to go out in darkness. Soon.

Herman Belling. No letters after the name, no resonant title before it. The fools. I'm the greatest mind since Einstein. They could have had unlimited power, energy to sculpt the face of deserts and shove mountains where they wanted them. Power to reach the stars. Power to turn the world into a paradise.

Not that they'd have done any of those things, of course. They'd have used it to destroy one another. You would have; I'm talking to you. The tape's going round and round its faithful, mindless circle in the pretty plastic Sony recorder. Lots of tape yet. Maybe I'll keep talking until it's run out and then press the button. The left button. The Doomsday switch.

You could have had it, but you would have perverted it. Better that I should make the decision for you, get it over in a clean single action of finality. Biafra and Vietnam and a hundred other hells are the testimony if you need one, and Hiroshima, and Dresden, Christ, and the Crusades and the whole of your stinking corporate history. Only the Bushmen and the Eskimos. In the whole recorded history of humanity they were the only ones who refused to slaughter their brothers. I'll be sorry to have to take them with me, but they're both dying breeds, they'll be gone or corrupted in a decade anyway.

I was prepared to offer my equations as a gift to mankind. What did you do, you crazy lunatics? Sent my papers back to me, back from *Physical Review*, back from the *Journal of Theoretical Mathematics*, back from the Institute of Advanced Studies at Princeton, not even the decency to return the copies from all the other centers of so-called higher learning. I don't expect many people to comprehend the equations, it's taken me thirty years to derive them and I'm probably the world's greatest living mind, but to reject what they couldn't understand! You don't deserve me. You don't deserve to live, any of you.

But I'm bigger than that. Every cent. Equations into hardware. Christ, when I count the electronics components I've snatched one by one and slipped into my shabby old coat in glossy bright stores? How many meals have I gone without, how many nights slept in this crumbling stench-heap of a garage amid half assembled test rigs? I don't regret it. I know now I was right. I've built my Quark Catalyst. Now I can do anything I want. So I'm going to destroy you. All of you, you cruel pitiless bastards.

It's incredible when you think about it. The Manhattan Project—how many years did they work to create the first miserable little atom bomb? And how many so-called "great minds" did they have, loaded down with government money, fed and clothed by the entire resources of America? Herman Belling had nothing. Not one cent of public assistance, unless you include the pittance of unemployment relief. Nothing but scorn, ridicule, loneliness. And yet what a thing of wonder I've achieved. What a work of genius and grandeur! A device to exterminate not thousands, not millions, but billions of human scum in an instant. Poof! The flame.

I'm weeping. Believe it or not, tears are gushing down my cheeks. Do you think I want to have to do it? You pigs, do you imagine that I hate you, that I am untouched by human pity and remorse? "Show me ten just men," Jehovah told whoever it was, "and I will reserve my wrath." I don't even ask that. One, one human being, that's all. And I'm not interested in justice. That's a harsh, cruel virtue, even if I intend to obey its laws when I destroy you all. Pity and kindness; that's all I ask. Compassion. Love. Ha!

They try to tell you your parents love you. The delusion of it! Parents hate. They resent their offspring, they make them with the fluids of their bodies to the glory of their own petty egos, then they demand worship for what grew out of their jerking spasm. They pay for your food, but they extract every cent a thousand times in return. Mother love? That fantasy. A pathetic lie to hide a woman's hunger for something to push around, mould, manipulate. At least they don't have the hypocrisy to talk about father-love.

If I had children I'd love them. Ah, God, God! I can't talk about that, it wrenches me all around inside. Ah, you're surprised? Herman Belling has feelings, knows pain, suffers? None of you has ever dreamt that might be the case. You really never guessed. Or did you? Was it your pleasure to goad me and shove me aside, knowing all the time the agony ripping my soul to shreds?

You bastards, of course you knew. I've read a few novels. Every one of you knows what misery is. Why else do you drown it out with your drunkenness and fast cars and bright lights and clamoring voices. You know what it's like but you're insensitive, you enjoy the pain of others. Here I sit, Belling the genius, the only lonely man in the whole bloody world, the funny little man you all laugh at. You fools, I'll incinerate the universe. Stop it!

Strange, sitting here muttering into the cool gray circling magnetic tape. Not a human ear to listen, just the flickering of electrons marking their invisible signals and pulsations on the winding plastic strip. It doesn't matter. My words are being caught there for all eternity so you can play them back, know that I've relinquished petty revenge and spared you. Maybe no one will ever hear these words. But just in case. It's wise to take precautions. The balance swings back and forth. The little button under my right thumb is seductive too, you know. A private immolation. A death by myself. Why should I give you the privilege of coming with me? Can you hear me? Are you listening?

Freda, Freda, Freda. God, my eyes ache. Why did you have to act that way, you bitch? You could have been queen of the world. You could have sat beside me in my glory and ruled the whole earth. No, damn that. You could have shared my bed, brought me that joy at least. Am I so repulsive? Freda, I'm not. I am not. Am I crooked, stunted, missing a limb, scarred hideously? No, God damn it! All right, so I'm no movie star. But I'm a genius! I can destroy the world!

Listen, you bastards. I'll tell you what she did. Oh, she'll deny it, no doubt, she'll find excuses and evasions. No, I won't let her have that satisfaction. None of you is innocent. Don't blame her, cunts, blame yourselves. You share her guilt. Every one of you.

Listen. I was twenty-eight-years old. Yes, as long ago as that. I'm not an old man, far from it, but that's how long ago it was. I'd never had a woman. Incredible, isn't it? I saw a copy of *Time* the other day, it said everybody's getting it now. Like rutting animals.

In their drive-ins, their lust palaces, their portable brothels on wheels. God, you deserve to die, you filthy depraved animals. The world quakes with the sound of your bodies plunging together. The air shrieks with mattresses creaking and crying. Damn you. Damn you all to hell!

I never thought of Freda in that way. I had respect for her womanhood. You've forgotten that now, haven't you? It's vanished, along with compassion and decency and...and...I—

Look, I can afford to be honest. I wanted her. Her hot slimy cunt. Her.... It doesn't matter now, you'll never hear this tape. Dead, all expunged in my final act of judgment. I wanted her, craved her flesh, hunted her in my thoughts and dreams, lured her into alleys and assaulted her, smashed her and raped her. In my dreams. Those foul thoughts. Trembling awake all hot with sweat, slimy in my own fluids, filled with loathing and disgust.

Freda, Freda, all I ever wanted was for you to look at me and see me, see Herman Belling, recognize me standing there and reach out and smile. That's all I ever asked. But you wouldn't lower yourself to do that. You were too lofty, too smug. God, you were beautiful. It made my mouth taste of salt and blood.

That's right, I remember now when my mouth tasted like that. Blood, running down my throat after the bastards had hit me and hit me and wouldn't stop hitting me. Where are they now? Enjoying their fine education and their beautiful women, no doubt, swilling their guts full of booze and food in their wonderful apartments. Jesus, it's exciting to know they'll go when I press the button. Their bodies will crackle and char like burnt pork.

Funny, I can't remember their names any longer. One thing I always thought'd be burnt forever into my memory. Webb, that was one of them, Jack Webb, or Jim or something. Who were the others? Blood, that's all I remember, the taste of my own body and the pain and the bruises and the gravel rash where I fell down trying to get away. God, it's dreadful being a fat schoolboy. You can't play any of their sports, you waddle where they run, you ooze in the hot sun with agony burning up from the sticky asphalt during Assembly, you jerk like a fly in a hook in your too-tight clothes. And they pick on you, bray and poke with their fingers and dance away, and hit you, push you into corners smelling of old apple cores and filthy banana skins and pull your hair and there's nothing you can do but cry, and run and run and run. But they always catch you. It hurts, Jesus, it hurts my chest.

Hands are getting cramped holding the control units. I must relax, it'd be ironic if I pushed the wrong one by mistake. Wasn't it clever of me to hang the microphone over my head so I could have my hands free? The tape's whining quietly down, too slow for recording music but it'll do for my remarks; the slower it is, you see, the more I can get on the tape. I'm not going to change the spool. If I haven't pressed the button before it runs out I will when it does, right away.

I've destroyed all my scientific papers, have you discovered that yet? I can be vindictive too. If I decide to kill myself instead of blowing the world up, you'll have nothing to go on except this tape and the Quark Catalyst. And that won't help you very much. It's too advanced, too superior. If you don't already know the principles you can't recover them by pulling the bomb to bits. An enigma. How do you like that? A dreadful puzzle for the so-called experts, and no Rosetta Stone.

I'll give you a hint. It won't do you any good, of course. Quarks. The basic stuff the universe is made out of. Six little particles. Put them together and you can make any atom in the whole goddamn starry void. Take them apart—in the right way—and you can blow the crap out of everything. Neat, isn't it? Tidy. You fart around with your nuclear weapons and piss yourselves waiting for the Big Nuke War. Small beer, pigs. The Quark Catalyst does it all with no effort. Press the black button and the quarks start kicking each other apart. And they don't stop. The effect spreads at the speed of light. Crump! Powie! Like they say.

I'm the King of the Castle. And who wants to be boss of that crap heap? You're scum. It'll be your finest fiery hour when I push my left thumb that half inch. They'll see the fire all the way to Alpha Centauri, if there's any intelligence out there, four years hence they'll see it like a flare in the sky, and they'll wonder. They'll have no way to be sure, though. It's a pity I can't work it so the earth's destruction spells out in letters of gold flame: HERMAN BELLING HAS DESTROYED THE WORLD. But they wouldn't be able to read English.

I mean, I tried to talk to Freda. But my tongue got caught up in the top of my mouth and felt like it had swollen to three times its size. Muttering, stumbling. Her scorn, her contempt, just saying in her soft bitter voice, "Yes, Mr. Belling? What is it? What do you want? Can I help you?" What could I do but scowl and crawl away. She saw nothing. She turned her face in blindness and went to the smirking bastards who waited in their cars and apartments.

You made me do filthy things, Freda. Sent me stumbling out of the building with anger and hunger boiling about my numb corpse, sent me raging past schools where the little girls scampered about in their scanty skirts, sent me on endless odysseys up and down escalators to press my yearning body against shop assistants and shoppers until the pressure was eased and they looked around in suspicion and horror. I ran, a thousand times ran and pushed into street crowds, waiting in dread for the shouts of accusation, the contempt for the molester.

I watched their wide eyes in dreams, the panic, the fear, the torment of wanting you Freda and having nothing but poisoned fantasy in elevators, the press of crowds, by schools, hiding in shadows to see them walk past with their hidden tits and their tight dresses.

My Ice Princess. I had no wish for those obscenities, those animal cravings, that heat purged in fleeting acts of loneliness. All I ever desired was the touch of your kindness. To stroke your brow, your soft smooth brown arm, your.... To, to...Freda, to hear you say that you loved me, me, Herman Belling. To hear that. So simple to say. How many times have I whispered those words, seen you sobbing at my feet in remorse for your careless callousness, forgiven you....

Damn you! May you blaze like a dried flower, ice melted, all your juices bubbling out, screaming in agony, flesh glazing and running greasy fat, may you die in the heart of the exploding world, Freda, die, die, die! It doesn't matter anymore what I say, does it? What an amazing relief, to admit all the loathsome things I've ever done, to state them publicly. Even if there is no one here but me; the tape writhes on and sucks in my every admission. I keep bursting into laughter. Light and floating, that's how I feel, buoyant and free. There are no chains any more. Nothing restricts me. Like God in the Void, before creation, or after He has finished with creation and seen it vanish back to nothingness.

What power. My God, what unlimited force resides in me. These hands. This focus of force and might. As God forged Adam from the muck with His Hands. A pressure from my thumb and it is all consummated. Credits by H. Belling. The End.

But not just yet. Not for a moment longer.

I could certainly do with a cigarette. No worries about cancer and coronaries now. It never really made any difference, but I felt consumed with guilt when l saw those brown filthy stains on my pudgy stumpy fingers. God, I loathe my body. Dross and disease, heaviness dragging me down into the embrace of gravity, heart laboring uselessly to push the blood around the looping fleshy tubes. I've often thought of castrating myself, hacking away those organs lusting in their private passion for replicas of myself, destroying all possibility that I should ever conspire with filth in the production of filth. It's called an orchiectomy. That's a laugh. Pretty unnecessary that would've been. Bitches, bitches, bitches.

It's quite dark now, except for the periodic flash of red and green from the neon advertisements. Cars skid around the corner. Crazy bastards, I hope they kill themselves. It's a bad corner for accidents but they never learn. Round they go, burning rubber off their wheels, filling the air with stench and noise to grate my teeth. I can't see the tape-recorder any longer but I'll know when it's run out by the noise it makes. The end of the spool flaps like a chicken with its head cut off. Blood spraying on the ground.

The dark makes me wonder if perhaps this is my Destiny. I mean, I wonder if this was all planned. Not by God—I don't believe in God, how could any divine Being possess the malevolence to create this botched universe? No, I think maybe I was produced by evolution to put an end to the disease called humanity. That's all you are, you pigs, a mistake that slipped through the Survival test, a vile blunder in the process. But Nature's wise; old Mother Earth has evolved Herman Belling to fix up the bungle.

I'm sort of a Prophet, in a way. Bringing fire and vengeance to all mankind for their sins. For their pride and their arrogance and their uncaring selfishness. And their lust. Their twisted, perverted thoughts. I am the Prophet of Fire and Death, waiting here in the gloom with my thumb poised over the black sweaty button. When will I choose, cast you all into the howling torment? Soon, soon.

Sparks are dancing in front of my eyes when the neon flashes fade away for a moment of blackness. The ache's gone from my chest. It...I almost seem on the verge of a vast revelation. I can hear all the voices of the world shouting their useless vetoes, crying to me for mercy and pity. Can.... Could.... I mean, is that really my purpose? Dear Christ, the blood is leaping through my veins again, I can feel it pounding in my forehead, in my temples.

Listen, hear this—could it be that I am intended as the New Savior? Is it my death and not yours which will win your salvation? Can I reprieve you, you pathetic slugs, poor blind stupid creatures, can I give you a further chance? Yes, yes, of course I can. The voices are clamoring for mercy and rebirth. I, Herman Belling, will not forsake you.

Well, maybe I won't. Just let me think this through. All the pity I never had, all the kindness and compassion you've never shown me, my birthright as a human being, I can give it to you instead in one glorious magnanimous act. Press the button in my right hand and I can die in your stead. I can burn one final time for mankind. Freda, Freda, do you hear me? Are you listening to those words in some superb cathedral built to my memory, some splendid memorial created in the highest mountains by the peoples of the world to honor their Savior? Ah, you'll be dead and dust in thirty, forty years in any case, and still these words will echo out over the bowed heads of the multitudes. They'll bring their sick and lame to the tomb where my poor scorched body will lie, hoping to touch the silver and gold of its ornaments, hoping for a miracle. And already you will have received the most extraordinary miracle that anyone has ever dreamed of—that I did not, when the opportunity was mine, destroy the world. Ah, God, God, the beauty of it....

Only don't bet on it. Sure, I'm up to your tricks. All my life I've seen that old shill game. Kid him along, promise anything only never pay out, laugh at the poor swine when he tries to open to you.

Listen, pigs, I'm not a child any longer. You can't put it over on me. I hold the trumps now. Oh brother. It's a choice. Right or left? Left for death, right for death. But don't push me, Mac. I'm bloody sick of people pushing me. I've had all the pushing and smirking I'm gonna take.

Tape must be goddamn close to running out now. My fists feel like acid in their nerves. Cramp from gripping the things so tight. But I can't let go. I don't dare let go. My arms are trembling. I think I'll make my choice now. On the count of three. Death for me, or Apocalypse for all you cunts.

Some choice, huh?

Any moment now.

Right.

Or left.

# INTERVIEW WITH DAMIEN BRODERICK, PART THREE

## QUESTIONS BY RUSSELL BLACKFORD

**Blackford:**

*Let's talk about your second novel,* The Dreaming Dragons. *It's been a success—with a Ditmar Award, Campbell runner-up.... How much is it a culmination of your previous work? (I'm thinking especially of its exploration of religion, mysticism, and science.) Or how do you think it compares with the earlier work?*

**Broderick:**

It's certainly a *continuation,* but evidence from order of publication is always risky. My forthcoming novel, the bloody old *Mandala,* was started in...aw, 1967? First plateau was 1970, when I sent it to the Scott Meredith agency (incredibly, they charged a fee!) and got it straight back. Rewrote it heavily around the waist, mailed it to Pohl at Bantam Books in the mid-'70s. Pohl found it a bit lopsided with esoteric words, but then again Bantam (he mentioned) had just done quite well with *Dhalgren* and *Gravity's Rainbow* (!), so he figured that with a smidgen of work he could maybe move half a million copies for me. I was getting the pool site measured when his next letter arrived, indicating a change of mind: on reflection, the rotten thing was just too difficult. Gloom.

I'd been in touch with Virginia Kidd by then and had the good fortune to be taken on as a client. She sold a bit of the book to *Galileo* (I'd actually sent "Growing Up" to her in her role as editor of *Millennial Women,* but she couldn't use it; women writers only), but kept getting rave rejection notes for the thing in its entirety from the great and near-great. Believe me, receiving enthusiastic rejections is infinitely more graveling than pulling a printed-form response. Eventually I wrote *Dragons*, which sold to David Hartwell and John Douglas at Pocket Books; it had a bit of success; they decided to take the plunge and try *Mandala*.

Which brings me to the point I want to make (hope you haven't been holding your breath): readers unaware of this quite ordinary tale of confused chronologies might easily draw the most demented conclusions about how my work has either improved or decayed following *Dragons*, when in fact *Mandala* is as much a product of my Delany-infatuated 1960s youth as it is a reflection of my present concern with power, feminism, and structuralism (which in turn are, of course, also of interest these days to Delany).

*Dragons* was, in the first instance, written as an act of despair. I had been attempting to sell "difficult" work such as *Mandala* for so many years, and earning such ambivalent response, that at last I took Lee Harding's advice to whack out something quick and nasty for Laser Books. Coupla thousand bucks, get your name seen at last. So I exhumed three stories written for *Man* magazine in the late '60s (and revised somewhat for publication in *Vision of Tomorrow* in the early '70s) and thought very hard about tying them up into what the Nicholls *Encyclopedia of SF* terms a "fix-up"—a quasi-novel of the sort van Vogt used to generate by merging a handful of different pieces and giving all the lead characters the same name. Actually it's even more circuitous than that: the seed of the project was a kid's version of the earliest of these stories, some 15,000 words, which Hamlyn had commissioned from me in 1971 (I told the whole horrid tale in the introduction to *The Zeitgeist Machine*) but which never saw print.

**Blackford:**

*How did you work out the main idea of* Dragons? *Developing the relationship between the Rainbow Serpent of Aboriginal myth, and feathered dinosaurs, seems like a considerable imaginative feat....*

**Broderick:**

I was living in an old brothel in the Sydney suburb of Darlinghurst at the time, just down the hill from King's Cross, hub of vice and drugs. I spent most mornings for six weeks strolling through the Cross mumbling plot ideas to myself, which made me appear inconspicuous in that place, and borrowing armsful of random volumes from the municipal library. I scoured their pages on my return for quaint and unusual facts or opinions and added these to the five or ten pages I wrote in the afternoon and evening. At the close of the period I had a book which seemed to me quite miraculously coherent given its genesis as a fruit pudding, and I titled it *The Gestalt Machine* and sent it off to Virginia. She was rather rude about Laser Books and tried it first on poor long suffering Fred Pohl, who rushed it back to her with a brittle cry.

Eventually Carey Handfield and I discussed the chances of doing novels in Australia, through Norstrilia Press. He and Bruce Gillespie and Rob Gerrand looked upon the words and found them if not good at least vaguely saleable, and dispatched the volume to the Literature Board for evaluation. (Without Australia Council subsidies, it is virtually impossible to publish here.) While that process was in train, Pocket bought the rights for a rather fatter sum than I had anticipated. By the time the Literature Board gave the nod, poor old Norstrilia were in the ludicrous position of having to buy back the Commonwealth rights from the USA. I'm very glad they went ahead; they did a beautiful job of hardcover production on *Dragons,* and redeemed some of their investment by flogging Australian paperback rights to Penguin.

This was hardly the end of the matter. Hartwell had indicated that he was not entirely pleased with the text, that certain changes were in order. He left the divination of these weaknesses pretty largely to me. There was a quantity of correspondence between the two nations on this score, but very little precise instruction was forthcoming. It seemed clear, however, that David approved of a certain marginal Aboriginal oil-man whom my white anthropologist stumbled upon in the middle of the Dead Heart desert. More of him, ordained Hartwell. After massive brooding, I went at it laterally and wrote the Aboriginal out altogether. This might seem counterintuitive, but of course my next step was a piece of drastic genetic and social engineering: Alf Dean the white anthropologist became Alf Dean Djanyagirnji, black anthropologist and grouch. Good thinking, Dave.

This might all sound unduly flip, even cynical. And God forbid that I should seem to be engaged in that loathsome practice which Robert Silverberg sometimes skidded on the edge of—the practice of boasting that one had produced yard-goods, only to see the ignorant suckers proclaim them pearls beyond price. *Dragons* was hard work, and contains a measure of passionate concern for the topics that form the narrative arena. But at root sf is sport, game-playing, ingenuity, cross-referential wit, adventure spiced with a blend of that comfortable awe which old-time religion ritualized quite nicely. At a recent Nova Mob meeting Lee Harding declared that writing was a life-or-death issue. Not so. Living on the dole is a life-or-death issue; writing, unless you are genuinely liver-and-lights-obsessed with forging the uncreated conscience of your race, is a species of decorative tatting. This is not to demean tatting; it is to insist on some degree of realistic proportion.

**Blackford:**

*You've told us a bit about your next novel,* The Judas Mandala. *What else are you planning, or working on? Are you still interested in writing for film* or *television?*

**Broderick:**

In 1980 I was granted a Literature Board Senior Fellowship on the understanding that I would spend the year hard at the typewriter, specifically with the aim of producing "a comic novel of contemporary Australian life, in which the machinations of the luckless protagonist's well-wishers precipitate the creation of a new religion; in treatment the book will move somewhere between Kingsley Amis and Jerzy Kosinski." This merry prank is still hovering between the cortex and the page; notes abound. It keeps going off into Phil Dick land. (To my chagrin, I recently read *VALIS* by Dick, which arrived in some of the same places I'd been heading.)

As well, I stipulated that I would write a cycle of sf stories embodying some of the techniques of Cordwainer Smith. One of these, *The Ballad of Bowsprit Bear's Stead*, had already been published in *Edges*, edited by Le Guin and Kidd; several others are under consideration in the States; yet others are to be written. I am a slow writer. Even if I did cobble *Dragons* together with some dispatch, I was reworking previous material, which helps enormously.

As well, I've written a screenplay for the NSW Film Corporation, a sort of "Hamlet-in-the-asteroid-belt." No one seems to have the faintest idea what it all means. I shall certainly be using the script as the skeleton for a longer work, maybe a novel.

Right now I'm packing my bags for three months in the States, with a week in Denver at the World SF Convention, and that's magic country. Anything could happen.

[August 1981]

# POSTSCRIPT, OCTOBER 1982

**Blackford:**

*Since I spoke to you last,* The Judas Mandala *has appeared in America. The reaction there has been less favorable than the reviews we've seen in Australia. Yet, ironically, the novel hasn't yet found an Australian publisher.*

**Broderick:**

As I mentioned, *Mandala* is a "difficult" book. Your own review for *Science Fiction* makes that point, I think, and I enjoyed the way you picked up my structural intentions and lots of the decorative elements from Yeats, Lévi-Strauss, Jung, and all over. When the reviewer in *Locus* said that it was "so overwritten as to be quite incomprehensible," my first instinct was to treat this as the reaction of a genre reader pushed by a heavy schedule.

If the book has any merit (which is not the point I'm arguing here), I don't really expect that it'll be picked up at once, except perhaps by a primed "academic" reader such as yourself. In time, the density of the puzzling parts of the book will either be generally accepted as boring incomprehensible old rubbish, or produce the effect I wish, which is concentrated pleasure of the kind you get from multiplex allusive poetry or intellectual game-playing like Hofstadter's logic/image/music thematics.

**Blackford:**

*Those "demented conclusions" about your development as a writer have started to appear: I was amused to see the* Analog *reviewer's comments on your improvement—apparently meaning from* Dragons *to the* Mandala.

**Broderick:**

Exactly. (laughs) Of course, it's true that I did a lot of work on *Judas Mandala* when I was staying in New York last year, but it was pretty much clean-up fine detail stuff. In essence, the book is the same one I sent to Pohl in the mid-1970s. There again, to be fair to Tom Easton, maybe he is referring to changes evident from my earliest US appearances, such as *Sorcerer's World* in 1970. I'm quite certain that I've improved since then; the test of that hypothesis will be seen when I do the rewrite I have in mind of that book, which will extend it and deepen it in much the way Michael Bishop and Gregory Benford have dry-docked several of their own early works.

**Blackford:**

*Let's tie up a few loose ends. Your story "The Magi" has appeared, though I haven't had a chance to read it yet. Anything I should look for? And what about the saga of your Hamlet-in-space film?*

**Broderick:**

"The Magi" is the longest piece in Alan Ryan's big fat anthology, *Perpetual Light.* I haven't been so excited for a long time; I ripped open the package from the States and gulped down my words like a drunken narcissist. Very strange...while I was writing that story I was in a kind of altered state of identification: my syntax is markedly different, in places, from the way I usually write. I find the story curiously moving, as if it had been produced by someone else. And yet the impulse behind it was almost technical—I certainly don't hold the same values as Father Raphael Silverman (indeed, I consider his moral repugnance to abortion as profoundly in error); yet, for the compass of the story, I as reader can identify with his shock and grief in just the way I as writer hoped to evoke empathy in the suspended consciousness of my readers. No doubt this moral suspension will get me beaten up in some quarters, but I can't avoid the conviction that a primary function of fiction is provisional moral empathy with positions which one as subject would find odd and even repellent.

**Blackford:**

*Hold it there! You mean you're expecting the feminist critics to act out a sort of Gene Wolfe title when they read it? You know:* The Slaughter of the Ironist.... *Or are you saying you've abandoned irony in representing values you find repugnant?*

**Broderick:**

Those critical buzz words have a habit of changing on you. Hang on, let's see what it says precisely in the *Oxford*....

"*Irony:* expression of one's meaning by language of opposite or different tendency, esp. simulated adoption of another's point of view or laudatory tone for purpose of ridicule."

So, no, I was not adopting Father Silverman's viewpoint in order to ridicule it, but perhaps to allow a kind of *reductio ad absurdum* that would blast the sympathetically resonant reader with genuine ontological shock in the conclusion of the story. Unlike Blish's *Case of Conscience*, which is one of the obvious sources of the style and concerns of "The Magi," I don't leave the big question open at the end. It turns out that traditional Catholic doctrine is true, and that's it, folks. As a thoroughly ex-Catholic, I find this a distinctly creepy postulate. Still, this "simulated adoption" is undertaken for purposes other than ridicule...so maybe "irony" is the wrong word. By the way, it's not the rage of feminists I fear, because I'm sure that my position with regard to abortion is straight down the feminist line; it's the anger of people who cannot distance writer or reader from text. As Sturgeon once had to say, "I wear no silken sporran." Or silver cross.

**Blackford:**

*Okay...back to Hamlet. Then you'd better tell us a bit about the new novel coming out from University of Queensland Press.*

**Broderick:**

Hamlet's working title now is *Besterman,* another self-evident *hommage.*

I dunno. There's a hint of interest in Sydney, but it's too soon to get my hopes up. If anything comes of it, it'll only be after the script has been utterly revamped by someone who knows film a hell of a lot better than I do.

The UQP novel is a collaboration between Rory Barnes and me, and its current working title is *Valencies.* It's a highly realistic work set in a rather bleak and rundown version of Asimov's Foundation Galactic Empire future, one in which the Empire was sustained indefinitely by Hari Seldon and the guys from the institute. As you can see from this thumb-nail sketch, it's actually about the relationship between Australia and the United States. Sf genre fans will almost certainly recoil from it with yelps and shrieks of loathing, and "mainstream" readers will have to pull on their rubber boots and hope for the best. I think it's a very funny book.

Right now I have to learn to master my new word-processor. Once I've got the technology out of the way, I have about three largish projects on the agenda, possibly including a transposition of *Besterman* from screenplay to novel. [Finally published as *The White Abacus*, 1997.] I still owe the Literature Board a novel of mainstream gloom, based closely on the life of Bruce Gillespie. [Published as *Transmitters* (1984) and recently given a different setting and reimagined as *Quipu* (2009).] I feel free to say this, because I have a little piece of paper here with his signature, swearing that he will never sue me for libel.... (Maniacal chuckle)

## AFTERWORD 2010

By the end of the 1970s and the start of the 1980s, then, I had transitioned from easy sub-genre knockoffs to more ambitious work like "A Passage in Earth," "The Magi," "The Ballad of Bowsprit Bear's Stead" and a number of novels that attracted a measure of attention. I was also editing sf anthologies in Australia: *The Zeitgeist Machine,* a gathering of reprints, *Strange Attractors,* with invited contributions of original work. I did not find it reprehensible to include samples of my own fiction in such conspectus volumes; I was, after all, one of the few sf writers in the country who had made any kind of larger mark, and anthologists such as Robert Silverberg had used their own work in similar gatherings.

With the following story, though, I knew I was pushing at the bounds of readerly acceptance. As I commented recently to my friend Barry Malzberg, "I intended this piece to be funny, ironic, and to some extent (with the Rirette thread) taking the piss out of Theodore Sturgeon in his most sentimental and self-help-bookish. Nobody noticed any of this, and probably took it for a manifesto of some sort. Sigh. (By the way, there really was an Aussie council worker named Laurie Hogan who came up with the grandiose plan I draw upon; that his name was 'hogan' was too much for me to leave it alone.)" A hogan, if you're wondering, is defined as "a one-room Navajo structure traditionally built with the entrance facing east, used as a dwelling or for ceremonial purposes." Barry replied with typical perceptiveness: "its careful poisonousness could be mistaken, I suppose, for sentiment but not by me. I can see the Sturgeon put-on (but maybe only because alerted); it's a clear chronicle of terminally self-delusive unhappiness lacquered over by Big Plans." Yes. Exactly.

# THE INTERIOR:
# A TALE OF OUTBACK RAPTURE
# (1985)

Oh, the dreams they have, the women.

All their dreams come true here, if they work at it.

Sally loves insurance. She'll never make another meal (John only used to pick at it, anyway). There are laws to learn, statutes and actuarial tables. Where would we be without those hands waiting to catch us?

Elaine's going to drive the tram she conducts. Fares will shortly be abolished. A flat tax, devised by Jane, makes that silly system uneconomical.

Dianne goes to meetings and is snide and loving by turns. Who understands her piercing intelligence? Who warms to her caring? Perhaps she will open a house for marginal loonies, outside the system.

All these things have come to pass here in the desert, in the hot gusts and new oceanic rains of the city of Restitution.

One or two of the blacks get drunk. They like living out there in their filthy humpies. There are always a few deadbeats, after all. Paradise can hardly be summoned by legislation.

In the morning the red land is darkened halfway to noon, in the west, by the shadows of the pyramids we put here.

Angela climbs the struts, putting on muscle mass now she's given up her nervy anorexia, climbs pantingly the four kilometers to the top and cocks her Leica, squinting cunningly at the readouts. This is magic. It is her soul she captures, sucking it into the banging nanosecond aperture. How she sighs. Here and there gawk people in family groups. She grabs a snap. How hard it is to breathe at this height. Still. Bliss.

Yvonne looks after her fractious daughter and on the tea-table edits books. In Restitution she has an official post but is permitted to work at home, of course. There is no point in Yvonne's friends complaining that she is not director of the firm. Her gift is the sensitive nuance of text.

Jackie is the firm's top dog, and rightly so. She loves it, though it's exhausting. They never see one another; Yvonne spends a fair bit of time keeping up with it all on the phone.

Lucy is a mogul of information. Jenny engineers the data flows. Neither of them digs ditches or washes babies' bums. There are babies squalling and snorting and radiating cuteness all over the hardy grass when it's not too hot, but none of the babies belong to Lucy or Jenny, or Russell or Damien or Bruce or John or plenty of the others. It's not totalitarian in the desert. Laurie's mountain is not a pyramid, in fact, but a wedge, a hollow concrete-lined earthworks higher than the Matterhorn. It's eighteen hundred kilometers long, splitting the continent at longitude 130 degrees, from the Great Australian Bight to the Joseph Bonaparte Gulf up North.

There's a little, unpretentious shrine in Artarmon in the house where Laurie Hogan used to eat his breakfast before he went off each day to work for the Willoughby Council. That was in the big depression, before we got the rains started here.

You can stand in the desert and see the snow up on the plateau. No wonder Angela is shivering, protecting her delicate camera lenses.

Not all the aborigines are shickered, naturally. Most of them work inside the Hogan, where it's kept cool. When you have those big nukes churning out the juice, air conditioning's no problem. Of course, the sheer mass of dirt helps keep off the desert sun.

The canal is on the western side, where the precipitation's forced by the Hogan's upward jut. Gillian sails there with her cousins. She leaves the portapak at work and lies there in the afternoon sun, adding melanin to her goldy skin.

Kim Phuc smiles across the lapping water at her from a dhow. She's got enough melanin already and keeps her face shaded, soft, fresh, lovely as a dream of courtesans. No jellied terror drifts.

There's romance and self-discovery in the sacred places of the Hogan. Under its colossal fin the bones of fifty thousand years lie, tenderly held. Rirette yawns delicately behind five exquisitely coral nails, musing spitefully on one hundred and eighty thousand farms, averaging two thousand hectares apiece. And hurls with vicious force one of the bottles from the table at her side. Fish-breeding farms have been made feasible by the 1,100 mm. of rain forced onto the desert from the high trans-oceanic winds, all God's plenty watering Restitution and the other forty-seven new cities of the inner plains, the secret places of the roo and emu. It is a whisky bottle, which splinters the glass and polished wood of her favorite clock, falls unharmed and gurgling to the white pile carpet. The slowly spreading rust stain holds her attention with a horrid fascination; just once she sobs. Laughter strains her throat eventually, hysterical perhaps, stretches her face and does not stop. How empty her life must be, even here.

Surely none of these men wish to drive great hot machines, run with sweat, scratch whiskers matted on exhausted faces, leave their babies unhugged for hours each day. Out come the babies in shaded strollers, and Jean sits in the high, shaking cabin to shove tons of earth while Peter and Klim listen to the kids' demands for eccentric purchases at the supermarket: no milky products for this one, nothing fibrous for that, special fish-pond-grown supplements for the third.

Claudia dances so hard her menses are confused and pinch her.

Carey chops vegetables into a wok.

Len listens to the complaints of the distraught, Berys organizes their troubled lives for them, drawing up lists. She has all the details on file for their benefit. Each remembers the old way of it, in the city, under the screw, with the yellow gasping sky and cockroaches sauntering in the kitchen. In Restitution there is no grease on the stove, and it is our tendency to eat in excellent Chinese restaurants where the children do much of the serving.

When Ki-in-jara arrives at the door, an hour later, Rirette's ruined clock is in the tidy, all the tiny shiny cogs and springs panned up; a Venetian statuette stands in its place, a Persian throw-rug covers the tawny stain.

Ki-in-jara is not unsophisticated. Through her glowing beauty (opposite of his dark) he sees her misery. Lightly he kisses her, comes without a word of greeting into her house.

"You are the mythic heart of Australia," she whispers to him.

She touches, without pressure, the welts of his burkan markings, the totemic whip marks that score his face.

Somehow, here in Restitution, they make a harmony; every meeting is a new unfolding, a new wonder, a fullness of joy. What can he guess of her emptiness, he who is so full of the joy of life?"

"I need you," she tells him. Yes, he knows that, but how can he know that her need is so different from his?

For Rirette, drifting here in the concrete, nuclear-lighted and airconditioned halls of the Hogan's six trillion dollar flattened truncated pyramid, Ki-in-jara is, she understands, the final glimmer of meaning in life.

Without him is...well, death. She plans to cut her throat and bleed as quickly as possible into the snow.

Up at the Top End, the man-made mountain swathes through tropical jungle screaming with birds of mad hue. In the dead heart, there's stone and willy-willies and tiny blue flowers when the rare rains come, every hundred years, though the Hogan's going to change that. The wind there drones like a corroboree of blacks blowing ancient blues down the misery and power of their hollow didgeridoos.

We love it here, by and large.

She who is empty listens, in their talking, and his voice speaks for both of them. He has not come like a savage clad for the desert, naked, his woomeras and boomerangs clacking at his belt of wallaby skin. She hears only one part in ten of what he says and what she hears infuriates the sick, tormenting thing inside her, but his voice is beauty and life and strength and a promise (if she can only find it at last) of meaning.

Why is he with her? It is duty, yes, vocation, yes, but for Ki-in-jara it is a sad gladness and a love powerful as the deep voices of his kin droning their strange sophistications in the departing deserts.

Some of the women have children. As yet it is difficult to arrange pregnancy in the men, but researchers from the Monash University Medical Centre are discussing its implementation and ethics. A reasonable proportion of the women abide in the love of their own sex. This is true also of a proportion of the men. Some, too, are quite solitary.

Now Lee's kids by his first association are grown, Irene and Lee have started again with a baby of their own. Isn't it nice to know you can always start again?

Dianne and Damien are infertile, one of them by the knife. Dianne exercises so hard that her menses have gone haywire.

Elaine and Bruce have a good number of pussycats. Gillian eats no milk products. They make her sick. So her figure remains shipshape without effort.

Jenny can't stomach the tiniest trace of farinaceous foodstuffs. It causes a kind of mimetic global depression, not conducive to advising big business in the flow structure of their computer databases.

☼

Ki-in-jara is pure, a virgin. Rirette, sated to the edge of emptiness and death, almost finds satisfaction in him.

She looks at his face, at the dark, pocked planes, and his eyes are light entire. She touches his strong hand with the exquisite manicured fingers which hours earlier had hurled the bottle in useless passion at the void of useless living. She takes his hand and leads him to the small oak table in the dining room, and rings a bell, and the caterer fetches in their repast.

As they eat, his silence is as rich as his conversation.

The fowl they eat (swan, from the ponds), and the Barossa wine in the crystal, and the joint with the dark coffee, are things shared. Before Ki-in-jara came to her out in the desert, Rirette never imagined herself other than a singleton, an isolate. She has been always Society, never her deep true self. In Ki-in-jara she has found a spiritual world opening beyond herself, a reverberation speaking to her from the mythic centre of a continent as dry and empty, until now, as her heart.

"You hold open the door," she tells him, "waiting for me to pass through."

She has never known love before.

Nigel writes poems of love and hate, epithalamiums to the Hogan.

His daughter dances to the night, changing her hair. Many women know Nigel.

☼

"Love," Ki-in-jara says, "is an echo, a pool where ancestors look up into us. Love is a place we may rest. It is a return from one to the other."

"Where have you learned these things?" she asks him, touching his scarred cheek.

"One-sided love is a hurt," he tells her. "Love is a giving, and a receiving. What you ask for is comfort," he says, and she has never heard this harsh truth from him before; it tears her. "What you need is reassurance, and love." He is a solid warmth.

Ki-in-jara is not self-sufficient.

He needs to give.

She sees that he offers his soul and she is too terrified to enter. Love is too big a thing, almost a myth, as the ancient place the Hogan bruises with its monstrous new weight.

All her life her givings have been inessential, untrue, selfish: witticisms, criticisms.

His shadow moves over her heart.

And she is weeping, freed, in his terrible desert arms, all his virgin desert mystery holding her, salt-wet tears like the great rains that have begun to crash into the secret red heart of the continent, tears lifted from some distant ocean and set down pure, cleansing and burning her eyes.

Ki-in-jara holds her, and strokes her pale beautiful hair, and sees that what the ancestors have told him is so, that she has been at the verge of self-destruction, that he must call her to their waiting places if she is to be spared the ruin which has been done to her.

Only native birds and flora are permitted here, in Restitution. Pets, though, are allowed inside the Hogan. Another plague of rabbits would be quite a set-back.

"Rirette," Ki-in-jara whispers, "this is not all."

Wonderingly, she gazes up.

"Not enough," he says. "Love comes from the spirit, from the Rainbow, from the sacred places, not from this world of machinery and images and babbling toys."

She is not surprised to hear him speak of his ancient faith, for his people were nothing if not religious, but she is surprised to find comfort in his words.

She draws back gently from his arms.

"Take me, Ki-in-jara," she says, "if it is permitted, to your sacred sites. I have...things...to think about."

Later, in her dream, it is never anything like the truth.

They go down the gaunt pillared solitude of a European cathedral, Rirette lost in a drift of years and incense. They stand in the arc of the altar's great stone tracery. They move into a pew and kneel. Her heart soars. She recalls, in her dream, the aunt and mother perfumes and the rustle of dresses and the crisp prayer books of childhood. The golden voices, the smug faces, the hurt and soft hands and hatred. The hatred. There is no hatred here, in her dream, only a tired age and an echoing silent blessing in stone, and Ki-in-jara.

The sun strikes through the new, heavy clouds, strikes hot despite them. A kangaroo lopes in the distance, golden as a coin. She hears the caw of a magpie. Can this be the Dead Heart? At the edge of the world the snow-capped Hogan runs forever, and the drumming of the turbines comes to her shoeless feet through the hard ground.

"A giving," she says.

He stands naked, made for the desert. She removes her light garments, stands as he gazes on her.

"And the longing to be wanted," he agrees. "Here, you'll get burned." He reaches into his pouch, sprays her shoulder, her breasts, her flanks, her trembling limbs with sun-screen. The insect repellent in the spray bites her nostrils, makes her sneeze and laugh. Beads of spray glisten in her blonde pubic hair. Their gaze is a deep, shared pool, mysterious as the place he will take her.

*He gains from me*, she thinks in revelation.

She runs after him, the new grass prickly under her bare feet. The place of stones lies ahead. They will dance there, in the ways ancient to the land, if he shows her how.

In her dream she could not recall it, not in its reality. Shimmering white lace of stone. The strong dark beauty of the man beside her.

"It is here," she says. "I feel it. How strange...."

Ki-in-jara's face, looking at her, flames with the imagined colors of stained glass, with the reflected radiance of the old, old wall paintings.

"I...love you."

And the bullroarer: "Hhhhrruuuuummmm, thhhhhhhrrrhhhuuuummm"

And the didgeridoos: "Booooonnnnnmmmm, ggggarrrrooommmmm."

Oh, the dreams they have, the people of Restitution and the other forty-seven cities of the inland.

All their dreams come true here, if they work at it.

This is Laurie Hogan's epitaph, written in letters of gold recycled from the Roxby Downs plant, written on the titanium slab high in the snow above the Bight, gazing down toward the useless icy wastes of Antarctica. (We're melting them.) Laurie taught us the way to go:

> *Sure, it's a Utopia thing.*
> *But we're capable of building it,*
> *why don't we build it?*

# INTRODUCTION TO "THE DARK BETWEEN *THE CITY AND THE STARS*"

In the second half of the 1980s, restless, I went back to university to find out what had been happening in the two or three literary-theoretical revolutions since the 1960s. Structuralism seemed interesting, in a rather algebraic way, but I was somewhat baffled by the opaque claims of deconstruction. Yet I was intrigued by the continuing fascination that this drastic form of critique held for one of my heroes, Samuel R. Delany, so I wangled a scholarship to pay for a bridging year from my patchwork bachelor's degree, plus three years of Ph.D. study and dissertation. (In the event, to my astonishment, the scholarship permitted me not only to live comfortably but to put down a deposit on a house, something I unconsciously sensed was needed as my long relationship with Dianne ground to a halt.)

The doctoral program—with supervisors Sneja Gunew and David Turnbull, at Melbourne's Deakin University—was entertaining, traumatic, successful, and yielded not only a fat thesis but three published volumes in different semiotic topics. One of these was *Reading by Starlight*, an overly compressed investigation of the strategies of modern and postmodern science fiction that seems to have slowly infiltrated the canon of sf criticism (I've seen it cited by Fredric Jameson, Adam Roberts and Istvan Csicsery-Ronay, Jr.), and helps account for my 2005 receipt of the Distinguished Scholarship award from the International Association for the Fantastic in the Arts. Australian newspapers continued to run my reviews of both sf and popular science books, and later I spent a couple of years writing review-critiques of new science fiction novels for *Locus*, the sf news monthly, and continued contributions to the *New York Review of Science Fiction*, the premier sf review monthly. By the end of the first decade of the twenty-first century, I'd published (rather to my surprise) an additional three critical volumes: *Transrealist Fiction*; *x, y, z, t: Dimensions of Science Fiction*; and *Unleashing the*

*Strange,* and had selected two gatherings of excellent essays by other critics, *Chained to the Alien* and *Skiffy and Mimesis.*

From the 1990s on, as these books and others began to appear, I realized that my technical competence had grown to the point where I can write almost anything I want to—from the first book-length study of Vernor Vinge's brilliant postulate, the technological singularity (*The Spike*), to a nonfiction investigation of the prospect of scientifically enhanced unlimited lifespan (*The Last Mortal Generation*) and of recent parapsychology (*Outside the Gates of Science*), children's and YA fiction sometimes co-written with Rory Barnes, and novels like *The White Abacus*, which I immodestly thought as good as any other book of its year. One novel I desperately wanted to write, until I ran into a brick wall with an obdurate agent, would have been a sequel to my favorite novel when I was a teenager. Recently I was invited to provide some hints on where such an expansion might have led me, and in the following essay I blend critique and wistfulness to suggest a path never followed...(so far, at least).

# THE DARK BETWEEN
## *THE CITY AND THE STARS*
## (2007)

Half a century ago, in the days when the first artificial satellites were thrown into the sky, when I was stretching like some gawky long-limbed thing emerging from its chrysalis, chalk dust and wood planings and hot turned metal in my nostrils, tumbled by the rush of hormones which make us giddy with dreams, I toppled a billion years into the future:

> Like a glowing jewel, the city lay upon the breast of the desert. Once it had known change and alteration, but now Time passed it by. Night and day fled across the desert's face, but in the streets of Diaspar it was always afternoon, and darkness never came. The long winter nights might dust the desert with frost, as the last moisture left in the thin air of Earth congealed—but the city knew neither heat nor cold. it had no contact with the outer world; it was a universe itself....
>
> Since the city was built, the oceans of Earth had passed away and the desert had encompassed all the globe. The last mountain had been ground to dust by the winds and the rain, and the world was too weary to bring forth more. The city did not care; Earth itself could crumble and Diaspar would still protect the children of its makers, bearing them and their treasures safely down the stream of time. (p. 7)

That is the exultant lamentation which opens Arthur C. Clarke's *The City and the Stars* (1956), a novel based upon a tale with the even more evocative title *Against the Fall of Night* (1948). Clarke's book was quite simply the most important novel I have ever read, will ever read. It guaranteed that I yearned to be a science fiction writer. When I was fourteen or so, I sat in class in my infinitely tedious trade school with the newly released Corgi paperback of *The City and the Stars* propped open under the desk and dreamed, and dreamed, until the stern Christian Brother whacked his cane down on my isometric projection and made the pencils jump.

Later I found Clarke's apocalyptic novel *Childhood's End* (1953), as I neared the belated end of my own. By then (as other children are turned towards painting, or composition, by some germinal encounter with a luminous canvas, compelling score) I knew that this wonderful blend of poignancy, aspiration, absurd adventure and odd beauty was what I wanted to create for myself, some day.

I wanted to know *what happens next*. I wanted to carry forward the misty collective enterprise I seemed to detect in these tales that everyone else took for tasteless tomfoolery. It was as if I had been invited to join some secret masonry of dreamers, to partake of their Gothic vision of a world where science really is close to magic, when everything has been known and done, and forgotten, when the world, failing in entropy, is kick-started back to numinous ignition.

But I don't wish to be solemn. This is pleasure I'm talking about. I was an inward, asthmatic child, and liked nothing better than pedaling in the cool afternoon air to second-hand swap shops (now long vanished) to exchange tattered magazines and books, with titles like *Galaxy* and *Astounding* and *Science Fantasy*, trading over and again the four or five I could afford as my stake. In all this, it was some haunting overtone from Diaspar which fugued through my unconscious, and forced me to become an sf tale-teller.

So much for the thunderclap impact in my late childhood. Decades later, does the novel retain its power, the transcendental shock of its cascade of conceptual breakthroughs (to borrow the useful coinage of my friend Peter Nicholls)? I think it does, even though many of Clarke's brilliant insights have now become commonplace not only in science fiction but in authentic science. But there are other ways to approach a book like this, richer than the bewildered excitement of a young reader. Theorists call one kind of reading the hermeneutics of suspicion (that is, a method of interpretation that takes nothing for granted and snuffles about in search of hidden agendas) and if that sounds ungracious or even paranoid it probably is, and faintly pretentious as well, since it places the reader in a loftier position than the writer. After all, critics have sometimes asked, what does the writer know? The death of the author was declared by Roland Barthes and Michel Foucault, after all, a good many years before Sir Arthur's physical demise in 2008. For all the suspicions an honest plain reader might harbor toward any hermeneutics of suspicion, startling discoveries await, tucked beneath the ancient sands that circle the timeless city of Diaspar, and the re-shaped constellations above her.

Such complexities became a matter of some urgency for me about two decades ago, when I asked Arthur Clarke for permission to write a sequel to *The City and the Stars*. Although Clarke favored the possibility, in the meantime his agent had agreed to a proposal by the award-winning writer and physicist Dr. Gregory Benford for a similar project based on *Against the Fall of Night*. Imagine my frustration. Later, in the introduction to their combined volume *Beyond the Fall of Night*, Clarke wrote that perhaps in another decade my proposal might bear fruit, but that never happened. Even so, I spent a lot of time thinking about the great novel, the implications hidden beneath its surface or folded into its structure, and where the logic of its argument might take a sequel. I did not attempt to create an entire plot or new cast of characters; my method of working is more organic than that, with problems and surprising solutions arising as much from my dreaming unconscious as from cool calculation and analysis. But here are some of the aspects of the novel I found, often to my own startlement.

Consider Diaspar, that brilliant city at the end of time. Clarke is exact in his opening description: "Like a glowing jewel." The familiar implications suggest that the city is beautiful, wealthy, resistant to change, like the jewels of a necklace or crown, and all this is so— but the description tells us quite literally that Diaspar is crystalline, brittle, the very opposite of a living world. If it persists despite its crystalline fragility, that is due to miracles of super science, or perhaps something stranger still. What Diaspar is not, most conspicuously, is a *garden* lying upon the breast of the desert. That alternative is apparently offered by the rural utopia of Lys, a bucolic closed economy a quarter of the way around the edge of the dying earth. In fact, a moment's reflection reveals to us that Lys is precisely as contrived and artificial as Diaspar. In a world where the last clouds are gone, the oceans evaporated away or sequestered beneath the crust of the earth, where, at best, the desert is dusted with frost, a paradise like Lys is not nearly lost but impossible—unless it is sustained by exactly the same super science miracle.

Or, shocking thought: are they both unreal contrivances, dream landscapes, virtual realities? It is a mark of Clarke's genius that the very term "virtual reality" had not been coined when he displayed exactly such a simulated world in the first chapter of the novel.

Today, that possibility is banal, as crude as a child's story escape clause: *And then he woke up—it had all been a dream!* At the same time, we are only now beginning to understand that something like this might be literally true on the largest possible scale, that the solipsistic fantasy familiar from a dozen stories by Philip K. Dick (*Ubik*, most explicitly) could describe the universe we inhabit (the universe as computational simulation in a higher cosmos). And if not that, then the constructed, simulated universes we or our uploaded descendants shall eventually live in when computing power has grown sufficiently. That postulate is now called the Vingean Singularity. A chilling literal reading of *The City and the Stars* might be that the entire narrative is a higher order embodiment of the adventure game simulation with which the novel opens. It explains a great deal—the impossible physics, the starship that travels faster than light, the coincidences, the innocent megalomania. That reading exacts an unacceptable price, however. It tears us out of the apparent frame, and dumps us into a tawdry contrivance. Still, in a sense it lurks behind the surface of the book (and, after all, all novels are indeed contrivances, machines for prompting dreams) like the imaginary Diaspars visible behind the fake mirrored walls below the Tower of Loranne:

> Whatever mechanism produced the images was controlled by his presence, and to some extent by his thoughts. The mirrors were always blank when he first came into the room, but filled with action as soon as he moved among them...perhaps it was not a real scene from the past, but a purely created episode. A careful balance of figures, the slightly formal movements, all made it seem a little too neat for life. (pp. 31-32)

What's more, simulation is embodied as the very key to the unlocking of the Master's last disciple by Central Computer, who (in a beautiful and terrifying scene) seduces the machine into a thoroughly convincing virtual Rapture at the end of time, breaking down programmed compulsions. Is there, finally, any difference between the unsleeping people of Diaspar dreamless in their millennium suspension between rebirths, and the sorry fate of humankind in my novel *The Judas Mandala* (where I seem to have coined the term "virtual reality"):

> For the first time, I understood the overwhelming lure of addiction, the honeys of transcendental art. I understood how it could be that the Dreamvats of the cyborgs contained the majority of the world's living human beings.... The hunt is done and bellies are full. In the flickering firelight the tribe lean forward to hear and tell their boasts. The old ones sing, at last, the sagas of their once and future heroes. In the Dreamtanks, at the apotheosis of art, the old ones live and sing forever.... (1982, pp. 154-55)

Clarke had been there ahead of me, of course. In his early novella "The Lion of Comarre" (1949), the sleepers of that abandoned future city dream trance hallucinations under the influence of thought projectors. Is this the true, hidden secret of Diaspar and Lys, of the omnipotent fantasy of Mad Mind and Vanamonde?

This would be a postmodern and reductive reading, the novel as trompe-l'œil, as a conceit by Magritte. Let us assume, however, that Clarke's paradoxes are less cruel—some chosen, some an accidental function of genre and period. For a start, let's return to that apparent binary opposition of city versus country. If the novel is a *Bildungsroman*, the coming-of-age of the supremely anomalous youth Alvin, his first cognitive shock is to discover that Diaspar is not the whole of the universe, that beyond its great walls extends lifeless desert as far as the eye can see, to distant eroded hills. His second shock is finding Lys, apparently the binary contrast to Diaspar. But, as noted above, each of these habitats is entirely unnatural and stationary, sustained by a science sufficiently advanced to be indistinguishable from magic. If Diaspar is crowned by a dome of force that hides the sky and keeps out the parched winds of the desert, so too must Lys be. If Diaspar's citizens have persisted unchanged for a billion years, why, so too have those of Lys, despite their superficial "naturalness." Evolution has been stymied. Neither Alvin nor the complacent, telepathic inhabitants of Lys recognize this deep identity. It is captured quite beautifully in the moment when Alvin first sees a creature in a lake:

The great silver fish that suddenly forced its way through the underwater reeds was the first nonhuman creature that Alvin had ever seen. It should have been utterly strange to him, yet its shape teased his mind with a haunting familiarity. As it hung there in the pale green void, its fins a faint blur of motion, it seemed the very embodiment of power and speed. Here, incorporated in living flesh, were the graceful lines of the great ships that had once ruled the skies of Earth. (p. 68)

We, as yet insufficiently denatured by technology, instinctively see an aircraft or spacecraft as copying the creatures built by natural selection under evolutionary pressure; for Alvin and his culture, more than a billion years old, life has always been shaped by desire and design, so the analogy operates in the opposite direction.

In short, the binary contrast is not between Diaspar and Lys, but between both and a blighted, corroded nature. That this is not accidental becomes clear in the terrifying finale, when Alvin escapes from both gilded cages to find a darkening, wrecked galaxy thinned out by the deliberate obliteration of stars. Many stellar systems have flung themselves away into the greater darkness, powered by the death of stars; others have been smashed and ruined by the psychotic frenzies of the Mad Mind, unconstrained technology at its nightmarish worst. So the contrast is not, either, between triumphalist technology and backward superstition, as so often in science fiction. Superstition is represented, in the compulsive delusions of the Master, but it seems to be a kind of ultimate superstition of technology, of super science. Nothing seems more suitable and appropriate than that its final bamboozled adherent is...a robot.

Consider another classic binary: the upper world and the lower, heaven and hell, the sky and the deeps, the stars and the earth. For Clarke, nothing is ever so simple or clarified, even in a tale that seems utterly translucent and artless. For Alvin to escape Diaspar, he must first sink into the depths beneath the city (a trainspotter's vision of harrowing hell and finding heaven). The wry gaze of Yarlan Zey, designer of the deathless city, looks neither to the stars nor to his fellow citizens but to the escape hatch at his statue's feet. To leave the earth entirely, a buried starship must be retrieved from the desert, caked with soil; it does not fall like an angel from orbit. These are interesting ambiguities. A Lévi-Strauss might speak of autochthones with their feet anchored in their native dirt (although with "matter-converters" [p. 87] available to them, able to build food from air). An obvious conjecture—and one Clarke himself raises, only to dismiss it—is that Alvin is Yarlan Zey redux. This seems very plausible to me. Once again, though, we confront a crux which might be no more than an artifact of the novel's history: why should Yarlan Zey have a Tomb? For the designer of Diaspar with its endlessly cycled reborn citizens, death should have presented no obstacle. Is this a clue to some mystery? Probably not; it seems to be an incompletely rationalized residue from the earlier novella, before Clarke had translated his novel from the mechanical age of the 1930s to the post-Shannon information age of the 1950s.

So: can I tell you *What happens next* beyond this complex, evocative, and searching novel? I'd rather not. I have my own ideas, but I fear I shall never be allowed to develop them in the sequel Sir Arthur almost permitted me to write. I'd be very interested to read the speculations of others. Is it really possible that Alvin turns his back on the denuded Galaxy, content to tend his own planet-sized garden, recovering the lost oceans and enlivening the soil with living creatures, the ultimate Green boy scout? Might not the nameless starship of the Master return rather sooner than expected, bringing transcendent news from the edge of the universe where the builders of Diaspar and the other bold geniuses of the dawn ages had gone in search of an awfully big adventure:

> All we know is that the Empire made contact with—something—very strange and very great, far away around the curve of the Cosmos, at the other extremity of space itself. What it was we can only guess, but its call must have been of immense urgency, and immense promise. Within a very short period of time our ancestors and their fellow races had gone upon a journey which we cannot follow. (p. 181)

I will reveal my suspicion that Diaspar—the city of Port Diaspora, as I read it—is, in reality, not merely an earthly conurbation, but a James Blishean city poised for flight, its internal structure proof against interstellar radiation and impacts, powered with the same engines that flung whole stars out of the Galaxy. Might Alvin awaken finally from his late adolescent billennial amnesia to see that he is, indeed, Yarlan Zey, reborn, ready to take the helm of the star-ship Diaspar? No doubt that is too crude a reading, even in this day of revived space opera. But I refuse to accept that the people of Diaspar and Lys will settle for anything less than the heroic, once they free themselves completely, as the Master's robot was emblematically freed, from their long delusional passivity.

# INTRODUCTION TO "COCKROACH LOVE"

At the start of the new millennium, I was restless again, fell in love during a long courtship conducted largely by email with Barbara Lamar, a Texan permaculture farmer, former commercially-rated pilot, and lawyer, married her in Melbourne, and moved to San Antonio. The books continued to roll from my word processor, and now I have more than forty to my name—paltry by the standards of a Silverberg, a Malzberg or an Asimov, but satisfying enough for the inner kid who wanted to be a science fiction writer, despite everyone's objections, and did so. I hadn't written any short fiction for quite a long time until one month in 2008, when I decided on impulse to try a series of *hommages* to some of my favorite SF writers: Philip K. Dick, Roger Zelazny, J. G. Ballard, Cordwainer Smith. I was gratified to see the editor of *Asimov's* science fiction magazine, Sheila Williams, announce the most recent of these (the opening story in this book) as part of my "unofficial series of *tours de force* inspired by classic SF talents." Several have been selected for inclusion in 2010's *Year's Best* anthologies, and appear as well in my collection, *The Qualia Engine*.

During this burst of graphomania, I came across an amusing comment by an Egyptian cultural critic and writer (quoted by Indian essayist Pankaj Mishra), regretting the surrealistic and playful tenor of his nation's recent fiction. An absurd idea popped into my head—why not write a story precisely of the kind he was denouncing?—and I decided to share the notion with my gonzo, wildly talented email friend Paul Di Filippo, who agreed to collaborate with me in the lunacy. The story was published at the end of 2009 by the humorous Australian periodical *Andromeda Spaceways In-flight Magazine,* which brought everything back home (for me, if not for Rhode Islander Paul) and completes this trawl through the history of my evolution as a writer with, I suppose one must say, a bang.

# COCKROACH LOVE
## (2008)

### WITH PAUL DI FILIPPO

"The problem with Arab literature has been that it forgot to tell stories and lost its way in experimentation. Too many novels that start with lines like 'I came home to find my wife having sex with a cockroach.'"

—Pankaj Mishra, "Where Alaa Al Aswany Is Writing From," *New York Times Magazine*, April 27, 2008

When Kay got home, tired and unhappy from her grueling flight halfway round the globe, she found her husband Elwood fucking a cockroach the size of a cocktail waitress.

She had longed only to kick off her sensible yet constricting Madame Ambassador high heels, and collapse on the couch for a foot massage from a considerate spouse. Unburden herself of all her diplomatic aggravations, with a cool drink in hand. Instead, that piece of furniture was now being creakingly abused.

Kay instinctively plucked off one pump, and heaved it at the insect.

In her blinding fury, she missed the bug by a good yard, and her husband as well.

The foul thing glanced at her and kept right on peeling an orange with its mandibles as her spouse of five years thrust at its hindquarters. Kay couldn't tell if the roach were male or female, not that it mattered especially.

"For the love of God, El!"

Elwood Grackle noticed her, finally. His face was flushed to a Clintonesque burgundy, and so was most of his bare chest. With a final shudder he jerked his useless fluids into the insect and fell forward, panting and dripping sweat onto the gleaming, jewel-toned carapace. The cockroach swallowed its final bright segment of fruit and chased it down with a tart bite of peel before throwing the curly remainder considerately into the faux fireplace.

Elwood detached with a squelch and a measure of insouciance. He pulled his ankled pants up awkwardly with one hand, reclaimed his shirt from the sofa back with the other. "How was the flight from Cairo, darling? You're early."

"I'm five hours late, you squamous fucker."

"Well, yes, strictly speaking, but I was factoring in post-arrival press conferences, debriefings, and the like. Allow me to introduce Emma. Em, this is Kay."

The roach's voice resembled a bandsaw working its blade through a wet sandbag. "Your wedded bliss. Madame boss. Most honored."

"My wife, yes." He toweled himself off with his shirt. "Em is our new Kaf."

"Christ, so now you're reduced to screwing a transgenic. The flight was gruesome, and so was Cairo. The noise of that place is indescribable."

"Really? What's it like?" He tucked himself away, donned the damp shirt, went to the bar to wash his hands lightly but firmly, and got out two tall frosty glasses from the fridge. He fished out a lime and slashed it. "A Margarita, darling?"

"What do you mean, what's it like? If I could describe it it wouldn't be indescribable. Yes, I'll have a drink, and why don't you tell this filthy thing to clear off, I'm sick of the sight of it."

"Your lovely bride is testy, Elwood. Felicitations, Madame, I was just leaving. I hope your mood is improved when next we meet." Boldly flashing the progenitive trademark of the Abu Dhabi University biolabs branded onto its shell, the roach was out the door in a darting motion that eluded Kay's swinging, still-shod foot with ease.

"I take it from your sour mood," said Elwood, "that negotiations with the Egyptians were not successful."

"My sour mood, as you so sympathetically phrase it, has more to do with your rutting."

"Oh, don't try to make me the villain. I sensed from your last phone call that you were already about as cheerful as a...as a drowning Micronesian. Your tiresome moodiness has been the status quo in our happy home for months."

Kay was suddenly immensely weary. It was true. She'd been a fount of black despair lately. Not that she could help it. So much was going wrong for the nation. For the world!

She sagged down on the couch, hit the glutinous wet spot, recoiled and shot up again—awkwardly, given her half-shod condition—and spilled her drink. Considerately, Elwood jumped to support her, and guided her to the safe haven of a dry armchair. Her façade of professional and wifely fortitude crumbled. His familiar, solicitous touch! She began to weep.

El patted her shoulder. He went to mix her a replacement Margarita, talking soothingly the while.

"There, dear, have a good cry. It's not easy, helping steer the ship of state through these perilous times. Never forget, I'm always there for you, darling."

"You're never there," she said, sobbing. "You're always here."

"Exactly, I'm always here for you. Look, you realize that my little impulsive moment just now has no bearing on our marriage, or my love for you."

"Are you *insane?* You were *fucking a roach!* What am I meant to think?"

El's mouth twisted a little. "She's a gift from the biolabs at Abu Dhabi University. For both of us. I was testing out all her advertised features."

"A Kafka, for god's sake. I've seen them in Cairo, you don't need to explain them to *me.* Fifteen percent human genes."

"Well, yes, but that's a feature, not a bug. Sorry." He raised his hands protectively in front of his face and tried not to grin. "But that's what they are, dear. General factotum and bug of all trades."

"What are *you* doing with one, that's what I want to know? Surely for something that expensive we should have discussed—"

"No, I'm telling you. A gift! For you, really. It seems they sent one to every high-level bureaucrat in the current administration. Some potentate's largesse, like the bestowal of the camel or virgin in days of yore."

"Oh. Right." Kay's expression hardened. "In gratitude for President McMurtry's new stance on Israel."

"Probably. But hey, Big Mac didn't exactly *disavow* American support, it was more a subtle shift in the—"

"Subtle! Subtle! About as subtle as getting home to find you screwing a *bug*. I'm going to bed. You can sleep on the couch. Oh, and wipe up the slime first."

She hoped he could tell she didn't mean it. He should be in the bed beside her. Because, really, there's no place like home.

The Kafka, Emma, sucked in her stout belly and scrunched behind the water heater. Her upstairs sleeping crate beckoned to her with its pheromone-laced organo-plastic shell, but she dared not approach it yet, given the hostility of the house's queen female.

Trembling with the aftershock of insemination, Emma was also seething with anger. The bitch had called her a cockroach! Em gnawed at the drywall opening, shoveling the unpleasant residue aside into a white powdery pile, and dragged her carapace into the wall space. She was no more a roach than that fool Elwood was a...a...tarsier.

Beneath her forward feet, the rough-cut joists tasted of mouse droppings and something less appetizing. A cat had been in here. Not recently, though. Alert for danger, she forced herself to relax. Cockroach, indeed! Cretin! Em had eaten enough roaches to know the differences intimately—they were flat, their legs stuck out grossly, most were wingless. *My* belly, she told herself, settling onto it in the soothing grime, is rounded and womanly. My back is strong and mounded like the dome of a noble capitol building. My legs are sensitive and petite. I am a *beetle,* you stupid human cow. Hear me roar!

At the quivering tip of her abdomen, in the protruding ootheca, her rows of eggs glowed under the attentions of Elwood's wrigglers. Babies! Soon! She yearned for motherhood.

Her irritation failed to subside. It wasn't meant to be like this. They'd promised so much more, in the hatchery, along with their cynicism and, simultaneously, their rather pushy warrior faith. In the dim light, Em poked about and found the battered Avon paperback half-copy of Nabokov's *Pnin* she'd been consuming. She managed three pages, gobbling them up as she committed the words to memory, before she fell asleep.

"I hope you're planning on a shower before you come to bed, darling," Kay told him, throwing off her underwear and moving in the dark. "I can't bear the stink of the thing on you."

Elwood's voice came to her, from the open bathroom door, in the unlighted bedroom: "Sweetheart, you know I always—"

Kay slammed her toes into something and yelped in pain. In a moment, El was beside her, naked, smelling of rancid sex, wide-eyed. He flicked on the overhead light. "What? What's the matter?"

"What the hell *is* it?" Kay cried, high-pitched. Her bare toe had struck a bulky off-white curved *thing* of some kind, as large as the kennel for a Bernese Mountain Dog and shiny as a polished egg, which it rather resembled. It had been squeezed in between her side of the bed and the sliding mirror fronting her closet.

"They brought it when they delivered the Kaf. It's where she sleeps."

"In my *bedroom?*"

"They abhor light, darling."

Kay stopped rubbing her toe, which still felt as if maybe she'd broken one phalange, and looked for a handhold on the carrier. Nothing—it really was like an egg, seamless, closed.

"How does it get *in?*"

"You really mustn't call her 'it,' sweetheart. There are provisions in the law now, I should have thought that you, of all people...."

Her questing fingers found a gap underneath. By main force she dragged the plastic shell to the end of the king-sized bed and tried to tip it over, gasping for air.

"I don't think she's in there," El said. "Look, let's just leave it there for the night, she'll probably come in later, they're very quiet and tidy, you know, we're both exhausted and out of sorts, you and I, I mean, everything will look rosier after we've had a good night's—"

Kay was not listening. Slamming the door between bedroom and hallway, she tugged at the old mahogany chest of drawers she'd inherited from Aunt Lil, dragging it, with a squawk of tortured Columbian structured parquet flooring, to jam the door shut, barring any direct or even furtive approach by the loathsome insect.

"Kay, it's— She's a *person.* This isn't like you. I thought we had an arrangement?"

"Yes! But the main contract preceded the fooling-around clause. To love and honor till death us do part! You're doing neither!"

El's expression indicated he had a ready marital riposte. But some imp of caution dissuaded him from venting the pithy reply. Instead, he wisely hung his head, retreated to the bathroom, had a short but energetically hygienic shower, then crawled meekly into bed, carefully keeping a DMZ of six inches between himself and Kay, whose quivering silent fury scared him fully as much as the world had been terrified of Kim Jong-Il just before that dictator had been assassinated in the very act of launching assorted ICBMs. A crisis Kay had a not-insignificant part in defusing, with hard-nosed realpolitik efficiency.

Lying tensely on his back, vainly inviting sleep, Elwood Grackle remained unaware of the newly introduced and cleverly designed spirochetes working their way up his urethra with their snicker-snack flagellae, heading with mysterious intentions much deeper into his system.

Professor Qutaybah Al Nahyan nervously fussed with his headdress in preparation for his interview with the Sheikh Khalifa. Although the Professor maintained a certain formally congenial consanguinity with the ruler of Abu Dhabi—fifth cousins once removed on a great-uncle's side—the hard facts of their relationship remained obdurate and inequal. One man was the living embodiment of their proud nation and its glorious destiny, Lion of the Prophet, while the other was a humble university instructor and researcher, educated at Oxford and Cal Tech, unmarried, living in a sparsely furnished bachelor's condo in the Mussafah Residential neighborhood. So today's meeting was hardly between peers, let alone friends. It would be a master's interrogation of his servant.

Drawing a small comb though his mustache and beard, Professor Al Nahyan sought to reassure himself that the Sheikh Khalifa would be pleased with what he had done, on his own initiative. True, he'd had to use some accounting sleight-of-hand to transfer funds from certain above-board projects to his own lab. And he had shamelessly passed off many of his classroom duties to his grad assistant, a stocky yet rather attractive American woman named Cayenne Sorbet, giving him time to work on tweaking the genome of his prized spirochete. Also true, he had unleashed his creations on the world—via the Trojan Beetle of the Kafs—without so much as an environmental impact statement. Yet was it not all for the greater glory of Islam, a most gentle and accommodating way of spreading the faith? Surely, with such motives and goals, no discredit could redound to him.

At last the Professor could dither no longer, but must make haste. Down to the condo's basement garage, into the air-conditioned comfort of his Chinese sedan, and out to contend with the impossible traffic of the island city-state. Subsidized gasoline prices encouraged auto use here, unlike most of the rest of their world suffering $200-a-barrel oil, despite the power beaming down now from orbit.

The meeting was scheduled to take place at MOPA, the Ministry of Presidential Affairs on the Corniche Road. As Professor Al Nahyan pulled into the parking lot, the sharp sparkle of the ocean waters nearby pierced his eyes and gave him an instant headache. He began to suspect that this meeting would not go well.

The Sheikh, however, seemed in a fine, expansive mood when Al Nahyan was finally ushered into the presence. Four or five men in tasteless western garb and an equal number of proud yet fawning cousins in their mid-twenties and early thirties attended the potentate as he sat at ease behind a desk as large as an aircraft carrier's launch deck. Holograms projected above the black glass desk displayed a magnificent assortment of prancing, head-tossing racing camels, presumably candidates for the Sheikh's fabled stables. Rumors suggested that the best of these coursers were genetically modified, enhanced against all the laws of God and man. If it were so, the result, the professor had to confess, proved the infraction worth the risk. His eyes moistened to see them, even at one-tenth scale, and his heart beat faster at the thought of mounting one and wheeling away into the desert, as his ancestors had ridden for centuries in the service of the Sheikh's own lineage. He came to his senses as the dealers in dromedarian flesh departed, puffing on large cigars, and his master faced him with a keen glance.

"Fine steeds, eh?"

"Yes indeed, sir."

"And what of your own little breeding experiments, eh? Eh?" The Sheikh laughed a booming, deep-chested laugh that rattled the professor's equanimity if not the bomb-proof three-ply windows. "Are we on target for the, uh, *transformation* of the infidels?"

Al Nahyan nervously found a chair, but dared not sit, though his knees knocked.

"Second stage insertion has begun, sir. A container of larvae has been ferried up the San Francisco de Quito skyhook, packaged for orbital transport by Virgin as solar cell panels. I anticipate shuttle deployment above Ecuador within the hour. We'll take down those Google power-sats in a matter of days."

The Sheikh's face set hard, considering who knew what complexities of realpolitik. He tilted his bearded head, then, and reached for the humidor.

"The Kafirs, the infidels, will not know what hit them. A cigar, doctor?"

☼

Melatonin-plus carried Kay through a night racked, in the deepest crevices of her jetlag-shocked body, by exhaustion and disgust. When the alarm beeped at ten in the morning she was still asleep—miracle of pharmaceutical science!—and when she flung her legs over the side of the bed she was hardly any closer to full consciousness. Her toes banged into the roach kennel as she stumbled to the bathroom.

"*Damn* you, El!" she shrieked, but the chest of drawers had been pulled ajar and he was long gone, into Beltway wonk territory, no doubt greasing his way along the corridors of D.C. power, such as it was any more. The pain in her toe seemed out of all proportion to the impact; maybe she *had* broken a bone. Shit! Now she'd have to fit an X-ray appointment in with all the rest of her impossibly burdened schedule. "Planner on," she shouted furiously to the system, and through the scrubbing and gurgling of her morning ablutions dictated her modified timetable. The odor of freshly-brewed automated coffee floated to her under the door from the kitchenette, and something more. Could it be a toasted muffin with orange marmalade? Heavenly! It made her laugh and brightened her mood. She'd surely put the fear of reprisal into the brute. For Elwood to stay home and make her breakf—

"Good morning, madam," the Kafka said, peering out from behind the refrigerator. "Would we care for an egg?"

Speechless, half-blinded by a rush of blood to her brain, Kay stopped on one foot (the uninjured one) and stared through squinted eyes at the gleaming kitchenette. One of her failings, she was prepared to admit, and certainly one of Elwood's, was to let the conapt pile up ever grungier with unwashed plates and cups and glasses, half-empty containers from the classiest takeoutlets in Maryland, a dead imported wine bottle or two from the Rhone Valley in Germany or the Illawarra in Australia abandoned on its side under the couch. The help were meant to deal with it, one day a week, but since Big Mac's punitive expulsions of the wetbacks it was impossible to get any help at all, let alone the good kind. Yet now everything in sight was redeemed, renewed, polished. Had the *roach* been bending its many elbows to the task?

"No egg," she said weakly. "Just bring me a cup of coffee and that muffin. I'll be in my study."

The creature turned away obediently, no hint of the saucy impudence of last night, but as Kay left the room she caught a glimpse of something horrible and disturbing. A kind of pulsing puce-hued bag protruded from the Kaf's hindquarters. An egg case? Dear Christ, was the thing *enceinte?* Was it about to *give birth in the kitchen?* She couldn't handle it. Her mind shifted sideways to the problem Sheikh Khalifa posed to the Free World from his seat of power in the United Arab Emirates. If only she had been able to make the Egyptians see that the Emirates were as much a threat to them as to the West—

In the hallway, her bare toes came down on something hard and sharp, something that scattered and rattled. White, stripped bones, with a quite largish crunched skull, as big as a—

Kay screamed at the top of her lungs, and ran for her iPhone, punched Elwood's direct link. "Get back here *this minute,*" she shrieked. "Your fucking sex toy has *eaten the cat.*"

☼

With the surname Stoner, a man was doomed from birth to a certain fate. Nominative determinism was a potent cosmic force, creating a Filipino Roman Catholic Cardinal named Sin, not to mention that top Harley Street neurologist, Lord Brain, Fellow of the Royal Society. So no-one among Jayant Vishnu Stoner's co-workers aboard Google PowerSat ☼9 was surprised at Jay's penchant for ingesting, smoking, injecting, popping, perfusing, snorting, or transcranially/magnetically inducing any illicit stimulant that fell to his questing hand. They regarded as just another workplace perk his amusing propensity for chatting with amiable hallucinations, a luser's gag, they assumed, meant to entertain them during their endless orbital days.

With his long funky dreads and his migratory subdermal flock of CGI tattoos, his fascination with jam-band music (his iQuant held 10,000 Phish tracks alone) and his slacker work habits, Jay surfed leisurely through his duties as solar-panel installer like a toasted postmodern peon of the space age. Only Jay's bosses were ignorant of his potentially dangerous non-compliance with management-approved modalities of employment. They were too busy surveying their stock options and charting the exact moment when they could prematurely retire.

Google's network of PowerSats was nearing the edge of critical mass, the ability to produce a quantity of non-petroleum energy able to rival—and eventually displace—old dirty sources like gas and soft coal, the bane of China's industry. These megawatts of clean power beamed by microwave to lacy terrestrial rectenna farms had already brought down the price of a barrel of oil from $250 to $200! Of course, as pointy-headed economists had warned, that cost reduction immediately led to an outburst of SUV purchases burning this cheaper fuel—but every solution has its drawbacks. Soon, the new paradigm of carbon-free power would be a reality, and the global economy would surge forward on a solid footing, no longer indebted to tyrants and dictators or greedy CEOs.

Not that Jay subscribed to any such high-minded idealism. It wasn't as if he had yearned or studied for this position. He had lucked into this job as part of a class-action lawsuit settlement. Google had failed to defend its search hog adequately against all the latest viruses, and the rogue program SnapDragon had snared the name and stats of Jayant Vishnu Stoner, and the randomly selected names and stats of several hundred other innocents. Their photos and full details immediately popped out whenever the search-term "FBI most wanted" was entered. In return for this gross defamation (and several false arrests, plus one fatal shooting), the victims were offered a choice: a job with Google, or a cash settlement. In a moment of sober practicality, Jay had taken the employment and training option.

So here he was, geared up in a nifty, sleek Dava Newman Bio-Suit against the unforgiving cargo bay vacuum of Google PowerSat ☼9, helping to unload the Virgin Galactic Ship *Victoria Beckham*, out of Quito Skyhook and now a good part of the way around the planet. In the satellite's microgravity, the bulky waffle-patterned organo-plastic crates were easy to shift and slot, allowing Jay to focus on the Widespread Panic tune pumping through his earbuds, and the low-level buzz created by his consumption of a morning fetal-cell-and-absinthe cocktail. Floating in a lazy haze, Jay was only a little surprised when Mr. Mxyzptlk showed up. The derby-wearing imp from the fifth dimension was a welcome confidante. Jay paused his iQuant and greeted him happily.

"Mxy, my man! What's down?"

Speaking around his cigar, Mr. Mxyzptlk told him, "Feast your peepers on the crate with the pliss scabbed on."

Jay focused blearily through the distortions of his merry high. Sure enough, one crate packaged as solar cell panels also featured an attached Portable Life-Support System. Weirdness! Why would dead power mechanisms engineered for the nullity of high-orbit require livestock temperature and atmosphere regulation? This shit had to be contraband! The PowerSat crew enjoyed frequent illicit shipments of porn, pets, alcohol, drugs, cigarettes and transfats, and this had to be one such—although the usually reliable grapevine had not alerted Jay in advance.

"Think I'll just skim a little off the top, Mxy! Thanks for the heads-up!"

"No grind," Mxy said. With a shouted "Kltpzyxm!" the imp vanished.

Exhibiting a druggie's exaggerated slyness, Jay guided the selected crate out of sight of his busy co-workers, through an airlock, and into the adjacent shirtsleeves environment of the large room where Manned Maneuvering Units were repaired. The workspace, festooned with spare parts, was luckily unoccupied, sparing him any need to blurt out an absurd excuse for his presence. Still in his suit, Jay cracked the seals of the crate with fumbling eagerness, anticipating familiar goodies.

For a full ninety seconds, his fogged brain failed to register what he was seeing, actually *seeing* in external reality. As far as he could tell. "They're immature bugs!" the voice of SpongeBob SquarePants whispered in his ear. "Giant fucking larvae, dude!"

He tore at his eyes, but sure enough, the crate was filled with squirming featureless maggots the size of microwave ovens. Several had begun to pupate, enclosing themselves in the shells that would crack to discharge the adults of whatever the hell gruesome species they were.

One of his rare bad trips kicked in. The wriggling flesh hassocks creeped him out. A powerful vision seized him: roaches expanding, multiplying, filling the station from wall to wall. "Yaargh! Gotta get rid of the suckers!"

Jay hastily re-sealed the crate, and removed its PLSS unit. All he had to do now was cycle it back out to the airless cargo bay, and the unprotected bugs would die.

He pushed the crate toward the airlock. At the last moment, SpongeBob offered counsel.

"Man, somebody went to a lot of trouble to get these up here. These things must be valuable! Why not save at least one...?"

"Good idea!"

Jay soon had a single grub hidden inside an empty suit, tethered by netting to the wall of the workspace. With luck, it would survive and not be found until he could get it back to his quarters. His humor was mellowing again. Hey, who knew what might hatch out of it? Something pretty cool, maybe.

"Great job!" said SpongeBob. "Let's hit the dining hall for a Crabby Patty now!"

"Yeah!"

"You son of a whoring bitch!" Kay shrieked, gazing at the pink-tipped strip of paper in her trembling hand with its pink-mauve + sign. A drop of urine dripped off of it, splashed her bare foot. If the kit did not lie, her uterus was flooded with chorionic gonadotropin. Was *invaded*. She rooted frantically through her packs of pills. A rushed count showed none missing. What the *hell*? Had the bastard purchased some exhausted stock from a crooked Bolivian recycling pharmacy, via Web2Bay? Substituted the past-use-by dud product for her own contraceptives? The print was too small to tell. "I informed you it was too soon for this! I have my diplomatic career to consider, you ridiculous sentimentalist."

In the living room, Elwood had his forehead pressed to the new patterned mat he'd extended over the parquet. Outside, the usual unearthly wailing rose from a plasticized carbon-bonded minaret erected with grudging city approval just across from the Farmer's Market. The Adhan rose and fell, calling the faithful to early morning salat prayer. "*Ash-hadu anna Muhammadan rasūlullāh,*" El murmured ecstatically. "*Hayya 'alā Khair al-'amal.*"

"Make haste toward the best thing yourself, you pig of a pig." Wasn't it enough that she had to put up with this ululating in Cairo, where she'd spent six weeks in a crash Arabic course using the powerful mnemonic principles of the Pole, Piotr Wozniak. "What's the idea? And get up off the floor, you fool, you're an Episcopalian and a third-degree Mason, not a Muslim."

El lifted his spirochete-laden head dazedly. "We are all part of the body of the Umma," he explained. "So mote it be."

"Well, something else is part of *my* body now, you sorry excuse. I'm *pregnant*!"

After a pause for pious thought, El told her, "I forgive you."

"Will you be taking breakfast, madam?" asked the roach, putting its head in from the kitchenette. "And congratulations on the baby—I'm in the family way myself."

Kay seized a bright green apple from a decorative bowl of wax fruit in the center of the table, flung it at the creature; the fake apple caught in the plates of its back. "And I know who the hell the father is! Elwood, you disgust me. How could you fuck a thing like that, and then bring your soiled seed to our marriage bed?" It's affected his mind, she thought. *In*fected his mind. And probably his body as well. She shuddered, feeling befouled.

"Verily," El expounded, "prayer prevents the worshipper from indulging in anything that is undignified or indecent. That's Surah Al-Ankabut, chapter 29, verse 46." He got to his feet, a look of crazed passion in his eye. "They can all grow up together. They can attend Naval Prep School, in historic Newport, Rhode Island, as I did, and my father before me. Imagine them in the rigging! Six legs good!" Foam was starting to seep from the edges of his mouth.

A hideous peeping came from the kitchenette, as of a nestful of baby chicks calling their mother. Kay's face drained of blood. No, not chicks. They probably hunted down chicks and ate them raw. And what the hell was growing inside *her*?

"I'm going to kill you," she told her deluded spouse. She picked up an ornamental brass poker from the set of Ralph Lauren accessories resting beside the ornamental fake fireplace, and hoisted it lustily above her head. "I'm going to fucking *murder* and *skin* you, and then I'm driving straight to the Prince George's clinic."

Elwood Grackle grabbed a defensive dining room chair by its cushioned back, but left it dangling. "Fight in the way of Allah against those who fight against you," he warned, "but begin not hostilities. Lo! Allah loveth not aggressors. Kill them whenever you confront them and drive them from where they drove you. Surah 2, verses 190-191."

"We're fresh out of eggs," Emma called in her abrasive voice. "Anyone for a sliced sausage?"

☼

Aboard Google PowerSat ☼9, Jay Stoner was entertaining a visitor in his private room, a room admittedly smaller than the average terrestrial capsule-hotel accommodations. Luckily, the visitor could be cradled and compassed completely within the circle of Jay's arms.

The gently squirming peristaltic mass of the lone surviving smuggled larva, retrieved from its hiding place, radiated a kind of numinous pet-like comfort into Jay's quiveringly drug-sensitized brain, traversing all interspecies communication gaps and barriers. Waves of wordless approbation laved him. Damn! This thing was just like a Tribble! Shame he had killed all the others, he could've sold them to his fellow crew members. Life aboard the solar-power station could be harsh and boring, despite both management-approved and illicit recreations, and any additional source of comfort was always eagerly sought. But all the other bugs were irrevocably gone now, and Jay wasn't one for crying over spilled bongwater.

Suddenly a floating copyright mark akin to Jay's own anime tats drifted up to display itself beneath the larva's epidermis, much like an answer appearing in the window of a Magic Eightball.

"N-5397-batch5," read Jay aloud. "Aw, is dat your widdle name-ums? Uncle Jay is gonna call you Enny. Enny-wenny-wenny-henny-penny!"

Jay began to tickle the bug, and gushes of telepathic gratitude swamped his senses. "What does Enny-wenny want now? Sugar water? A widdle sweater to stay warm?"

The flood of love pouring out of the larva almost instantly transmuted to hate. Jay was stunned and saddened. But then he realized that the hate was not directed against him. Oh, no! Enny's anger and pain represented a lashing-out against the bug's creators, the men who had placed Enny and cousins on a one-way trip to space, away from all familiar earthly pleasures, to carry out their greedy schemes like disposable grunts on the front lines of corporate wars.

"Tell me, tell me, Enny! Who did it to you! Who must suffer your sweet, sweet ichorous revenge!"

Images marched through Jay's brain. Arabs in their robes, state offices, a seaside city, signage—

"Yes, yes, Enny, I know who they are! Bastards! We'll make them pay! Soon, soon, just when the shift's about to change—"

Jay smooshed his face into the warm pulpy haggis of the larva and smothered it with kisses.

Enny seemed content to wait.

☼

"Nothing has gone *wrong, qua* wrong," Professor Al Nahyan assured Sheikh Khalifa. His glowering master did not look especially assured. "The package was intercepted somehow. We had no way of perceiving in advance—"

"Quiet." The Lion's fingers, scented and beautifully manicured, drummed on an acre of black glass. The great office, blue lit, was refrigerator cold, its master wrapped in a fur-lined *dishdasha*. Qutaybah shivered. "One larva is still minimally responsive, you say?"

"Yes, yes—within certain unpredictable limits. But there are very many more on the ground, naturally. Ready to give birth, if the induced mutations hold steady. Some have already been through parturition." He checked his babbling tendency to persiflage under stress. "They are very...compulsive animals. The second generation individuals are even more potent. With sixty-five percent human genes, thanks to the maternal and paternal contributions, they are more anthropomorphic, and completely irresistible to either human sex. The Westerners will go extinct, wasting all their lusts on the bugs instead of breeding strong sons and modest daughters."

The Professor neglected to add that the hybrids would be fully Islamic in their outlook, due to the onboard spirochetes of his devising—Plan B, as it were. He was still unsure of the legitimacy of conferring Koranic knowledge on another species.

"So I understand." The Sheikh failed to fly into a rage, which was at once a blessed relief and a phenomenon beyond all understanding. Al Nahyan wrung his sweating hands, fearing for them. But the sheikh merely lifted one of his own and flicked his fingers. Begone, said the fingers. The endocrino-entomologist scrambled gratefully from the room, reeling with the vertigo of terror. Clearly, geopolitical and theological factors were in play here well beyond his narrow, specialized knowledge. Beyond his need to know. He crept past crisp guards in military uniform and languid courtiers arrayed like peacocks by languid couturiers. The sun, when finally he escaped into the open, beat on his naked head like a cruel blessing. Like the justice and mercy of Allah.

In the distance, a voice called from the muezzin, called the Faithful to prayer.

But contrary to all his past devotional humility, all that Professor Al Nahyan could think of was the image of his plump and attractive grad assistant, Miss Cayenne Sorbet, locked in carnal embrace with a second generation Kaf.

*What a waste. I've completely thrown my life away....*

Jay oozed stealth as he air-swam down the corridors of the satellite, mingling with the dispirited workers swapping posts. Enny rested hidden in a courier's bag strapped to Jay's back.

"Soon, Enny, soon," Jay muttered, drawing no suspicions from his co-workers, who were certain he was merely addressing the ghost of Phil Silvers or John Lennon or Yogi Bear, as was his wont.

At the beam-control room, Jay encountered Bob Hazzard, itching to leave, and knew he had beaten Bob's replacement to the door. Unquestioningly eager to leave, Bob allowed Jay inside.

Jay locked the door.

Fully automated, the cybernetic mechanisms that kept the output beam of PowerSat ☼9 focused on the rectenna farms in the deserts of the American west needed only to be monitored for freakish drift. But of course, manual overrides existed to allow a complete shift in target.

Unpacking Enny and allowing the larva to float beside his shoulder, Jay set to work.

Plugging in the GPS coordinates of Abu Dhabi took only seconds.

Fingers poised to stroke the touchscreen and send gigawatts of searing microwave radiation down upon the unsuspecting, unprotected emirate, Jay paused and turned to Enny.

"Is this really what you want, Enny?"

The savage surety of the bug's response was unmistakable.

Jay stroked.

In a D.C. townhouse, a man and a woman lay insensible on the floor, while dozens of second-generation infant Kafs swarmed over them, spreading mutagenic slime trails across their skin.

Emma watched with pride and pleasure. Like the heroine in one of The Master's best books, *Lolita*, she knew that innocence was much deadlier than cunning any day.

☼

The Sheikh Khalifah relaxed in his chair. He touched hidden contacts on his great desk; the doors locked with chunky authority. The smoky, polarized windows transitioned to complete opacity. He stroked a last button, and a brocaded, gilded basket rose from beneath the floor. Within the basket, a gleaming, jewel-crusted mutant bug turned her sleepy gaze upon him, preened her antennae.

"My lord," she said.

"Come to me, you lovely bitch," said the Lion of the Prophet, parting his blue-silver trimmed *dishdasha*.

The Sheikh was suddenly forced to shield his eyes. What unexpected nova could leak through the window films?

Only a city instantly aflame.

The contents of the office burst into flame, and for a final mortal second, the Sheik Kalifah learned that roasting Kaf smelled like lobster.

# WHERE TO NEXT?

Here I am, then, exactly half a century after I fled my family in search of purpose and God and found science fiction instead. I've been thought retarded or at least slow, and a prodigy. My first extended stint of writing, done when I was seventeen, researched in the university library, was a short history of St. Joseph—husband of Mary, and about whom almost nothing is known except his cuckoldry by the Creator—that I wrote hoping it would be published as a slender pamphlet by the wonderfully-named Catholic Truth Society. It was my whimsy to title it *The Man God Called Dad*, and to nobody's surprise it was declined.

Four years earlier I had auditioned for a role in a serial broadcast in the early evening as part of a children's show from the Melbourne AM radio station 3DB (no FM back then). I was terrible, but they allowed me into the studio to watch the rehearsal and then the five or 10 minute live-to-air reading, sound effects done by rustling paper or hitting gongs or blowing across a microphone to mimic a storm, and I kept coming back night after night, as my parents worried frantically. I carried home with me as many of the discarded scripts as possible, like passports to a finer world of the imagination. I was besotted by the lovely young middleclass girl actors in their expensive school uniforms, and envious of the strapping boys. The serial had a bizarre title—the Fakermagangees—named for the fictional kid adventurers' club. How I wished to join such a club! At thirteen or so, horny for the first time, how I wished to frolic with those juicy girlets on their expeditions around the world, into space (if only in an extended dream sequence) and through time! Instead, I rode home to the outer suburbs on the jolting train through the winter night and turned for consolation to the lurid sf comics and magazines my parents deplored, sublimating my envy into dreams of, you know, voyages to other worlds, time travel to more exotic epochs, mental communion with welcoming gestalt super-beings. And in time I turned all this to advantage, making up stories of my own, even a few radio plays that I attended during rehearsal and performance, knowing that the words these actors mouthed (brilliantly or clumsily) were finally, truly, my own, come back to me, transformed and audible across the whole continent.

So I live out the destiny of a kid who disliked homework and now does it all the time, pouring out articles and reviews and short stories and books instead of school essays. How did that happen? Just lucky, yes. My obsession with the possibilities of the future, grim or beckoning or utterly transformative by turns, finds its expression in the fictions of science, but also in the sciences at the edge of fiction: explorations of the deep future (*Year Million, Earth Is But a Star*), parapsychology (*Outside the Gates of Science*), radical life extension (*The Last Mortal Generation*), runaway exponential technologies (*The Spike*), the literary semiotics of science fiction itself (*Unleashing the Strange*). Meanwhile, there are short story collections (*Uncle Bones, The Qualia Engine*), a screwball *noir* crime novel with my old pal Rory Barnes (*I'm Dying Here*), our UFO abduction novel (*Dark Gray*), and a near-future immortality thriller with my dear wife, Barbara Lamar (*Post Mortal Syndrome*). Even as I complete this book looking backward, marveling at the strange journey so far, I've begun another, *Wild Science*, that will again consider psychic phenomena from a practical viewpoint, and the possibility of time machines. The technological sublime lures me far from the safe pastures of the known. And that's okay, surely, because the unknown is where we are headed, always, climbing into the future up the green or icy slopes of Mount Implausible.

# ACKNOWLEDGMENTS

"Dead Air": *Isaac Asimov's Science Fiction Magazine*, February 2010.

"Walk Like a Mountain": *The Australian Messenger of the Sacred Heart*, August 1963.

"The Mirrors of the Sea": *Orpheus: Monash University Magazine*, 1964.

"The Sea's Furthest End": *New Writings in SF1*, ed. John Carnell, Dobson, 1964.

"Interview with Damien Broderick," Questions by Russell Blackford: *Science Fiction: A Review of Speculative Literature*, ed. Van Ikin, Issue 12, Vol. 4, No. 3, September 1982, pp. 94-105.

"Exorcism": *Man,* June 1966, here slightly revised.

"Murder Is in the Eye of the Beholder": *Man*, January 1967, here slightly revised.

"Incubation": *Man*, August 1967, by Damien Broderick and John Romeril (with kind permission of co-author), here slightly revised.

"Symbol of the Serpent": *Man*, January 1973, as by Philip Jenkins.

"Drowning in Fire": *Dreamworks: Strange New Stories*, ed. David King, Norstrilia Press, 1983.

"The Interior: A Tale of Outback Rapture": *Strange Attractors: Original Australian Speculative Fiction*, ed. Damien Broderick, Hale & Iremonger, 1985.

"The Dark Between *The City and the Stars*": adapted from an essay in *Arthur C. Clarke: A város és a csillagok*, Metropolis Media Group Kft., Galaktika Fantasztikus Könyvek, Budapest, 2007, as "Túl városon és csillagokon," trans. Attila Németh, and in *New York Review of Science Fiction*, Number 239, Vol. 20, No. 11, July 2008, and forthcoming in *Sentinels: In Honor of Arthur C. Clarke*, ed. Gregory Benford and George Zebrowski, Hadley Rille Books, 2010.

"Cockroach Love": *Andromeda Spaceways Inflight Magazine*, 41, 2009, by Damien Broderick and Paul Di Filippo (with kind permission of co-author).

Thanks to Dr. Russell Blackford for his splendid foreword, to Gary Livick and Spike Jones for proofreading, to Barbara with love for her company, wit, and endless help, and to the School of Culture and Communication at the University of Melbourne, where I am delighted to remain a Senior Fellow even at this planetary distance.

# ABOUT THE AUTHOR

More than enough has been said in the preceding pages "About the Author", but briefly: Australian science fiction and popular science writer, editor and critic **DAMIEN BRODERICK** has won a number of Ditmar and Aurealis awards for his fiction, was runner-up in 1981 for the John W, Campbell Memorial Award (for *The Dreaming Dragons*), and received the IAFA Distinguished Scholarship Award in 2005. He holds a PhD from Deakin University. Currently he lives in San Antonio, Texas, with his wife Barbara Lamar, their Border collie Rufus, and three semi-wild cats, one a Savannah who spends most of his time above the ceiling.

www.ingramcontent.com/pod-product-compliance
Lightning Source LLC
Chambersburg PA
CBHW020445270626
47155CB00022B/1518